THE MONK
AND HIS
MESSAGE

THE MONK AND HIS MESSAGE

UNDERMINING THE MYTH OF HISTORY

GEORGE WOODCOCK

Douglas & McIntyre
Vancouver/Toronto

92 93 94 95 96   5 4 3 2 1

Douglas & McIntyre, 1615 Venables Street, Vancouver, British Columbia V5L 2H1

Canadian Cataloguing in Publication Data

Woodcock, George, 1912–
  The monk and his message
  Includes index.
  ISBN 1-55054-005-X
  1. Historiography   2. History —Errors, inventions, etc.
I. Title.
D13.W66 1992   907'.2   C92-091057-2

Editing by Saeko Usukawa
Design by Eric Ansley & Associates
Typeset by Vancouver Desktop Publishing Centre Ltd.
Printed and bound in Canada by D.W. Friesen & Sons Ltd.
Printed on acid-free paper ∞

To William Toye,
who did so much
to turn me
into a Canadian writer

CONTENTS

THE MONK AND HIS MESSAGE

The Reconstruction of History

A merry road, a mazy road, and such as we did tread,
The night we went to Birmingham by way of Beachy Head.
　　　　　—G. K. Chesterton, "The Rolling English Road"

There has been a great deal of talk and writing recently about the deconstructionist study of literature, which breaks down barriers of form and function and calls the reader into the heart of the process of creation and criticism. The book which you, the reader, are now invited to enter is a kind of deconstructionist treatment of history. It sets out to undermine the conventions by which so much formal, especially political, history has been written and exposes the authoritarian relationship between rulers and conservative historians that has existed almost from the time when Hecataeus and Herodotus, those relatively pristine pioneers, started on the task of chronicling the past in the hope that it might offer lessons for the present. This book also confronts the apparatus of determinist laws of history, of providential plans, of eschatological prophetic visions, emanating from many of the most powerful minds involved in the study of history, from Zoroaster and Plato and Joachim de Fiore, from Vico and Hegel, from Marx and Lenin, and shows that they have not only been false prophets but also, in their effects on human societies, ultimately and universally harmful. In place of the grand misleading structures of such determinist historians, I am offering an approach to history based on a recognition of the world of contingency that operates not according to certain occult laws of destiny

1

but according to the limitations of our mentality, our physical and mental powers, and our environment. This is a world of process and change, a world of chance (but chance of course is a kind of Janus—one of whose faces is called opportunity) and, above all, of choice. Determinist history, as I shall show, makes people see themselves as the slaves of destiny; free history, true history, offers them the challenge of chance and choice.

At no time, in fact, has that challenge been stated more clearly, in social and political terms, than in the years between 1989 and 1991, when people in Europe and in Asia, including the great late Soviet Union which belonged to both continents, demonstrated their rejection of the totalitarian realms that had been justified by historicist ideologies. The challenge failed in China but succeeded in a number of European countries, liberating them from the realm of false—or prophetic—history into that of the true history of events which gives lessons from the past to the present.

This is the view of history that has determined a Chestertonian strategy which will not be unfamiliar to literary deconstructionists. The book starts with a Tibetan monk in Norway proposing what many people considered impossible but continues with people in Europe in the 1990s achieving something almost as impossible.

Then the book plunges to that point in the past, round about twenty-five centuries ago, when history first began to detach itself from ancient myth and shows how authoritarian religions and political interests early seized upon history as a potential weapon. Eventually, with the totalitarian regimes of this century, the narrative emerges into the present, descending from the malign and abstract heights of totalitarian ideology to life as humanity prefers to live it, to the realm of change and chance and choice, to East European peoples shouting their governments out of existence, and to Canada facing an internal political crisis that national myths cannot solve.

The arrangement of the book illustrates that history is only significant when it brings the past forward into the present and leaves us to discover its lessons, sailing at our peril. Perhaps we can take ironic consolation from the last lines of Chesterton's poem:

> For there is good news yet to hear and fine things to be seen,
> Before we go to Paradise by way of Kensal Green.[*]

---

[*] Kensal Green was the great North London cemetery where many notable English writers were buried.

PART I

·

THE

·

MONK

·

CHAPTER I

The Monk and His Message

In the early 1990s, when the bases of our world are once again in question and our sense of history is changing shape, it seems appropriate that this book dealing with such matters should begin with the statement of a man who has lost all temporal authority, and who owes the undoubted moral influence he wields to the vision and the virtues he has cultivated as, to use his own description, "a simple monk," a man who, by definition, has stepped outside of history.

I refer to Tenzin Gyatso, the fourteenth and according to many Tibetan prophecies, the last of the Dalai Lamas, once both temporal and spiritual rulers of Tibet. One of the last memorable events of that *annus mirabilis,* 1989, when peoples who had lived in darkness found their voices and *vox populi* in Europe sounded amazingly like *vox dei,* was the presentation in December of the Nobel Prize for Peace to the Dalai Lama.

On the day after the Dalai Lama made his brief acceptance speech for the prize, he gave a much longer lecture, in which he began by dwelling on the past sufferings of his Tibetan people and their present plight, living under Chinese oppression or scattered over the world as exiles. But he went on very quickly to consider the situation of Tibet in the context of a world where, whether willing it or not, humanity has become a global family. For what has happened in Tibet, and what is still to happen, is no longer isolated in a mediaeval realm hidden behind mountain barriers from the modern world.

Tibet was never a great power, even though a thousand years ago its

5

armies poured into Chang'an, the imperial capital of ancient China. In recent centuries it and its people have been wholly without political or economic influence. But the lack of such forms of power does not necessarily mean the absence of the power of moral examples, and moral examples begin with visions. It was a vision that the Dalai Lama presented in Stockholm that December day when he suggested that, for the good of the Tibetan people and of the world in general, his country might be transformed into what he called "a Zone of Ahimsa."

Ahimsa is a word used by the Jains, a nonviolent sect of small numbers but considerable moral power in India. *Himsa* is "harm," and *ahimsa* "the negation of harm." The concept had been taken up by Gandhi to inspire his great campaign against the British Raj. While Gandhi had proposed a political struggle "without harm" to his opponents, the Dalai Lama was proposing that a Zone of Non-Harming be created, a zone of peace to be achieved on three levels: peace among human beings by the transformation of the Tibetan plateau—the legendary "roof of the world"—into a militarily neutral zone; peace between humanity and other species by turning the Tibetan plateau into the "world's largest natural park or biosphere"; peace between humanity and the earth by forbidding technologies that produce hazardous wastes.

As I read this speech, I was reminded of the day thirty years ago, not long after the Dalai Lama had fled from Tibet, when my wife and I went up to the Indian village of Dharamsala in the Himalayan foothills and first met him, a young man still in his twenties, dressed in a plain maroon robe. He was sitting, on a chill December afternoon, in the old British bungalow, with langur monkeys pattering over the corrugated iron roof, that then served as his "palace" in exile.

He described himself even then as a simple monk, shyly pushing aside all the journalistic nonsense that had exalted him as a "God-king." And already he was thinking of plans to liberate Tibet and transform it into something different from the mediaeval, obscurantist country, ruled by abbots and aristocrats, which it had been up to the disaster of the Chinese invasion in 1950. "We must get rid of the drones," he said, referring to the parasitical ruling class of Tibet's past, and he talked of a democratic society in which the true principles of Gandhi, whom he greatly revered, would be developed in a land without an army, where all living beings would be respected, and his own role would be redefined by the will of the people.

He has been consistent over the years since then in his work for Tibetan liberation, in his efforts to sustain Tibetan culture in exile. Yet as I read his Oslo speech and remembered that conversation long ago, and other conversations when we had met again over the years, I could not but think at first sight that what he was advocating sounded like an insubstantial and escapist vision unrelated to the world of today. Did it not call up echoes of the faraway refuge of Shangri-La, the romantic earthly paradise in the Tibetan mountains that James Hilton invented in his best-selling novel of the 1930s, *Lost Horizon*?

But how near in fact to reality is this vision so long treasured by the Dalai Lama? Appearances indeed suggest that it may be remote from actuality in the 1990s. His country is now one of the most militarized parts of the world, occupied by no less than 250,000 Chinese troops. Recent Tibetan manifestations of rebellion have been ruthlessly suppressed at the orders of the power-avaricious gerontocrats in Beijing. The Chinese have been systematically ravaging the earth of Tibet for more than four decades, felling forests and mining sacred mountains to tear uranium and other rare metals from their rocks.

As for the idea of creating a vast natural park, that seemed until very recently an impossible hope, given the reports of the fate of the once abundant wildlife of the Tibetan plateau. Travellers who visited the country before the Second World War, and even during the 1940s, gave fascinating accounts of the great herds of deer, antelope and wild asses, of the bears and snow leopards, that moved fearlessly through the mountains, and of the flocks of birds—rare elsewhere—that frequented the great upland lakes. Tibet, in those days before the Chinese invasion, had the most successful system of environmental protection of any inhabited region of the world. There was no legal code that forbade the killing of wild animals; there were no parks or wildlife reserves formally constituted in the Western sense. Such forms of protection were not needed in a land where devout Buddhist compassion for all living things reigned supreme.

Recent reports from travellers in Tibet were not nearly so idyllic; they described a countryside that has been ravaged, its wildlife massacred and hunted into distant refuges. An article on the subject by writer and photographer Galen Rowell in *Greenpeace* magazine as late as March/April 1990 described in most pessimistic terms the steady destruction not only of wildlife but also of wildlife habitat, including even the great rhododendron forests on the slopes of Everest.

Yet when Rowell visited the Dalai Lama and talked of these matters with him, the latter seemed strangely unperturbed:

> He commented on the way his people used to coexist with
> animals and humans before the invasion. "Some of that har-

7

mony remains in Tibet," he told me, "and because it happened
in the past, we have some genuine hope for the future."

And in fact there emerged, shortly after the Dalai Lama's speech and just
before Rowell's article appeared, the extraordinary news that one vast area
of wildlife habitat in far northern Tibet remained virtually unspoiled and
that less than three weeks after the Tibetan leader received the Nobel Prize,
a letter of intent to preserve this great enclave of mountain wilderness had
been signed between the Environmental Protection Agency of the Chinese
Government and Wildlife Conservation International. The Western signa-
tory of the agreement was George B. Schaller, a zoologist of high repute
ever since his remarkable studies in the 1960s of the social life of gorillas.
In recent years, since 1984, Schaller has been conducting wildlife surveys
in the high Tibetan plateau where he penetrated a region—the Chang Tang,
or Northern Plain—"so barren and high that only a few people live on its
periphery." Even the Chinese poachers who have so radically reduced the
wildlife of the blander areas of Tibet have not reached this region in any
considerable numbers. As Schaller says:

> The Chang Tang is bleak, with vast expanses of gravel and
> wind-blown soil, its plains and rumpled hills covered with
> herbage so scant it leaves only the vaguest impression. Yet at
> this elevation of 14,500 to 16,000 feet exists a unique large-
> mammal fauna; wild yak, Tibetan argali sheep and Tibetan
> brown bear, as well as wolf, snow leopard, blue sheep and
> others. Not only are many of these animals found nowhere
> else, but also some occur in large numbers.

Thus what happened and was revealed in public after the Dalai Lama's
apparently optimistic statement in fact seemed to give it authenticity. It also
revealed patterns of hesitation and loosening conviction among Chinese
political leaders in the very year of 1989 when Communist regimes were
washing away throughout Eastern Europe, inducing us to look again at
events in Beijing during that summer. The newfound willingness to consider the lives of wild animals, to regard them as honorary comrades, fitted
in with the totally unanticipated month of hesitation on the part of the
authorities that allowed the student demonstrations and that fostered the
feeling of solidarity between intellectuals and populace. Panic rather than
firmness induced the men of Beijing to carry out their massacre. They
realized that power was slipping away from them, but by their very actions

they placed a time bomb of resentment in the heart of the last major Communist dictatorship.

So the voice of the people in Beijing and the other great cities of China may, sooner rather than later, usher the ancient leaders and their ageing cadres out of power, and in the process change the future of Tibet and its people as well as that of China itself, as the people of so many other countries did in the annus mirabilis of 1989 and the hardly less miraculous year of the disintegration of the Soviet Union in 1991. The Dalai Lama may in the long run be right.

I have brought forward the Dalai Lama and his "impossible" proposal with a broader intent: to challenge the historical assumptions under which we have tended to live for many centuries, and especially the assumption that outside written history, which is the selective recording of actual events, there exists a shaping force with its own laws that is called History (with a capital H) and that has been invoked by totalitarians everywhere. These assumptions were accepted until the last decade, when people—as individuals coming together into articulate masses—overthrew tyrannies and in the process destroyed the icons of political traditions and regimes considered as the manifestations of determined destiny, destroyed them decisively and for the most part without violent revolution.

For such an inquest it is necessary first of all to examine how the concept of a determined and foreseeable future took hold of historians and produced the super-myth of History. And this means beginning where the writing of history starts, in archaic Greece about the sixth century B.C., to reveal how almost from its birth history tended to be appropriated by rulers and political leaders and transformed for their purposes. Then I show how, through the visions of the great Iranian sage Zoroaster, the eschatological idea of the world and humankind moving onward to a great and predetermined final struggle between good and evil emerged in the Middle East and was transmitted to the religions of the Book, Judaism and Christianity and Islam, giving them a dynamic urge towards a millenarian future that had not existed among the more truly Asian religions like Buddhism, Taoism and Hinduism. This urge was taken over by secular historians, both liberals who turned it into the myth of progress and totalitarians who associated it with their own doctrines of racial superiority (in the case of the Nazis) and class warfare (in the case of the Communists). Finally, I show how the myth of historical inevitability became entrenched in the minds of people both outside and within the Communist bloc during the half-century since 1917, so that anything less than Armageddon seemed unlikely

9

to dislodge the totalitarian monolith.

In the concluding chapters, I turn my attention to the events of the 1980s, and especially the two marvellous years of 1989 and 1991 when, in an apparent double miracle, people suddenly lost their fear and discovered that the will of their rulers had rotted away with their ideology. The myth of "revealed" History no longer dominated people's minds; the "truths" of Marxist-Leninism were shown to be empty dogmas exploited by ruthless men of power. The prophecies of which Karl Marx and his successors had made so much had long been invalidated by the survival of capitalism and the decay of communism as economic systems. The rulers had neither the reason nor the will to exist, and their doctrines were discredited by their inaction.

In the process, as I shall show, the whole myth of a force directing events in a foreseeable way, called History by its protagonists, was finally discredited. History can now return to its proper role, that of a written art searching for some comprehensible but necessarily arbitrary form in the chaos of events. There is no point in searching for laws; the only law of history is that there are no laws of history. History consists merely of the muddle of events, the unpredictable flow of process, and the historian's selecting and arranging eye is what gives shape to it. But each work of history is only one individual's shaping of the past, and by the very nature of true history it can tell us nothing about the future. The marvellous events of 1989 and 1991 have in fact put history in a position analogous to that of physics, whose theoreticians have recently felt obliged to create their concept (an anti-law one might call it) of chaos. We need now our historian's anti-law that will help us redefine what history is, and also, more importantly, what possibilities are open to humankind in a nondetermined world. We need to regain the innocent, intelligent eye of Herodotus, gathering and judging facts in the dawn of history, writing twenty-five centuries ago.

I end by returning to the Dalai Lama and his "impossible" proposals, and to the suggestion that a new view of possibility rather than inevitability as the central characteristic of history may open up to us all, as Canadians and world citizens, avenues we have never dared to explore because of our fear of History, as distinct from history.

PART II

HISTORY

AND

THE

NECESSARY

LIE

CHAPTER II

Necessary Lies: The Birth of History

In this book I am proposing what is essentially an anti-theory of history, a deconstructive examination, in the light of recent events, of the ambiguous spectre that has long overshadowed with its great nineteenth-century beard our consideration of human achievements and hopes—the determinist view of history.

History, as it affects and often afflicts the mind of post-Renaissance humanity, can be seen in the image of one of those dual monsters so favoured by ancient myth creators and by modern heralds. A centaur, perhaps, with a head of human reason and purpose and a body of animate unreason, of endless process. Penetrating the image, we recognize that "history," as we conceive it, has become two things at once. It is written history, the narration and interpretation of events; but the same word is also used to dignify the process of events itself, the "march of history," and even to personify History—as political theorists as well as poets have done, into a kind of titanic force that speaks with dire impersonality to mankind. As W. H. Auden put it in the celebrated lines of "Spain":

> History to the defeated
> May say Alas, but cannot help or pardon.

In the confusion of narrative and process lies the cause of those forms of historicism which turn the process of events in determined and prophetic directions, as Marxism has done. But events contradict the efforts of historians, and of the leaders they often serve, to arrange the past in ordered ways in the hope of perceiving and being able to control the shape of the future. For history, in fact, can be concerned only with events as they have unfolded and continue to unfold; as prophecy, it is as useless as reading the livers of Roman animals or the collarbones of Chinese sheep.

Writers in the past have addressed this question, notably Karl Popper in *The Open Society and Its Enemies* (1945) and especially in *The Poverty of Historicism* (1957), to which I have been greatly indebted in my earlier encounters with Marxist determinism. I return to it here because recent events, building up astonishingly in 1989 and 1991, have reinforced the arguments of writers like Popper and have thrown into doubt the validity of any laws of history. I return also because these events, by releasing us from a fatalistic view of history and from a crippling sense of inexorable destiny, may also liberate us to shape the flow of process being directed by the dead hand of the past or the marshlights of futurism.

The confusion between narrative and events that occurs when we treat History (suitably capitalized) as if it were a determining force, or at least an inspired oracle, can be traced back to the beginnings of recorded history in those years between the eighth and sixth centuries B.C. when the myths that had supported the great tribal kings of the Mycenean period were given the permanence of writing, as were the chronicles of mundane events.

"Toutes les histoires anciennes . . . ," remarked Voltaire, "ne sont que des fables convenues," and it is true that the art of history (which the scholars of the Hellenistic period gave its own muse, Clio) was from the beginning a combination of chronicle and myth. In so far as it was created by the imagination to overcome the inveterate chaos of mere process, it was already, as it has remained, a kind of facilitating fiction; rarely a downright lie but equally rarely the statement of mere fact which recent "scientific" historians have so palpably failed to achieve. In this sense it is not entirely unjust that Herodotus, first of the major historians, should have been called the "father of lies," for he indeed sought those plausible fictions, constructed largely out of facts, which are necessary for the human mind to penetrate the sheer disorder of actual process and existence.

The earliest true historian, however, was not Herodotus but Hecataeus of Miletus, who flourished a generation earlier at the turn of the sixth and fifth centuries B.C. Hecataeus was a boy when the Persians under Cyrus the Great invaded the Greek world in 526 B.C., destroying the great Hellenophile kingdom which Croesus sustained in Lydia and subduing the Ionian and Dorian colonies along the shores of the Aegean. Unlike the other Ionian colonies, Miletus managed to make special terms with Cyrus, so that

14

for a time its philosophers and scholars continued their enquiries and speculations undisturbed, and Hecataeus worked among a group of proto-scientists—Thales, Anaximander, Anixemenes—who were busily trying to make up for the dissolution of the world of myth by inventing their own ordered and often fantastic cosmologies.

Sheltered though they might be from immediate Persian tyranny, the thinkers of Miletus could not fail to be conscious of the way in which the Persian invasion had altered their world. Their contemporary, Xenophanes of Colophon, gave expression to the prevalent sense of major change, of a society in dislocation, when he remarked in one of his poems:

> Thus should we talk around the fire in winter, with a strange guest among us, all bellies satisfied, sweet wine beside us, and filbert nuts to chew. Then we can ask: "Pray tell us, sir, your name? How old are you? How old were you when the Persians came?"

Xenophanes himself had fled rather than accept the tyranny of a culture so different from his own and survived into late old age as a wandering bard, reciting his philosophically inclined poems about the nature of God and the origin of fossils in the agoras and tyrants' palaces of the Greek cities scattered on all the shores of the Mediterranean. The great conflict that developed between Hellas and Persia, as the sixth century B.C. drew to a close and the Greeks won their astonishing victories at Marathon and Salamis, not only created the gulf between East and West, between Europe and Asia, that has never really been filled to this day. It also provided a splendid subject for a new narrative art to grow up on, and this is why history produced so early in its development one of its great classics, *The Persian Wars* of Herodotus.

History began to separate itself from the grand racial epics like the *Iliad*, the *Odyssey* and their lesser rivals in what were essentially the first attempts at chronicle. These were the local chronologies that tried to make sense out of the founding myths of communities (or at times to invent them) and the genealogies that sought to establish family or community lines of descent, preferably from gods or heroes. They show fact detaching itself from group fantasy, the recognizable beings of actual persons taking their places at the ends of lines stretching back into the archetypal mists.

In his own way Hecataeus embodied the ambivalence of this stage of proto-history, for there is a tale, which Herodotus repeats, of his humiliation as a self-proclaimed aristocrat by the priests of Egypt. Travelling there, he visited one of the great temples of Thebes and made his claim to the priests that his ancestor sixteen generations before had been a god. Thereupon the Egyptian priests showed him the great wooden statues which each high priest ordered to be made during his life and which were later preserved to commemorate the succession. There were 345 statues, representing more than twenty times the generations of human ancestry to which Hecataeus laid claim, and not a god among them.

Whether or not Hecataeus felt humbled by his encounter at Thebes—and he may have told the story against himself—he pursued his enquiries with the same kind of regard for the ascertainable truth that was the mark of his Milesian contemporaries, the pre-Socratic scientist-philosophers. He was much interested in the world of his own time, and indeed is perhaps best represented by his writings as a geographer, notably the *Periegesis*, or *Tours Round the World*, a survey of the known world, bounded (as so many Greeks thought) by the encircling River of Ocean. He travelled far himself and used as well the accounts of other contemporary travellers, like Skylax who ventured into India and centuries ahead of Alexander followed the Indus to the sea, and like the Phocean mariners who founded Marseilles and sailed beyond the Pillars of Hercules to the Atlantic coasts of Spain and Morocco. He also drew the most accurate maps then known of the ancient world, and in his painstaking accounts of the customs and characteristics of various cultures, he was one of the first writers to use the emergent form of prose, with its tendency to literal exactitude.

Neither of the known books of Hecataeus—the *Periegesis* and the *Genealogia* (or *Historia*)—survives in more than fragments, though it seems obvious that Herodotus knew and drew heavily on the full works. The *Periegesis* shows already the inclination towards the environmentalist interpretation of the development of national or racial characteristics that later Greek historians adopted, notably Herodotus in his explanations of the local characteristics of peoples and realms in the world of the Persian Wars. Hecataeus was already a practitioner of that process which the archaic Greeks who first followed it called *historia*, meaning "an inquiry." Developed originally by Thales and his successors among the pre-Socratic thinkers, it was really an early form of the inductive method, consisting of observing a phenomenon or problem, collecting whatever information on it could be accumulated, and reaching an explanation based on such data. The great travels that both Hecataeus and Herodotus undertook in order to understand their world qualified them as historians in the earliest sense of the term. This was the sense projected by Thucydides, perhaps the greatest of Greek historical writers, when he described his own attitude and method:

16

And with regard to the narrative of events, far from letting myself derive it from the first source that appeared, I refused to trust even my own impressions, and combined what I saw myself with what others said to me, the accuracy of the final conclusion being tested in the most severe way possible. All this cost me considerable labour because of the differing accounts of the same happening by various eye-witnesses, sometimes because of failing memory, sometimes from a lack of impartiality.

This—the painstaking and objective enquiry, the patient checking of facts—has remained one of the essential components of history as it has been written. Both the most factual of "scientific" historians and the most eloquent of "artist" historians, the sons and daughters of Clio, have set out to provide accurate and sufficient information in fields where it is available and—like Hecataeus and Herodotus already—enlightened conjecture where it is not. It is the larger framework within which such observations and conjectures are presented that gives history a more ambivalent and ambitious role.

Hecataeus, the distant predecessor, already introduces that other aspect of history. His *Periegesis* is an empirical compendium of facts about the known world gathered by him and his contemporaries on journeys motivated by trade and curiosity. It tries, judging from numerous surviving fragments, to get as near the literal truth about the behaviour of peoples and the nature of their environments as any modern ethnological treatise. Even the tall tales, including his classic tale—which Herodotus stole—of the strange life cycle of the phoenix, are part of the lore gathered by many men on journeys and are presented as something told the stranger rather than as proven fact. The two aims most evident in the *geographical* writing of Hecataeus are to base what he says as far as possible on first- or secondhand observations and experience, offering what does not come directly from such experience tentatively and critically.

If the *historical* writing of Hecataeus seems different from his geographies, the difference lies in the material rather than the approach. The material of geography is the world as it exists, here and now, just as the material of ethnology is the social life of people in their contemporary setting, and the authenticity of information is relatively easily established so long as the regions described are open to travellers. But the material of history, with which Hecataeus began to deal in his *Genealogia*, is a matter of the past, and is present either in the written record, which before

Hecataeus himself hardly existed, or in the oral tradition, carried in memory, which in a few generations becomes diffused into myth.

Despite the attempts of Jungian psychiatrists and of certain literary critics, notably Northrop Frye, to present myths as emanations from a collective unconscious which have little relation to the chain of events known as history, there is no doubt that, for the preliterate peoples who developed them, myths were history. Actual remembered events were incorporated into a structure dominated by primitive religious and cosmological concepts that were shaped by the changing and creating hand of memory. Even modern civilized people have done the same, for at least until the end of the Victorian era a majority of Christians took the book of Genesis, myth crystallized in writing, as an account of actual events to which Bishop Usher was bold enough to add a chronology. At the same time historians of this period relegated non-Christian myths to the world of folk poetry, as having little relation to what actually happened. Hecataeus took a different approach, whose wisdom many modern historians now recognize; he examined the myths without wholly rejecting them.

It is true that he opened the *Genealogia* by boldly declaring: "Thus speaks Hecataeus of Miletus: I write such things as seem to be true, for many and foolish—I believe—are the tales told by the Greeks." But he was not in fact so sweepingly critical as these remarks suggest. He maintained the Hellenic myths, which united Greeks everywhere, as a basis for history while seeking to find rational explanations for their more unlikely aspects. He believed that what Homer asserted contained the germs of true history and that, rather than rejecting the ancient tales outright as mere figments of the primitive imagination, readers should view them critically, seeking the core of fact in each of them. For many centuries, while historians regarded Homer's works as mere romantic invention, Hecataeus seemed discredited. But the finds of archaeology, from the maverick grocer-archaeologist Heinrich Schliemann at Troy and Mycenae onward, have shifted our view of prehistory in Greece to something much nearer to what the archaic Hellenes believed. We now know that the Trojan and Theban wars—or something resembling them—occurred. We know that the high king who ruled in Mycenae and whose golden mask now rests in a modern museum—whether or not he was called Agamemnon—was the *primus inter pares* among a cluster of Achaean chieftains very much like the heroes of the *Iliad*; and that the command of the Dardanelles was even then crucial to the politics of trade, since Greek merchants had already begun to penetrate the Black Sea and establish their colonies in a development that

18

had its own myth, perhaps even a pre-Homeric one, of the Golden Fleece and the Argonauts.

So Hecataeus takes his place as the first of the critical historians whose works we know, and it was evidently thus that Herodotus, for all his jesting asides, regarded him; on several occasions he paid him the compliment of extensive and not always recognized borrowing. Hecataeus parallelled the efforts of his fellow Milesians to find an ordered structure for the universe by seeking to give order to the unordered past, on the assumption that tradition and authority were subject to critical examination. The critical examination of myth and legend, which is now a respectable branch of history—and at times the only way we have of making sense of archaeological discoveries—began with him, for he was not seeking to establish a theogony like Hesiod but to discover the roots of human society by bringing the myths, the only history the Greeks had before his day, to the earth of probability. Rather than Herodotus, he was the true "father of history." Paradoxically, in investigating the myths, he helped ensure that they would become an element in history exploited by the men of power who were his contemporaries.

At this point we come to another dominant figure in the sixth century B.C. Hecataeus was important because he initiated the process of disentangling the fact of history from the poetry of myth. Pisistratos, the tyrant of Athens, was important for the way he helped to make history serve as a new kind of myth, so initiating a process of manipulating the past that would develop into the leading subject of this book.

By the beginning of the sixth century B.C. the ancient Hellenic monarchies of the Homeric era had vanished except—curiously transformed—in conservative Sparta and in one or two remote colonies like Cyrene. They had been replaced by oligarchic or fragilely democratic city republics, in which ancient social rivalries revived once the traditional patterns of authority were superseded. The tyrants who emerged from this situation were in some ways similar to the dictators of the left and the right who cast their shadows over world and particularly European events in the mid-twentieth century. Like them, they built their power on popular discontent, and Pisistratos, who was perhaps the most intelligent of them all, based his regime on an adroit combination of respect for the rights of commoners and glorification of the embryo nation-state of Athens.

There were two ways in which the glorification of Athens, and of Hellas generally, affected the development of history and historical views. One was the remythification of the Greek past, linked to the celebration of the

Olympian gods and the definition of epic values. The other, linked with the emergence of newer and more populist gods, was the use of drama not only to celebrate human—even if mythical—heroes but also the amazing triumphs of the Greeks in the ongoing history of their conflict with Persia.

Pisistratos maintained his tyranny with a skilled populist hand when he deliberately and extensively encouraged manifestations of the arts that, by involving all classes, would reflect not only the greatness but also the cohesion of Attic society. He arranged great publicly funded displays like the splendid civic processions that took place during the Panathenaic festivals, which he developed to celebrate the city he ruled and its wise tutelary deity, grey-eyed and owl-attended Athene, and he encouraged the myth of the Athenian hero Theseus, who broke the ancient power of Crete. However, we owe to Pisistratos, as by-products of his acts of civic glorification, not only the drama but also the Homeric poems as we read them today.

It was Pisistratos who gathered together the *rhapsodes* who recited the epics and transmitted them orally, and sat them down with scribes to commit the great poems to writing. For the Greeks, the *Iliad* was history, even if already the *Odyssey* seemed a fantastic story, and of course much that the epic of the Trojan war contained was fact, so that its writing down provided one of the bases from which historians could proceed critically. It also, incidentally, gave an early opportunity for the manipulation of history, for most scholars believe that the inclusion of Athens among the communities sending ships to Agamemnon's great fleet was actually an interpolation made when the epics were written down to legitimize the Athenian claim to a leading role in the Hellenic community.

The epics and the Panathenaic festivals related Athens to the grand Olympian mythology by which rulers generally legitimized themselves. But the populist strain in the rule of Pisistratos was manifested in the rise of mystery cults, like that of Demeter of Eleusis, which not only anticipated Christianity with its teachings of redemption but opened its ranks to people of all classes. It also found expression in the cult of the Thracian god Dionysus. And if Athene had her festivals, so did Dionysus, in the Greater Dionysia, which was first observed in 535 B.C. when Thespis wrote the earliest of the Greek tragedies and initiated the dramatic tradition. The stage was set for Aeschylus and his great successors; fifth-century Athenian drama flowered on a stem planted by the sixth-century tyrant, and in the great cycles of Orestes and Oedipus and the Theban kingdom, the myths of men and women in the grip of fate—the founding myths of Hellenic society—were offered to the populace.

20

Writing about human heroes rather than the gods, who were rarely more than peripheral characters in the Greek tragedies, the dramatists were moving through myth towards history. The process was encouraged by changes in Greek forms of government and warfare, as Athens moved from tyranny towards democracy, a democracy protected by its citizens—the small, well-trained groups of soldiers called *hoplites* and the small, well-sailed navies which gained victories that seemed miraculous against the vast but poorly co-ordinated levies of a Persian empire already in decay. Myths mingled with actual hard-to-believe events; men imagined they saw the heroes of legend, like Theseus, fighting beside them at Marathon, when it was their own courage and soldierly skill that won the day.

All who took part in those battles seemed touched with a special glory resembling that of the legendary heroes, and "man of Marathon" was a description of the survivor that amounted almost to a title. Aeschylus was typical of a whole generation as he composed the epitaph to be carved on his gravestone:

> Planted in the rich cornfields of Gela,
> This stone shelters the body of Aeschylus,
> Euphorion's son from Athens.
> The glorious ground of Marathon
> Can tell of his bravery;
> The long-haired Persians felt its edge.

Aeschylus not only took part physically in the making of history that became national myth; he and the other early Greek dramatists also undertook the task of making the grandeur of such history as well as the real ancestral myths available to the populace whose military deeds made it a power in city-states like Athens.

Almost from the start, alongside their heroic cycles, Athenian tragedians were observing historical events that were dramatic and contemporary, notably those following the most dramatic of ancient events, the Persian invasion. No play, so far as we know, was written about Marathon; the best ancient account remains that of Herodotus, who was not an Athenian though in his own way a Panhellenist. But two plays were written about the battle of Salamis, *The Phoenician Women* by Phrynichus and *The Persians* by Aeschylus.

Of the plays of Phrynichus, the older contemporary of Aeschylus, only brief fragments survive, but we are told his plays about contemporary incidents and issues generated powerful emotions among their audiences.

21

When the city of Miletus eventually turned against Persia and took part in the Ionian revolt of 499 B.C., the Persians, in revenge, sacked and destroyed the city. To this event Phrynichus devoted a famous tragedy, *The Capture of Miletus*, whose laments were so striking that audiences fell weeping uncontrollably. Yet far from praising and rewarding him for his eloquence, the Athenians fined Phrynichus and banned his play for "reminding them of a disaster that touched them so closely." It was their guilt he had stirred; after encouraging the discontent with Persian rule among Asian Greeks, Athens had withdrawn its support of the Ionian rebels and left them exposed to the vengeance of Darius, a less merciful King of Kings than Cyrus. Still, Phrynichus continued writing, and the victory of the allied Greeks over the fleet of Xerxes at Salamis stirred him to write *The Phoenician Women*, performed in 476 B.C. Four years later, in *The Persians*, his first surviving play, Aeschylus returned to the theme of Salamis, and though the text of Phrynichus has not survived for comparison, the direction of influence is evident; Aeschylus paid his predecessor the compliment of opening his own play with the first lines of *The Phoenician Women*.

Both playwrights worked with masterly indirection; in each case the action central to the play is presented by a messenger informing a lamenting chorus. It is also probable—judging from the example of *The Capture of Miletus*—that they resembled each other not only in stirring the pride of Greeks in their achievement but also, as Aeschylus certainly did, in arousing pity for the defeated. Describing the sea covered with wreckage and the slaughter as the Greeks killed the Persians and their allies like tunny fish all day long while the light lasted, Aeschylus was writing the first poetry of war. He wrote with triumph. But he also wrote with a sense of the pity of it all that is not in the *Iliad* or even in the *Odyssey*. And that pity showed the new consciousness of a common humanity which was emerging during the sixth century B.C. and colouring the work of the first historians as well as of the first dramatists.

In another direction, drama comes close to history in the immense masterpiece of Thucydides, *The Peloponnesian War*, written at the very end of the fifth century B.C. and completed some years after the dramatist Euripides appealed to the conscience of Athenians with his play of pity, *The Trojan Women*, which echoed the women plays of Phrynichus and Aeschylus. While the earlier playwrights were referring directly to the tragic aspects of a great contemporary battle which they named and may well have witnessed, Euripides drew myth further into history by using a war of the mythical past, when the Trojan women were said to have been deprived of

22

their menfolk and subjected to the whims of their conquerors, to refer to the wars of the present; for shortly before his play was produced, the Athenians had massacred the menfolk of Melos and enslaved the women because that Cycladean island republic wished to remain neutral in the great conflict between Athens and Sparta.

The massacre at Melos sent shudders of horror through the Greek world, just as the sacking of Miletus by the Persians had done, and much of that horror enters into Thucydides' pages. His history is essentially a dramatic document, concerned with the dynamics of conflict between adventurous Athens and conservative Sparta. The great leaders who inhabit it are almost theatrical characters, with their pathetic or tragic flaws, rather than heroic. A further dramatic element was introduced by the speeches Thucydides composed for their lips, anticipating in this way the dramatization of figures in English history by William Shakespeare.

But the most important element, which showed that even in its early centuries—the sixth and the fifth B.C.—the writing of history had gone beyond the mere primary purpose of extricating a credible chronicle from the myths and legends of the past, lay in the emergence of great historic themes uniting and directing the facts. One, as in the case of Herodotus, was the theme of the differences and the eventual conflict between the known European world and the fascinating and largely unknown world of the East: Persia and Scythia, the realms of the Nile and Euphrates valleys. Many of the Greeks regarded with an amused scepticism the world of wonders that Herodotus offered them. (Now we know how accurate he often was when he seemed most fanciful to his contemporaries.) But they were stirred by the vision of an epic struggle that he presented and also, despite themselves, by the extraordinary unity of the Persian empire as contrasted with the political disunity of the Hellenic world.

This theme of political disunity was of course greatly enlarged on by Thucydides in his account of the particular series of conflicts between leading city-states which showed the disunity in its most tragic aspects. It was hardly surprising that Persia, which the sixth-century Hellenes regarded with the enmity proper when facing ruthless barbarians (as Xenophanes showed in his poems) became transformed in the minds of many Greeks into a model for political organization by the late fifth and early fourth centuries B.C. Indeed, even in the early fifth century Herodotus had already shown himself full of admiration for the efficiency of communication and bureaucratic procedure with which the empire of Cyrus and Darius worked over vast distances and among widely differing peoples.

An even more interesting and perhaps in its own way more influential case was that of Xenophon. Xenophon wrote a history of the Hellenes that carried on for another fifty years (up to about 363 B.C.) after the point where Thucydides left off, and he was highly conscious of Greek cultural unity without denying the merits of other peoples. He had served as a mercenary officer in the internecine war when the rival Achaemenians, Cyrus the Younger and Artaxerxes, competed for the Persian throne. When Cyrus was defeated, Xenophon led ten thousand surviving Greeks on a great march across Asia Minor to the Hellenic colonies on the Black Sea and described the experience in that classic narrative, the *Anabasis*. He had been a disciple of Socrates, and the conservatism implied in that association and in his un-Athenian admiration for Sparta was reflected not only in his friendship with the younger Cyrus but also in his admiration for Cyrus the Great which led him to write the *Cyropaedia*, a eulogistic portrait of the Persian conqueror. It was a highly tendentious work that praised Cyrus for unifying the Iranians into a powerful nation and carried a message for the Greeks which was followed and understood by the semibarbarian rulers of Macedonia.

For Philip, and even more for Alexander, it became an inspirational text; from his youth onward Alexander studied the book (perhaps with the encouragement of his tutor, Aristotle) and took it with him when he set off to invert the achievements of Cyrus by conquering the Persian empire with a Hellenic army raised through the temporary union of mainland Greece and the Ionian and Dorian colonies of Asia Minor. Of course, Greek unity disintegrated after Alexander's death, and the Hellenic communities became fragments scattered in the empire of the Romans, a people who—like the Persians—had less fissiparous political traditions than the Hellenes.

But in terms of historiography, as distinct from history-as-what-happened, a pattern was established, and in this development a less familiar Greek writer than Herodotus, Thucydides and Xenophon may have been more influential than they. Isocrates was a rhetorician who established a school in Athens which rivalled Plato's Academy in its popularity. He was also a great writer of speeches, though he rarely spoke himself because of his shyness and his weak voice. But, as with many orally diffident men, he had the talent for expressing strong opinions strongly, and the orations he wrote for others declared in very emphatic terms his concern for the disunity within and between Greek city-states, and his sense of the need for a strong leader, views he shared with his fellow student of Socrates, Xenophon. The speeches were circulated as handwritten pamphlets and had their influence not only on public opinion in Athens but also on the Macedonian kings. In 338 B.C., shortly before Isocrates died at the age of ninety-eight, Philip asserted his power over mainland Hellas by defeating the Athenian and Boeotian levies at the battle of Chaeronea. (There is indeed a story that Isocrates starved himself to death on hearing the news of Chaeronea, in sorrow that the unification of the Greeks was not of their own seeking but had to be imposed on them from outside.)

Two years later, Philip died. Alexander succeeded him and, after consolidating his power over the Greek cities, crossed the Hellespont in 334 B.C. as the leader of a Greek and Macedonian army, reawakening the great rivalry of Europe and Asia, of which Herodotus and the dramatists had written, by reversing and avenging the Persian invasions of Europe. Although a non-Greek he had been given a kind of naturalization by acceptance at the Olympic Games. And there is no doubt that, in his vision of uniting the Greeks to redress the offence of the Persian invasion, Alexander felt himself sustained by the arguments of Isocrates as much as by the political hagiography of Xenophon, though he was also moved by that sense of destiny, of proceeding towards a divinely ordained goal, that is one of the parents of historicist thinking. The relationship between history as a written record and history as an attempt to order the flow of events was becoming complicated.

Isocrates cannot be regarded as an actual historian; his works were after all mainly polemical, speeches that were incidents in a political process. But as a rhetorician he did teach the writing of history, and all his efforts in this direction seem to have been aimed at establishing it as a literary art. In other words, he was one of the first to realize, without explicitly saying it, that no amount of strict adherence to the facts such as Thucydides advocated would alone make the chaos of existence comprehensible to the human mind. Form was for him the essence of history, as of any of the other arts presided over by the Muses. Among his pupils in rhetoric, apart from the Athenian general Timotheus, who made history in the sense of events, were the two most important Greek historians in the century after Thucydides and Xenophon: Ephorus was a universal historian and Theopompus wrote on the life and times of Philip of Macedonia. The writing of history had been proceeding from the beginning towards formalism and towards dominating literary structures. But it was in the fourth century B.C. that it assumed two of the characteristics that would lead to the glories and deceptions of historicism.

First, the proliferation of facts led inevitably, as it has done in every age when history has been valued, to rigorous selectivity and to the arrangement of the selected material into comprehensible shapes. The already developed major literary forms of epic and drama offered formal devices that could be applied to actual episodes just as easily as they had been to mythological or fictional ones, devices that encouraged the necessary process of extracting history from the primal magma of events.

One such device was characterization. The emergence of the individual as an idiosyncratic personality, a character rather than a type, hardly seems to predate the Homeric epics, though in the *Odyssey* it is strikingly developed in the character of the humanized hero, Odysseus. During the eighth century B.C. the idea of character had been filled out by Hesiod's extraordinary evocation of the rustic personality in *Works and Days*, and during the seventh century Archilochus in his poems completed the shift from heroic ideal personality to credible human personality with its weaknesses complete in those verses—remarkable for their time—on the life of a mercenary who mocks the formalized heroics of the epics by revealing his own cowardice and petty rascality.

The dramatists and the historians alike drew on this recognition of the individuality and infinite variability of human beings to construct characters largely according to the rhetorical requirements of their time. After establishing their historical actors, they sought—as the novelists many centuries afterwards were to do—the element of plot, the selection and arrangement of fact and incident in such a way that a comprehensible pattern emerges. This necessity has borne down on historians ever since and has frustrated all the efforts of "scientific" historians, as of realist novelists, to offer life "as it was." For no more than the novel or the play is history an "authentic slice of life"; it is an imaginative reconstruction of events that is more comprehensible and has clearer verisimilitude than any conceivable literal narrative could have.

Finally, transferring from drama the element of character and from epic poetry the element of plot, the early historians added the didactic element of theme. History, as even the highly entertaining Herodotus seems to insist, is not written merely to interest us or divert us with exotica, or even to instruct us regarding our proper place in the world. It subjects the condition of humanity—that chaos of unrestrained particularity—to the generalizing process, which may also lead to lessons about the past that will result in instructions in shaping the present, so that it is conceivable we may actually "make history." (Though Herodotus might have been one of those to agree with the maxim that "The one lesson of history is that nobody learns from history.") Seeing their own lives being patterned by birth and maturity and death, observing the cycles of the seasons, watching the recurring phenomena of the heavens, even recognizing the periodic manifestations of lunar time in the sky and the tides and in women's wombs, people are also liable to see the mainly human-created events of history in some way linked in an ordered sequence. And particularly people try through history to detect in events the great tendencies of their times and to adapt their individual and collective lives to those tendencies. The need for prophecy dies hard, and the historian tends to become, whether willing it or not, the haruspex even in a rational age, isolating the major trends, the major anxieties, the major symbolic issues of an age, and if necessary inventing them. And here of course is another contributing factor to the eventual rise of historicism with its promises and what Marx so fraudulently claimed were its "scientific" discoveries.

CHAPTER III

Plato: History and the Utopian Vision

From the beginning, the Greek historians—their minds concentrated on the Persian invasion of Hellas—were sketching out, consciously more than subconsciously, two main and complementary themes. First, the deep and perhaps irreconcilable rift between Asia and Europe, East and West, which Cyrus's irruption had made manifest and which Alexander's expedition failed to mend. And second, the extraordinary fact that while the Persian "barbarians" had developed an imperial political system that seemed able to overcome many cultural differences, the Greeks, possessing an essential cultural unity—of language, of religion, of myth, of democratic evolution—had been entirely unable to unite or confederate for any length of time even in the interests of their own peace and security.

At this point the study of past history inevitably drew close to the necessities of contemporary politics, which had been shaping themselves for some time into a polarity of democracy and autocracy, represented by the tyrants and the rhetoricians who served them, as Plato served the unworthy Dionysius of Syracuse. The discovery that history could offer a plausible and convenient explanation of past and present and thus at least the hint of a lesson for the future, lent itself—like all historicist inclinations—to vulgarization and to the conclusion that history could be a tool to a political end. We have already noted the possibilities for political propaganda that were developed through the recension of the Homeric epics under the patronage of Pisistratos in Athens and in the building up of the drama as a means of glorifying that city, as the historical play was built up in England to glorify Tudor rule.

In the case of Herodotus, that native of outlying Halicarnassus who spent most of his life wandering in the Persian Empire, there is no evident political partisanship, no consistent axe being ground, though the picture of the great rivalry between Hellas and teeming Persia is constantly built up. Thucydides, considering the fact that he was dismissed from his generalship and lived twenty years in exile from Athens, wrote with a remarkable lack of grievance or partisanship or undue local patriotism. Yet, implicitly, his history is as much a criticism of inter-Hellenic war as was *The Trojan Women* of Euripides.

The didactic intent, which Thucydides does hardly more than sketch out, becomes much stronger in both Isocrates and Xenophon. Isocrates set out to subject history to the formalities of an art, and in such a way he prepared it as an instrument for the didactic and even polemical purposes of the Macedonian kings. Xenophon, with his open conservatism and his admiration for strong leaders, made history the instrument of a view of personal and social existence very close to that of his authoritarian and utopian contemporary and fellow student of Socrates, Plato.

And here perhaps, in a writer not generally thought of as a historian, is the first manifestation of true historicism, the creation of a utopian vision as a goal for human aspirations. Of the same group of patrician students of philosophy as Xenophon and Isocrates, and the greatest of all the sanctifiers of the old reactionary, Socrates, Plato saw no hope in democracy, Athenian or other, and at a time when tyranny was declining as a favoured institution among the Greeks, he still put his faith—as Isocrates did—in the enlightened ruler.

This involved him in what at the time seemed a splendid opportunity to try out his ideas of political organization. Dionysius I, the violent and powerful tyrant of Syracuse, died in 367 B.C., having given tyranny the bad name it has ever since endured. His son, Dionysius II, was a spoilt and corrupt young man, but the powerful Dion, who eventually deposed him, was an admirer of Plato. Dion tempted the philosopher over to Sicily in the hope that between them they could turn the new tyrant into an enlightened ruler, a philosopher-king. For a time Dionysius seemed an apt pupil, but he quickly lapsed into his old ways, and Plato's second visit to Syracuse brought no improvement. It may well have been the greatest disappointment in the philosopher's life except for the judicial murder of Socrates by men who—rightly or wrongly—disagreed with him.

Whether the *Republic* was written before or after the misadventure in Sicily is uncertain, but the confidence with which Socrates (Plato) advances his arguments in the great authoritarian dialogue suggests a man not yet disillusioned by experience. It is likelier that his more pragmatic and cautious later dialogues followed his return from Syracuse to Athens, dialogues like the *Politicus* with its discussion of the attributes of a successful statesman, and the *Laws*, which is a very practical discussion of how best to run an ordinary Greek *polis* in a better way than most. By this time he had been conducting at the Academy his courses in jurisprudence, and it seems evident that the day-to-day practicality of these studies and the disillusionment of the Sicilian experience led to the rather mundane practicality of these later political dialogues.

Overtly, the *Republic* has nothing to do with history, for what Socrates offers to his friends is a hypothetical structure, an ideal and therefore timeless and ahistorical community. It is in one sense an abstract discussion of the potentialities of the state (still an undeveloped concept in fourth-century B.C. Athens) and of the nature of a just society, given a touch of other-worldliness by the way in which Plato interweaves with some highly practical thoughts on social problems his theory of Forms or Ideas, the archetypes he presents as the only true realities in a world of ever-changing actuality. But in the other sense it is the demonstration of how an ideal society might work, operated by regenerated tyrants perhaps, but also more just than democracy has yet worked out to be. Here it offers the image of a utopia, a perfect patriarchal society in which change has come to an end and men and women still live together in a condition of perpetual controlled happiness.

Ever since Plato, the history of political thought has been scattered with utopian visions, offering patterns of life varying from the appallingly regulated uniformities of Sir Thomas More's *Utopia* and George Orwell's *Nineteen Eighty-four* to the genially eccentric ties of Charles Fourier's Phalansterian world (where water will be turned to lemonade if not to wine and the lamb will literally lie down with the lion) to the amiable artiness of William Morris's *News from Nowhere*. These were the speculative utopias, diabolical or innocent visions of worlds where change had ended and a kind of eternity had settled down. The key phrase for all of them is "for ever," most sensationally pronounced in O'Brien's remark to Winston Smith in *Nineteen Eighty-four*. "Imagine a boot stamping on a human face, for ever." In utopias of this kind, history has come to a stop, time has ended, and a kind of eternity, as in T. F. Powys's *Mr. Weston's Good Wine*, has at last begun.

Plato's *Republic*, like More's *Utopia*, remains ideal in the sense that it was never intended as more than a speculative model. Neither of the creators of these models envisaged a historical process by which their utopias would be attained in the world of time and the ideal be manifested in the quotidian sphere. No Platonists and no readers of Sir Thomas More set out to give the *Republic* or *Utopia* physical shape, as the disciples of Etienne Cabet did in the early nineteenth century when several hundred of them went with their master to realize his vision of Icaria in the American Mid-West.

Cabet had his predecessors. In the same century as that in which Thomas More lived so quietly and so dramatically died, Tomasso Campanella actually plotted an uprising in Calabria against the Spanish overlords with the intention of establishing the utopian and communist state which he later—in prison—outlined in *The City of the Sun*. Even earlier, in 1534, the year before More died, John of Leyden and his Anabaptist followers had established in Münster their "thousand-year reich" (it lasted only one year, even less long than Hitler's later imitation); with a great deal of zealous brutality, they set out to turn the city into an ideal Christian commonwealth ready for the millennial reign of Christ.

The change that had happened in the time between Plato and the Reformation period nearly two thousand years later and that led men to give concrete actuality to the Ideal was the emergence of radical millenarianism, first religious and then political, in which lay the beginnings of the historicist concept of a necessary series of events leading towards a predictable and of course desirable destination for humanity and its world.

To understand fully the development of historicist thinking between the archaic Greeks and the nineteenth century, we have to return to the relationship between Asia and Europe that so preoccupied the Hellenes of the sixth and fifth centuries B.C. For, though militarily defeated and unable to extend its political rule over Europe (except for the Balkans in the Ottoman era and southern Spain when the Berber kings ruled so splendidly over Granada and Seville and Cordoba), Asia came nevertheless to exercise an immense philosophic influence over the West through the Judaic and Christian religions with their heritages from more ancient creeds, notably those of Persia. And we can perhaps pick up our first clues to this change by turning back to that enigmatic man, Pythagoras, who in some degree was Plato's master.

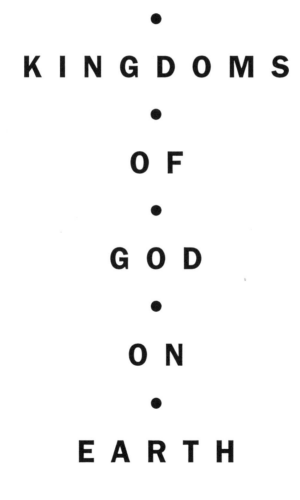

PART III

· KINGDOMS

· OF

· GOD

· ON

· EARTH

CHAPTER IV

Passage from Asia

Not very much is known about Pythagoras except that he was born in Samos in the sixth century B.C. and probably gained his preoccupation with mathematical proportions through contact with the architects and ingenious engineers—notably Theodorus—whom Polycrates, the ruler of the island, gathered around him. He seems to have fallen into the ill graces of the tyrant and found his way into exile at Croton in the heel of south Italy, then a notable centre of medicine and of experimentation in the nascent physical sciences.

For school children, Pythagoras is a name in elementary geometry, and his monochord is one of the basic primitive instruments in determining the numerical qualities of sound. Indeed, he tried to describe all the workings of the universe in numerical patterns, but it is for other reasons that he is important here.

Partly it is because he achieved before Plato what Plato only talked about, the creation of a community in which men would live by philosophic laws, and thus was perhaps the first of the practical utopians. His highly secretive community at Croton actually set out to give lessons in the contemplative rather than the social life, but it was not successful in terms of survival; the people of the city seem to have found the self-righteousness of the Pythagoreans beyond endurance, for they rioted against them, killing many and sending Pythagoras to a final exile in Metapontum, where he is said—like an Indian sage—to have starved himself to death.

It was not only in his death that Pythagoras resembled the philosophers of Asia, and here lies his interest in the present context, for he represented in a striking way the side of the Greek archaic consciousness that was drawn towards Asia while rejecting the political domination of Asian rulers.

At no time was there ever a sealed barrier between the Greek world and the Asian world. The alphabet, which the Phoenicians invented and put to such unimaginative commercial use, was developed by the Greeks into a vehicle for splendid poetry and noble thought; and the Lydian invention of coinage provided the basis for the vast network of Greek commerce that was established so firmly in the archaic age. Thales, the great Greek ur-scientist, seems to have been of partly Phoenician descent, and there are possibilities that he had links with Babylon; he certainly learnt a great deal from the Phoenician mariners' lore of the stars, while his conception of the shape of the universe strongly resembled that of the Babylonian priest-sages. Hecataeus went to Egypt if no farther. The brother of Sappho was a wine merchant in Naucratis, and the brother of her fellow poet of Lesbos, Alcaeus, claimed to have served as a mercenary for the ruler of Babylon and to have killed in his service a giant eight feet tall. Many Greeks served as mercenaries for the Saite kings of Egypt and also, like Xenophon, for Persian rulers, and the splendid relief carvings at Persepolis were mostly executed by Ionian sculptors. Herodotus extended his travels beyond Egypt to Babylon and the Iranian plateau, and also across the Black Sea into Scythia; other enquiring Greeks proceeded to the Urals and beyond, and brought back shamanic teachings and practices. Democritus, who with Leucippus developed atomic theory for the first time in the West, is said to have got as far as India, where a century before the sages of the Ganges valley—contemporaries of the Buddha—had developed their own concept of the atom as the basic unit of the physical world.

Pythagoras also is said to have made the journey to India, and whether or not he did reach that country, he seems to have been aware of many aspects of Indian religion. Notably, he developed a theory of reincarnation and metempsychosis strikingly similar to that sustained by contemporary Brahmin thinkers. He taught that the soul could not only live many lives but also that it could inhabit animal bodies and even more unlikely vehicles. One of the most curious rules of his community at Croton forbade the eating of beans, not because they induced flatulence but because, according to Pythagorean theory, a soul which had not chosen a permanent vehicle for its next existence might take temporary refuge in a bean. But though Pythagoras created a kind of historicism of the soul, by stressing its necessary continuity as a fragment or facet of the divine soul, he does not seem to have in any way developed a theory of collective necessity, of the life of humankind as a whole continuing in certain defined directions.

In bringing Pythagoras forward, therefore, I am not suggesting that he had a direct influence on European historical thinking, though the cyclical implications of his reincarnation theories are worth noting for their relation to Indian cosmology. But he is an example of the way in which the Greeks, eager to resist the military or political dominance of Oriental barbarians, were nevertheless willing to accept the influence of Asian religious concepts, which eventually would profoundly change European thought and create the tradition of determinist historicism.

Individual philosophers and thaumaturges may or may not have reached India and penetrated to the shamans east of the Urals, but the movements that gave Asian religions their transformatory powers over classical Western cultures, and even their concepts of history, operated on the level of popular faith. The Olympian religion of the ancient Greeks, far from being an exclusive creed as those of the Book later became, had something of the absorptiveness of the Hindu religion that was developing at this period from simple Vedic beginnings. Indeed, the original Vedic pantheon was so similar to that of Homer's warriors that the gods and goddesses can be ticked off in pairs. Always, in Greece as in India, there seems to have been an under-layer of localized plebeian belief, derived from earlier inhabitants, in the chthonian deities of earth, in the Furies, in the nymphs that guarded particular places, and in local nature deities like Pan. In India they came from the conquered Dravidians and lesser tribal peoples, and in Greece largely from the barbarian borderlands.

Like Hindu mythology, that of the Greeks was constantly absorbing new deities: Aphrodite was originally a Cyprian goddess, clearly related to the Semitic Astarte, and Dionysus, like Orpheus whose cult was closely related to his, originated in Thrace. Pan was the god of shepherds in the remote and primitive pastoral region of Arcadia, whose name has ever since seemed synonymous with bucolic distance and contentment.

None of these gods meant much to Homer and his patrician audiences, as he described the way in which the older gods and goddesses interfered in the battles their heroes conducted, and the few mentions he makes of them may have been added at the time of the Athenian recension of the epics, by which time there were strong cults of both Aphrodite and Dionysus, while the rural deities like Pan and Ceres had come out of the fields to take their places, particularly in the plebeian mystery cults.

The mystery cults were devotional rather than propitiatory; instead of seeing the gods as aloof and majestic presences in their sanctuaries, they encouraged a sense of congregational participation among their initiates in which, ritually at least, the gods took part. They were religions of hope through spiritual transformation, and they offered a beyond-death condition very different from the grey Hades of which the spirits of the dead complained to Odysseus when he called them to his pool of blood. For the poor and oppressed, the mystery religions offered surcease from their bitter lot. They gave them a future, and in this sense they introduced in its first nebulous form the concept of progress as well as that of freedom, even if neither took an earthly form.

From the fourth century B.C. onward, Asian countries began to be incorporated into European empires, first that of Alexander and then that of the Romans. Alexander reached India and then retreated, and the Romans never did make their way over the Hindu Kush, though after the death of Cleopatra the Greek trade down the Red Sea to India continued, and Buddhists were known in Alexandria. But the great area now known as the Middle East, from Iran to Egypt, lay under European control or in constant contact with Europeans until the last of the Caesars vacated Constantinople in the fourteenth century. Not merely were gods adopted but also whole cults, like that of Isis which became popular in Rome round about the end of the republic, and the Persian cult of Mithras which spread so widely among the Roman legions.

At one time, during the last generations of paganism, it seemed indeed that Mithraism might become more popular than the other cult of Christianity, which a number of Jews were actively propagating as a radical and proselytory variant of their own religion. But Christianity, through Judaism, had itself absorbed the essential dynamic of Persian religion and would transmit it in good time to the writers of history.

By the time the Greeks in the archaic period were creating a new relation between myth and history, as well as developing the political aspects of chronicle writing, their Asian congeners, the Iranians and the Aryan warriors and their priests who had conquered the Dravidians of the old Indus civilization and eventually those of southern India, were already mingling history with cosmology and seeing it in the vast cyclic or sequential patterns on which Western historians would eventually seize.

Iranian philosophers and teachers inclined to a strongly linear and progressive concept of the religious destiny of humankind as presented in myth and history. It was an active and dynamic concept, based on a dominant dialectic of choice and struggle. The Brahmins of India, perhaps drawing on a pre-existent pool of Dravidian wisdom, developed a more passive concept of history and human involvement. By a complex series of legends, in which the dreams of Vishnu and his symbolic stirring of the sea of milk played their bizarre parts, history was presented as cyclic and the human as its helpless creature. The life of the universe revolved in vast time wheels or *kalpas*, each of them more than four thousand million years, in which the world would be destroyed and reabsorbed into Brahma, the divine being, and emanate in a new creation; the cycles were virtually repetitive and conveniently long enough for it to be impossible to check them against events. Within them, human beings—and indeed all beings—lived in their own karmic circles of repetition, from which release was possible by extreme spiritual discipline, but rarely.

From Giambattista Vico in the early eighteenth century, many Western historians began to respond to these beliefs as they were opened up to Europeans through the scholar-merchants of the various East India trading enterprises. Most strikingly developed by Friedrich Nietzsche with his doctrine of everlasting return, and by Oswald Spengler and Arnold Toynbee in their splendid visions of the life cycles of civilizations and cultures, the cyclic theories which Europeans devised represented an aesthetically attractive way of arranging the rough shapes of actual history. Spengler's *The Decline of the West* and Toynbee's *A Study of History* are immensely appealing books which have greatly influenced artists and writers through the striking patterns they offer, and they have stirred the imaginations of those who seek evidence of the collective identities of nations. What they present is a circular rather than a linear pattern of history, history as form within chronology rather than history as duration.

For many Western minds, such cyclic histories, however formally attractive, have lacked the kind of logic that sees a straight line (*pace* Einstein) as the shortest way between two points. Yet they have appealed at times to totalitarians who think in terms of going back to the past and re-enacting it. Even radical thought, with its traces of millenarianism, tended often towards cyclic thinking. Both the authoritarian Karl Marx and the libertarian Peter Kropotkin, though their vision was predominantly linear, directed towards a future utopia, tended to loop back in their thought to the golden ages of primitive tribesmen and mediaeval guilds, and partly at least based their visions of the future on past models (they had after all no other models); and the socialist poet William Morris's *News from Nowhere*, with its deep nostalgia for the mediaeval world, was a strange example of regressive thinking in a movement whose open aims were progressive.

Cyclical history-making will not occupy us greatly in this book, except as an example of the less influential trend in historical determinism. Nevertheless, the distinction between linear and cyclical determinism is not so clear as might be imagined, for all linear vision ends beyond history in the stasis of a perfect order. We should not ignore the implications of Adolf Hitler's concept of the "thousand-year reich" (borrowed from Reformation millenarians) or of Benito Mussolini's attempt to recreate the imagery and ideals of imperial Rome in a twentieth-century world. The recurrence of millenarian visions, in evangelical religion and evangelical politics alike, has always varied the generally progressivist direction of determinist historicism; a kind of millennium in the form of a utopia, heavenly or earthly, lies at the end of every future imagined by historians, whose real task is of course to give order to our knowledge of the past and our intuitions about the present.

The deepest and most lasting lessons learnt by Western historians from the wisdom of Asia came from the Iranian rather than the Indian tradition. Like so much in history considered as the actual sequence of events, this came about quite accidentally through the dramatic conjunction of the Babylonian captivity of the Jews with the acceptance by the Achaemenian rulers in the tiny realm of Persis of the teachings of the Bactrian magus, Zoroaster.

Zoroaster gave to pre-Islamic Iranian culture a religion that, in its teachings as well as in its actions, was strongly activist in comparison with the quietism that permeated the other religions then (and ever since) dominant in Asia. It was a doctrine admirably suited to the forcefulness and vitality of the Achaemenian empire as its armies swept in the sixth century B.C. over western Asia and into Africa, overwhelming the ancient empires of Babylon and Egypt.

Little is known about Zoroaster, and there have been long disputes even over his dates. Some historians have actually placed him in the middle of the second millennium B.C. But a teaching that had shaken itself so notably away from mythological trappings could hardly have appeared so early, long before the Homeric epics and the Hindu Upanishads. There are good reasons for accepting a much later date, not least of them the fact that the traditions of the Parsees in India, which preserve an unbroken continuity from the Achaemenian age, declare that he lived between 660 and 583 B.C., the period when the great Iranian cosmological poem, the *Zend Avesta*, was rendered into its final form.

Zoroaster's name has also been associated with that of Vishtaspa, the early sixth-century ruler of a small Bactrian kingdom that was eventually absorbed into the empire of Darius; this would fit him into the pattern suggested by the Parsee tradition. The fact that Zoroaster is said to have originated in eastern Iran and to have done much of his preaching in what is now Afghanistan makes this identification all the more plausible. A final reason for accepting the end of the seventh and the beginning of the sixth century B.C. as the time when Zoroaster was most probably active is that his thought reveals an intellectual daring, a desire to present a rationally acceptable view of the universe and its processes that fits well with the spirit of that time. He was clearly in the same company as the pre-Socratic philosophers of Ionia and the heretical teachers among whom Buddha and Mahavira appeared in the Ganges valley. Like them, he tried to impose the acquired disciplines of human thought on the actual chaos of existence.

Yet, also like those philosophers, Zoroaster emerged out of his own social tradition, and if they were reacting against an unquestioning acceptance of the ancient Greek theogonies and against the Vedic teachings of the Brahmins, he in his turn appears to have been intent on changing the traditional religion of the Iranians. This was associated with the Magi, an order of priests in origin similar to the Brahmins. The original gods of the Magi, which became the official deities of Iranian rulers, were personifications of natural forces very similar to the gods of sun and sky and earth that dominated the Vedic pantheon. The links between the religion of the Magi and that of the Vedas are shown most clearly by the importance both of them attached to the cult of fire, which, when he devised an almost monotheistic religion, Zoroaster still retained for its ceremonial and symbolic value.

The two elements of Zoroastrianism that made it so influential in later times were its virtual monotheism and a paradoxical dualism which saw cosmic process in terms of a dialectical struggle between the powers of good and evil that must eventually end in the victory of Ahura Mazda, the principle of good, over Ahriman, the principle of evil and the true ancestor of the Satan of the peoples of the Book; to use more Zoroastrian terms, the victory of truth over the lie. In this vision the eschatological principle, the doctrine of an ineluctable progression towards "the last things," enters into religious thinking and into our view of the process of history, for the struggle was seen by Zoroaster as ending in a final battle and a cosmic conflagration in which the lord of darkness, the prince of lies, would ultimately be defeated. Light would triumph, the process of history would end, and the kingdom of Ahura Mazda, of truth and goodness, would continue unchanged forever. In that struggle each individual must make a free choice between the god of truth and the god of lies.

Described in this way, the teaching of Zoroaster seems to leap the ages, for there appears no doubt that the process by which Yahweh was changed in the eyes of the Jews from an exclusive and jealous tribal deity into a universal One God began at the end of the Babylonian captivity when they came into dramatic contact with their Persian liberators. At the same time, the imaginative and highly original model which Zoroaster developed became the pattern not only for the Judaic but also for the Christian and the Islamic visions of the destination of world history, terminating in the last of the great eschatologies, that of Marx, with its dialectical progression towards earthly paradise or utopia, where all struggle ends and all progress withers away. Thus it was from imperial Iran that emerged the concepts which would largely mould the world of the West over twenty-five centuries and distinguish its dynamic ways of thought, with their manifestations in progressive action, from the cyclic, unprogressive and destinationless concepts of cosmic change and human destiny that survived in the farther east of India and China.

The basic ideas that Zoroaster incorporated into his vision were not entirely unknown to Greek thinkers. Xenophanes presented a vision of the One God even more uncompromisingly monotheistic than that of Zoroaster, while both Anaximander and Heraclitus saw the interaction of opposing forces or elements as essential to the cosmic process. The fact that the Ionian historian Xanthus and some of his contemporaries spoke of Zoroaster early in the fifth century leaves little room to doubt that the Greeks who stayed in the Aegean cities after the fall of Lydia in 546 B.C. learnt from their conquerors the basic elements of Zoroastrianism, and it is tempting to think that the imagination of Heraclitus was stirred by the Iranian cult of fire when he made that element dominant in his vision of cosmic progress. But none of the pre-Socratic Greek philosophers developed anything resembling the vision that Zoroaster offered, of a progression terminating in conflagratory end of the world of change and the triumph of the principles of good and light. Among the legends of the Pythagoreans was a tale that their master discoursed with Zoroaster in Babylon, but there is nothing in what we know of Pythagorean beliefs that resembles the major teaching of the Persian magus.

Meanwhile, the Jews, descendants of a group of wandering pastoral tribes, probably very similar to the Bedouins, who had conquered the rich lands of Canaan and settled there, came to a crucial point in their history as a people. Backing, with almost fatal consistency, the wrong sides in the endemic wars between the great pre-Persian powers of the Middle East— Assyria, Egypt and eventually Babylon—the heirs of Solomon failed to sustain his kingdom. It split apart into Israel and Judaea, and the ten tribes of Israel vanished from history when the Assyrians in 772 B.C. dispersed them so efficiently that, ever since, eccentric and usually reactionary visionaries like the British Israelites have been trying to trace and identify their descendants. The minority kingdom of Judaea, centred on Jerusalem and consisting of the two tribes of Judah and Benjamin, survived the Assyrian assault. But a century and a half later, despite the loud exclamations of Jeremiah—sound political warning in the shape of religious prophecy—the rulers of Judaea dabbled in local political battles by supporting the Egyptians. Babylon was the winning power, and Nebuchadnezzar laid siege to Jerusalem; in 587 B.C. the city was captured and its fortifications and the great temple of Solomon were destroyed. In the next year many, though not all, of the Jews were taken into captivity in Babylon, where they and their descendants remained until Cyrus captured the city in 539 B.C. and made it a Persian satrapy.

On the whole, compared with the lot of modern political prisoners, that of the Jews beside the Waters of Babylon seems to have been relatively easy. When the captivity was ended, many Jews preferred the prosperity of Babylon to the austerity of their own arid land and stayed to establish a long-lasting community beside the Euphrates that finally disintegrated in recent years after the seizure of power in Iraq by Saddam Hussein. For all these Jews in Babylon, the captivity was a period of intense return to the fundamentals of their religion, of re-examining it in the light of the alien Babylonian and Iranian creeds with which they came into close contact, and reshaping it into the Judaism we know today, the creed that fathered Christianity and Islam.

In Babylon, the scattered writings of the Jews were edited, rewritten in so-called Classical Hebrew, which developed at this period, and assembled into something very like the Old Testament of the Christian Bible. The Psalms and the Pentateuch (Greek for the basic five books of the Old Testament) were given their definitive form, and the historical books of Kings and Chronicles were either revised or rewritten. The dominant tendency among these editors—as assiduous as they were pious—was in keeping with the spirit of the sixth century everywhere, the rejection of polytheistic myth in favour of the more rational concept of a single creating and sustaining First Cause or Deity.

Some of these changes had been foreshadowed, particularly in the statements of the prophets, during those years of self-searching which the Judaeans underwent between the annihilation of Israel by the Assyrians and their own defeat and captivity. During that period the remnants of the pagan cults that had still flourished during the reigns of Solomon and his successors were finally eliminated, and Judaism emerged from the Babylonian captivity as a monotheistic religion. Yahweh, the tribal deity, had been progressively transformed into the Jehovah we know, the one and universal creator and ruler of the universe. But if polytheism vanished, the powerful dualism of the Zoroastrians cast its shadow over the changing religion of the Jews, and Satan grew in stature as a principle of evil, so that, even in the successor religions of Islam and Christianity, God would continue to have his challenger until the last days of Armageddon, a challenger who would even become the hero of religious epics, as in John Milton's *Paradise Lost.*

At this period too the sense of a group destiny, which would become so important a component of historicist thinking, began to emerge, and the early conception of Yahweh as a tribal god was reinforced by the idea of Jehovah as a universal god who had picked the Jews as his own people. Out of this would come the most negative of all the tendencies among the religions of the Book, to divide the world between the faithful and the infidel, the chosen and the rejected, which was yet another version of the great irreconcilable struggle between Ahura Mazda and Ahriman, the truth and the lie.

Combined with the growing sense such notions projected of opposing spiritual forces—which would reach its apogee among the gnostics of the early Christian era and their successors among the mediaeval heresies, like Catharism and Bogomilism—ran a fragile but constantly renewed vision of the world moving towards a better future, whether here and now or in some superior future state. The early Jews seem to have had as grey and indistinct a view of life after death as the ancient Greeks did before the mystery cults began to develop, and the word "paradise" was first borrowed from the Persians (for whom it meant a great royal pleasure park) to describe Eden, the lost world of innocent happiness. Only later—perhaps around the time of Christ, who told the thief, "Tomorrow shalt thou be with me in Paradise"—would it be adapted to describe Heaven, the home of the virtuous dead and the destination of churchly eschatologies, though the idea of an "earthly Paradise," a replica of Eden inhabited by living people and somewhere far off in place or time, lingered through the Middle Ages to be taken up by the millenarian heresies and via the Reformation to become incorporated in the secular myths that end in utopia.

Even before the Babylonian captivity and certainly during that period, Jewish thinkers were already developing two ideas that would be important in later eschatological and also historicist attitudes. Jeremiah, a man much aware of the political realities of his time and endowed with a degree of historical feeling, began to talk of a "new convenant" between God and man, in which the links would become direct rather than mediated through priesthood, a notion that parallelled the abandonment—shortly afterwards during the Babylonian captivity—of a religion controlled by priests in temples, for a religion of scattered congregations in synagogues. This was but one manifestation of the tendency to elevate man as an agent in the great struggle between good and evil that began to take new forms as it emerged into the major Semitic religions, Judaism and its successors.

Zoroaster had stressed man's power as a free agent when he exhorted him (we are talking of a very male and paternalistic view of reality) to make his voluntary choice on the side of the great light-bearer Ahura Mazda, in the struggle against the powers of darkness. And though Jeremiah emphasizes that Jehovah is not just a better god, as the earlier Jews thought, but the only god, nevertheless man's submission to him must be freely willed. And the combination of submission and the sense of freedom is a paradoxical situation in all eschatological movements, whether religious or political. We must will the future, for the convergence of many wills is part of its inevitability, but we must also obey the force—the direction of destiny and eventually history—that the combination of our wills creates. This development of a will to choose, and the subsequent abdication of that will after the crucial choice is made, is part of every conscious eschatological movement from the Essenes down to the Communist party as organized by Lenin.

From this point, of man assuming the responsibility of a conscious choice, even if it implies the choice of not choosing, emerges one of the most constant elements in eschatological movements, in the millenarian cults that spring from them, in the historicist beliefs that arise when messianism is turned to political ends, and in the totalitarian parties that devote themselves to applying in practice the visions of progress towards an ideal future. That is the concept of the man who, in amassing and directing power and changing the world by his conquests, approaches deity and personifies history.

Here is a profound shift in the nature of the relationships between myth and actuality. The typical case is that of Heracles, whose legend is generally supposed to have originated in the feats of an actual Dorian chieftain who flourished even before the Homeric wars and from whom many of the dynasties of the Peloponnesus claimed descent. The Heraclides remained men; their ancestor was accepted—at least by the mythmakers—into the hierarchy of Olympus, where, like Dionysus, he remained always an outsider.

But the shift had been made. The gods were no longer remote celestial beings or nature spirits. Man could aspire to divine status, and dynasties able to trace their genealogies from gods were held to have special access to conquest and power, though of course the process worked two ways, and conquest and power could just as often lead to deification. Following on the mythical Heracles, this happened to the historical Alexander, who took on the persona of the Egyptian god Ammon. His successors also assumed the divine role, in the case of the Ptolemies by taking over the sacerdotal role of the Egyptian pharaohs. Some of the monarchs of the Hellenistic successor dynasties assumed the title of Soter, or saviour, and there is a challenging parallel here with the appearance of the Saviour concept in Judaism and—much developed—in Christianity; and also with the emergence, among the Mahayanist Buddhists of the early Christian era, of the concept of the Bodhisattva, the enlightened being who sacrifices nirvana—release from the wheel of life—to work for the release of all other living beings. The Bodhisattva was never seen as divine, because in Buddhism the gods also were seen as prisoners on the wheel of existence; the glory of the Bodhisattva lay largely in his essential humanity, for his wisdom was greater than that of the gods. At the coming of the Maitreya, the Bodhisattva of the future, as at the Second Coming of Christ, the world would be transformed; the belief was essentially eschatological.

In the case of Christianity also the human element was crucially important. The essential factor in Christianity was not that the god in some way condescended to man, as Yahweh did to the old Jews and the Olympians to the heroes of the *Iliad* and the *Odyssey*. It was that divinity entered into man and *became* human, and lived through the condition of being human to the bitter end of rejection and death. By a god having lived through the trials of being human, man had acquired the touch of deity that would make it possible to talk of the divine rights of kings, though the kings themselves were human and demonstrably mortal, as Augustus Caesar was when he turned Caesar's laurel crown into a sign of divinity and demanded worship at his altars under the pain of death.

This tendency to validate royal powers in divine precedence not only encouraged the inclination to see a divinely predestined direction in history but also helped to create another component of historicist thinking, the so-called "Great Man" theory of history. According to this theory, which Leo Tolstoy denounced and perhaps exaggerated in *War and Peace*, history was directed by men of more than ordinary abilities and powers, geniuses if not demigods. It was a convenient theory, turning history into a series of dramas rather than a series of chronicles, and eventually it became incorporated into the major trends of totalitarian historicism, according to which leader-figures—a Hitler or a Mussolini, a Lenin or a Stalin—came to personify the forward drive of history. Great men were seen as the supreme

46

instruments of historic change, the agents of destiny or the tools of God. One of the earliest celebrations of the Great Man in this sense was Isaiah's representation of Cyrus, the conqueror of Babylon, the great liberator of the Jews, as an instrument of Jehovah:

> Who raised up the righteous man from the east, called him to his feet, gave the nations before him, and made him rule over kings? He gave them as the dust to his sword, and as driven stubble to his bow.
> He pursued them and passed safely even by the way that he had not gone with his feet.

But if the shifts of this time, the remythification of history during the Hellenistic and Roman periods, led to the elevation of great men, Caesarean figures who took the place of the gods and so preluded the aristocratic societies of mediaeval Europe and Asia, there was a further strain to the religious ferment, which added yet another component to the pattern of historicist thinking. There undoubtedly existed in Judaea (perhaps with a succession of Isaiahs at its heart) a prophetic brotherhood of men who were not interested in power for themselves yet who were often politically very astute. There also seems to have grown up, judging from the Book of Isaiah and also from the Dead Sea scrolls and archaeological discoveries, a pattern of world-renouncing communities, ancestors of Christian monasteries and contemporaries of early Buddhist ones.

These were the counterparts of the Greek mystery cults. They were relatively little concerned with the task of blending secular custom and holy law into a religious code of behaviour that the orthodox Jews had already assumed and for which Christ mocked them. They developed a form of worship that stressed at the same time community and meditation. Yet while—like Christian monks—they often withdrew into remote places, as the Essenes did in the desert parts of what is now Israel, they did not withdraw themselves from history. Rather, they carried within their traditions the seeds of millenarianism, that primitive forerunner of historicism, for though they did not yet state it in terms of the thousand-year reign of the Messiah or of Christ, they looked forward to the apocalyptic end of conflict and the emergence of some kind of earthly paradise.

The early chapters of the Book of Isaiah appear to have been written down in the eighth century B.C., when it was merely the shadow of disaster but not yet the reality of dispersion and exile that fell over the Jewish people. They include the famous utopian prophecy of a renewed Eden, "where the wolf also shall dwell with the lamb, and the leopard shall lie down with the kid, and a little child shall lead them" and "the earth [not merely Judaea] shall be full of the knowledge of the Lord as the waters cover the sea."

By the time the later chapters of Isaiah were written nearly two centuries afterwards, the Persians had invaded Babylon, the captivity of the Jews had ended, and Cyrus had been hailed as the triumphant scourge of God. But for Isaiah, and for the writers of the Dead Sea Scrolls some generations later, the Lord had another servant as well as the Great Shah, a variant of the messianic agent of the deity who appears at various times in the Jewish tradition. The later Isaiah projected, in some of his most striking passages of prophecy, the appearance of a suffering servant of God. His misfortunes, clearly inseparable from his role, were described in the poignant words that inspired Georg Friedrich Handel to some of his most sublime music:

> He was despised and rejected of men; a man of sorrows, and
> acquainted with grief; and we hid as it were our faces from
> him; he was despised and we esteemed him not.

It is made clear that the servant is performing or enduring an atonement—that he is suffering not for his own sins but for those of others, as the well known verses run:

> All we like sheep have gone astray; we have turned away every
> one in his own way; and the Lord hath laid on him the iniq-
> uity of us all.
>   He was oppressed and he was afflicted; yet he opened not
> his mouth; he is brought as a lamb to the slaughter, and as a
> sheep before her shearers is dumb, so he openeth not his
> mouth.
>   . . . he bare the sins of many and made intercession for all
> transgressors.

Some time after the last chapters of Isaiah were written, on the eve of the Christian era, the communitarian sect of the Essenes appeared. Their emphasis on a self-abnegatory simplicity of living as well as on purity of doctrine distinguished them from the orthodox Jews, intent on imposing the details of religious law, whom Christ would later mock and castigate as the "scribes and Pharisees." There are good reasons to believe that the Dead Sea Scrolls, with their strong emphasis on the teachings of Isaiah, were Essene documents. These manuscripts agree with Isaiah in their insistent redemptorism. They talk of a Teacher of Righteousness who suffered for his beliefs and for those of others; the resemblance between what is supposed to have happened to this teacher and what the New Testament says about Christ is remarkable, even down to the passive willingness to be destroyed.

Theologians seeking to make their points have tended ever since the Fathers of the Church to look at Isaiah's statements in hindsight and interpret them in terms of later events. Christians see them as a prophecy of the suffering and death of the teacher Jesus, unmentioned in the chronicles of his times. Many religious leaders among the Jews put a collective interpretation on the statement, and see the sufferer as a person-ification of their people whom God or history has finally brought home to Israel.

But if we try to see the notions expressed by Isaiah and the writers of the Dead Sea Scrolls in terms of their time, and relate them to the teaching and life of Christ as recorded after his death, an interesting and different pattern emerges: the beginnings of an eschatology of the disinherited. All three— Isaiah, the Teacher of Righteousness, Christ—are concerned with a pro-gression whose destination is clear in the prayer that Christ gave to his disciples: "Thy kingdom come, thy will be done, on earth as it is in heaven." The destination, like that of the later Christian millenarians and their secular successors, is the kingdom of God on earth, towards which history implicitly moves and whose advent is hastened by the deaths of the willing martyrs, for "greater love hath no man than this, that a man lay down his life for his friends!"

A brief dip through James Frazer's *The Golden Bough* is sufficient to establish the number of sacrificial figures—gods like Dionysus and mythical personages like Orpheus, Atys, and Adonis—whose mainly plebeian cults became prominent in the age between Isaiah and Christ. The origins can be traced, as Frazer does, to the fertility cults of tribal antiquity, but when those cults moved into the urban settings of Greek and Roman cities, their nature began to change. They became to a large extent cults of the underdog in which all devotees (as they were theoretically in early Christi-anity) became equal, with class ignored and moral effort the criterion of initiation. (In a famous instance, Nero, even though he was emperor of Rome, was refused initiation into the Eleusinian Mysteries.) In Rome, by the time of the empire, the mystery cults and imported Middle Eastern religions, like those of Isis and Astarte, became elements in the fashionable life, as they had done to a certain extent during the late Hellenistic period; patrician ladies would take part in the eroticized Asian cults and also dabble in the more plebeian mystery cults, where they might very well find themselves celebrating with slaves.

This movement generated a historical perspective entirely different from that of the patrician historians of Rome whose works have come down to us, like Livy and Tacitus, and who deliberately fashioned their narratives for political ends: to develop and support with selected evidence the great myths of the Roman state, its past and its present. Since the reign of the self-deified Caesars was held to be the pinnacle of human endeavour, the best of possible worlds, the sense of events moving progressively towards a utopian goal did not exist here. The Roman ruling class were too pleased with themselves, at least until the empire began to break apart, to think of progress as a desirable or even possible goal.

The utopian element was, however, strongly present in one of the mystery religions, the literally underground cult of Christianity, sustained in the catacombs. The early Christians, between the first and the third century, lived in expectation of the proximate Second Coming of Christ, when he would establish the kingdom of God on earth. To a great extent they attempted to live the simple, communitarian, pacifist life that Christ had enjoined on them, rather like that of their predecessors, the Essenes, except that now Gentiles were accepted among them. Their sense of the world moving through struggle towards a paradisal condition was enhanced by the appearance about the end of the first century of the Revelation of St. John of Patmos, with its apocalyptic vision of the defeat of Satan and the thousand-year reign of Christ. With their unique view of all that happened on earth as part of a great plan centred on themselves, which is the burden of the Old Testament, the Jews had already prepared the way for such an approach; when the Book of Revelation, by very definition, took its place as one of the revealed texts in the Bible, a complete eschatology was finally in existence, from which all later millenarian or chiliastic movements, whether religious or secular, would ultimately derive.

Yet this did not mean an immediate triumph of historicism, within the Christian church or elsewhere. In the first generation after the appearance of the Book of Revelation, Christianity tended to be apocalyptic. But the long delay in the Second Coming, and the growing social and political acceptance of Christianity, tended to sap the zeal of the millenarians. Many patrician families had been converted by the early fourth century, and Christian beliefs were spreading even among the legions, overtaking in popularity the cult of Mithras. Therefore the conversion of the Emperor Constantine in A.D. 312 had its relevance in terms of *Realpolitik* as well as religion, giving the transplanted empire a new lease on life in the Christian city of Constantinople.

Christianity, which once had seemed synonymous with community, now became, for the long millennium of the Dark and Middle Ages, virtually inseparable from authority, granting "divine right" to reigning monarchs and seeking to share out the government of Europe between the Holy Catholic Church and the Holy Roman Empire. It was appropriate that the great early Christian theologians, the Fathers of the Church led by St. Augustine, should have begun to interpret Revelation allegorically rather than literally, and that the City of God, like the postmortal conditions described by Dante in his *Divine Comedy*, should promise joy in a non-terrestrial eternal paradise, rather than, as all millenarians have believed, on this earth and within the temporal dimension.

Apocalypticism, the ancestor of historicism, had flourished most in conditions of persecution when a promise as well as a faith was needed to sustain the converted. It began with the Old Testament Book of Daniel, probably written in the second century B.C., when the Seleucid ruler of Syria, Antiochus Epiphanes, was persecuting orthodox Judaism. Daniel himself, the last in the great Jewish prophetic tradition, went outside Judaism for much of his inspiration, for this is the book of the Old Testament in which the influence of Iranian religious traditions is strongest. Here, for the first time among Judaeo-Christian texts, the whole panoply of Zoroastrian conceptions is displayed: the battle between the forces of light and darkness in which men and angels will fight together on both sides; the Last Judgment, and the great eternal Fire consuming evil-doers while "the Son of Man" establishes a righteous earthly kingdom, very much like Plato's *Republic* actualized.

John of Patmos transferred these concepts into the canons of Christianity at a time when the new religion had undergone its first great persecutions under the Emperor Nero. Already St. Paul and Mark the Evangelist had spoken in apocalyptic terms, but it was John who gave eloquent and complete expression to Christian apocalypticism and initiated its eschatological tradition.

Down in the catacombs, the persecuted Christians compensated for the terror under which they lived during the reigns of Nero and his successors by their dreams of a very concrete earthly paradise in which their sorrows would shortly be relieved. The chiliastic tradition which emerged at that time never wholly vanished, for there were always Christians who were too underprivileged or too idealistic to accept the church as a justification for the earthly status quo. Yet as Christianity became more accepted in Roman society, the apocalyptic urge died down, and something prefiguring the Anglican balance of church and state began to take form, leading ultimately to the Constantinian accord between the emperor and the bishop of Rome which preluded the vast period—itself a millennium in chronological terms—when the papacy and the Holy Roman Empire in the West, and the patriarchate and the Byzantine emperors in the East, ruled over a Europe and not a little of Asia where time had been virtually halted in realms that conveniently separated the City of the World, where the power of Christian kings was unchangeably assured, from the City of God, to which the entrance gate was called Death.

In these circumstances the millenarians retreated underground, particularly since their doctrines gradually acquired the edge of mediaeval John Ball's earthly paradisal egalitarianism ("When Adam delved and Eve span,/Who was then the gentleman?") and veered towards the politically subversive as well as the heretical. The influence they ultimately wielded on historical thinking remained latent for most of the Middle Ages. During the long period from the Dark Ages to the Renaissance, written history became the occupation of monks and literate gentlemen, showing virtually no sense of historical development in any direction. Heaven was the other realm, attained by virtuous behaviour here on earth, but such behaviour had little effect in the present world except on those who had decided to withdraw from it into those halfway houses to Heaven, the monasteries. This meant that there was no sense of a progression in history, or even of epic themes like those of the Greeks, since man no longer had a sense of living in times of great historic cataclysm. History became related closely to the local and the contemporary, and the early Middle Ages showed a reversion to mere chronicle. The most striking example is probably *The Anglo-Saxon Chronicle*, whose lack of temporal consistency—and lack of concern for factual accuracy or even probability—demonstrates how the sense of history as flow, or even of the importance of grand overarching issues like the unity of Hellas or the effect of the Persian invasion, had died away. Even in Greece the great Byzantine historians like Procopius and Psellus were concerned mainly with the often amusing but often disgusting ephemerae of court life in their time. In the later Middle Ages in Western Europe, there were also some splendid writers—as vivid in their prose as the monkly illuminators of the books of hours were in their painting—about their own times, like Jean de Joinville, Jean Froissart and Geoffrey de Villehardouin, whose insights have been of vast use to later historians.

But it was not until the Reformation that the divisions between the twin concepts of the City of the World and the City of God would break down, and history—dragged by political intent—would take up its illusory progress from one to the other, as the millenarians emerged from the darkness of the Middle Ages and returned to Christianity its revolutionary potentialities. Essentially, the Reformation—John of Leyden's rather than Martin Luther's—saw the birth of the greatest of all rebellions against faith and reason alike, the authoritarian concept of a determined course of history.

CHAPTER V

Kingdoms of God on Earth

It was no accident that Friedrich Engels should hail Thomas Müntzer, the millenarian reformer and leader of one of the great peasant revolts through which Europe emerged from the Middle Ages, as an ancestor. For the doctrines of historical necessity developed by this Lancashire mill owner and his Rhineland friend, Karl Marx, derived not merely from the politically progressive movements of the Enlightenment, not merely from the ruminations of the romantic and reactionary philosopher Georg Wilhelm Friedrich Hegel. They were also deeply rooted in religious tradition, and mainly in the eschatological tradition that began with Zoroaster and was carried on within Jewry, finally taking secular shape in the Marxist version of the Hegelian dialectic; here the thesis of working-class revolution and the antithesis of tyrannical capitalism struggle together in the process of a history inevitably worked out by the laws of economic development, and the synthesis is achieved, not by the new heaven and new earth of the allegorical apocalyptics but by the utopian transformation of life on this earth. It was precisely at such a transformation that the millenarian Christians of the Reformation, of whom Thomas Müntzer was the most striking example, aimed their prophecies and their practices.

These millenarians, like most historical determinists, based their aims and their practice on a pattern of self-fulfilling prophecy that would be inherited and developed by the nineteenth-century determinist historians and their totalitarian allies. They embraced a desideratum, the earthly kingdom of God of the godless utopia, and pronounced its inevitability. Then they would work towards it, and their efforts would be blessed as part of an ineluctable process of which they would be the agents.

Some of the millenarian movements of the Reformation, like Müntzer's followers in Mühlausen, like the Anabaptists in Münster, like the Fifth Monarchy Men in England, aimed to achieve their ends by insurrection, violence, even a dictatorship of the saints. Others, like the Anabaptists in Germany led by Menno Simons, and the Diggers and Quakers in England, were pacifists. They believed that the struggle for the earthly kingdom of God must not be sullied by blood but that they must proceed by moral suasion and the example of peaceful communitarian living. It was they who first experimented in the methods of civil disobedience that Henry David Thoreau and Leo Tolstoy later advocated and Mahatma Gandhi put into practice in India.

The striking examples of millenarian historicism that emerged at the time of the Reformation in no sense represented a new development. Despite the capture of the Christian church by Constantine and its subsequent development as a bulwark for existing and continuing structures of earthly power, the "invisible church" as many have called it, the view of Christianity as a movement of the poor and disinherited seeking a new order in this life continued. The Catholic church, over its long centuries of power, sought to counteract this plebeian trend in various ways: by creating a vast company of Christian saints to take over the role of the pre-Christian local deities and—especially in the Mediterranean countries—to keep alive the hedonistic spirit of paganism among the peasants; and also by encouraging, with initial misgiving, movements like Franciscanism that stressed the spiritual power of humility without addressing in any fundamental way the physical needs of the disinherited.

But the millenarian cults continued, more often among peasant populations than in the cities, and became linked with the great heresies of the age which the church sought to suppress as dangers to its authority as well as to its dogmas. One of the great early millenarians was Montanus, a teacher who lived and preached in Anatolia during the second century A.D. As in the case of most of the early Christian heretics, we know of Montanus mainly through the writings of his orthodox enemies, who say that he founded an ecstatic and ascetic movement in the old kingdom of Phrygia, whose influence spread into North Africa and even Europe. Montanus taught what he called a Third Testament, that of the resurgent spirit of God which was to be made manifest in the imminent Second Coming of Christ. Montanism was suppressed in its time, but it has recurred throughout the history of Christianity, particularly since the Reformation, with such sects as the Jehovah's Witnesses, the Seventh-Day Adventists and the Latter-day Saints. All of these recent groups have clearly defined systems of belief and schedules of the holy life and of foretold events, which believers are expected to follow in order to achieve the historical and apocalyptic destinations anticipated in the sect's prophecies. In their own way and among their own faithful, they are totalitarian organizations whose sense of the certainty of their historical direction sustains them, often in spectacular good works that in some way anticipate the millennium. On this fundamental level the historical thinking of the Montanists or, say, the Seventh-Day Adventists, is not different from that of Communists or Nazis; the prophets read into the future a course of events that the faithful work to fulfil.

In the late eleventh century, when the mediaeval order was beginning to show the first signs of the breakup that preceded the Reformation and the Renaissance, the messianic millenarians began to reappear after a long silence during the Constantinian period. A self-styled messiah named Tanchelm led a broad movement in the Low Countries; this area of the lower Rhineland and what later became Belgium and Holland remained a centre of political and religious unrest and played a notable role in providing leaders of the Reformation. It was also a region in whose densely peopled industrial communities radical working-class movements would flourish during the early nineteenth century and in which several of the noted radical thinkers of the time originated, such as Moses Hess, and of course Marx and Engels.

History had not yet escaped the theology that dominated thought in a religious age, and the peasant revolts and other movements of the poor, with their millenarian hopes, were related to a kind of populist left that developed within the church in the twelfth century, located mainly in the radical ranks of the begging orders from the Franciscans onward. Such groups were regarded by the leaders of the church with a mixture of esteem and distrust; their leaders were often men of saintly life, like St. Francis, and they sustained—even in the ossified institution that was the mediaeval church—an area where zeal might operate and provide the church with the enthusiasm it needed to renew itself and survive. At the same time, their teachings encouraged a literalist kind of apocalypticism that verged on the heretical. Even St. Francis was suspect among the orthodox, and despite his importance as a theologian and his influence over the common people of twelfth-century Italy, who often regarded him as a prophet, that important churchman Joachim de Fiore was never trusted by the more cautious ecclesiasts. Significantly, despite his vast reputation, his great learning, his ascetic life and his rather demonstrative piety, Joachim was never canonized.

56

Joachim is important to the arguments of this book for two reasons. He reordered the concepts of millenarian apocalypticism, which by this stage, a thousand years after the Book of Revelation was written, had become somewhat disoriented. But his *Liber concordia Nova ac Veteris Testamenti?*, in the writing of which Pope Lucius III encouraged him, was a great deal more than a sophisticated millenarian tract. It was, even though it relied on revealed sources rather than objective research, a genuine work of world history, an attempt to interpret the past and the present through biblical exegesis, and in this way to justify a reasoned as well as a visionary view of the future.

His was the first book in which History appeared as a shaping and commanding presence, though not so openly personified as Marx would later do. And it was the first work in which a determined pattern of history was clearly and thoroughly developed. As Norman Cohn showed so well in that remarkable book, *The Pursuit of the Millennium*, it not merely represented mediaeval millenarian thought at its most intelligent; it also stood at the beginning of the tradition of totalitarian historicism, the long slope that led down to Hegel and Marx and the theoreticians of nazism.

Joachim's treatise was based on a combination of mediaeval theology, which placed the Bible at the heart of religious thinking, and religious numerology, which probably saved him from persecution as a heretic, since his obsession with the number three marked him off as a kind of trinitarian. No trace here of Monophysitism! Or of the neo-gnostic dualism which the Catharists and the Bogomils were beginning to spread in the Languedoc and the Balkans!

Joachim arranged his historical pattern in a triad, with three great dispensations, or testaments. The first *status* (as he called his eras) was the past from the creation to Christ, corresponding to the Old Testament; the second consisted of the Christian era, up to the Middle Ages. Now, in the twelfth century, the world was moving into a new status, an "age of the spirit" proceeding out of the earlier historical (in fact pseudo-historical) ages. It fitted neatly into the trinitarian pattern, for first came the status of the Father, then that of the Son, and then that of the Holy Ghost; the three became one in the wholeness of history. While the general plan won the approval of the church and perhaps saved Joachim from the stake, the third part appealed to religious enthusiasts and particularly millenarians, perhaps saving him from canonization, though many believed him to be a saint.

The third status would be a time of tribulation and triumph in which Christians would have to endure physical and spiritual privations, like those of the Israelites in their generations in the wilderness. But out of this dire

57

pilgrimage would emerge the collective saviours, orders of spiritual athletes whose role suggests the reviving influence of Platonism in the twelfth century. Two new holy orders emerge. One group consists of hermits, who contemplate the problems of the world from their distant caves, like Karl Marx ruminating in the British Museum Reading Room. The other consists of mediators, rather like the preaching orders of Joachim's time, dedicated to leading men on to the new spiritual plane. The general population, having in their turn been spiritualized, can perhaps be regarded as an improved version of the lay tertiaries attached to twelfth-century orders of friars. It is strongly reminiscent of the commonwealth envisaged in Plato's *Republic*, with its orders of guardians and auxiliaries guiding the general population. Unlike some of the other apocalyptic visions of the millennium, Joachim's Third Age is not ruled over by Christ but by a supreme teacher, a philosopher-king called *novus dux*, who will—after the fall of the Antichrist—lead men away from earthly preoccupations into the spiritual realm. For though this kingdom of God in the spirit will be on earth, the spiritualization of humanity will go so far that men and women will need no physical nourishment and so will be freed of the need to own property or to work.

On the turbulent verge of the modern age, Joachim went beyond the historians of classical antiquity to devise the first of the determinist patterns of history based on Zoroastrian-Jewish-Christian eschatological concepts. His triadic pattern would even re-emerge among the post–French Revolution historical philosophers of the nineteenth century.

There is a further stage to be considered beyond the spiritual millenarians—that of their socially minded successors of the pre-Reformation and the Reformation itself. For Joachim's prophecies of an earthly paradise of spiritualized beings were soon replaced by the visions of men like John Ball and Thomas Müntzer and John of Leyden in which the inhabitants of such a paradise would be natural and physical men and women fulfilling their appetites according to the anarchic beliefs of groups like the Brethren of the Free Spirit in the Low Countries. In these visions, the humble would be exalted, the saints would live in luxury, and their enemies—the priests, the aristocrats, the Jews—would either be exterminated or subordinated to the elect, as they were in the cities that did in fact temporarily constitute themselves earthly paradises, where terror ruled rather than peace.

There is no doubt that the millenarian commonwealths as they existed, with their sense of history fulfilled, their fury against the privileged, and the communist economies dominated by the new elect, bore a resemblance to what Marx would envisage, and an even closer resemblance to the actual totalitarian orders, so much broader in extent, of our own century: those of the Nazis and of Stalinist Russia. It was not inappropriate that Engels and the ideologues of nazism should have shown such an interest in the millenarian *prophetae* of the late Middle Ages and the Reformation. Even Hitler's plan for the extermination of the Jews as part of the fulfilment of history was anticipated by almost all the early millenarian leaders.

During Jan Huss's pre-Lutheran reformation and rebellion in fifteenth-century Bohemia, a group of millenarians led by Jan Zizka built the holy city of Tabor, where they proclaimed the proximity of the Second Coming of Christ and established a realm of the faithful, anticipating the Anabaptists, who later seized the city of Münster and expelled all but the elect. Both movements failed, and their leaders were destroyed by the church and state which they had threatened. But their tradition lingered in small dissenting sects which paid lip service to the millenarian ideals that were diffused in the memories of working people.

The leaders of peasant revolts of the Middle Ages were often at the same time preachers of heresy. John Ball, the hedge priest who supported Wat Tyler in the English peasant revolt of 1381, was such a leader; one of his speeches is recorded by the contemporary chronicler Froissart:

> Things cannot go well in England, nor ever will, until all goods are held in common, and until there will be neither serfs nor gentlemen, and we shall be equal. For what reason have they, who call themselves lords, got the better of us? How did they deserve it? Why do they keep us in bondage? If we all descended from one father and one mother, Adam and Eve, how can they assert or prove that they are more masters than ourselves? Except perhaps that they make us work and produce for them to spend.

Heretical radicals like John Ball and the leaders of peasant revolts like Thomas Müntzer saw their activities taking place under divine promise with a kind of proto-political eschatology, a rudimentary historical pattern leading to the earthly paradise of equality and brotherhood.

But, as historians have pointed out, not all peasant revolts were dominated by the millenarians; there were others that were more social and political than religious. John Ball's following was only part of the insurrection that Wat Tyler led. Perhaps the majority in the English revolt, in the French jacqueries of the period, and in the somewhat later German peasant revolts, were concerned mainly with making sure of their rights at a time when the feudal system was disintegrating. The growing importance of the socio-political element was emphasized in the English Civil War period, when a whole variety of mass discontents were projected, and the millenarian element, though present, wielded a relatively minor influence.

Even those who at this time saw the future of Christianity in the establishment of an earthly paradise were concerned less with the rule of a liberated elect than with practical egalitarianism. They tended to advert from the apocalyptic view of a historical destiny consummated by blood, fire and the destruction of the hated classes, to a simpler pre-apocalyptic view of the millennial destiny of Christianity, the conquest of evil through gentleness and love. This was the attitude towards which the Anabaptists inclined after the bloody assault on Münster, when the followers of Menno Simons formed themselves into a movement of pacifist communitarians. (It was a pattern that would be followed by many of the Russian sects that appeared after the Raskol, the great seventeenth-century schism in the Eastern Orthodox church, particularly the Doukhobors and the Molokons. In England it would appear among the more radical of the Quakers, who probably derived much from the short-lived group called the Diggers, who developed an early form of the civil disobedience that would later become the cornerstone of Tolstoy's social programme and of Gandhi's satyagraha movement.) These groups were no less eschatological in their attitude than the violently minded apocalyptics. They too were historicists who saw the destiny of the world working out according to their beliefs and with their humble assistance. Their difference lay in two factors: they did not separate the potential inhabitants of their earthly paradises into the two sharply defined classes of the elect and the damned. Their paradise would be for all, and so it was to be egalitarian as well as communitarian. And they believed, as Gandhi would do later on, that no one was irredeemable, and that even the worst enemies could be won over by love rather than force.

Perhaps the most interesting of these groups, for their awareness of social needs and also their inclination to set up reason as a guiding and forming principle, were the Diggers, and it is worth pausing to consider the clues they offer to the origins of the liberal and progressivist historicism which for many years shared the dominant trends of history writing with the totalitarian historicists of the left and right.

The Diggers, some of whom had already been Levellers, extended the religiously tinged radicalism of the group into the social field. They sprang up—during the period of economic depression that followed the defeat of the Royalist forces and the establishment of the Commonwealth—not as a movement of discontented soldiers like the Levellers but as a group of poor men ruined by economic circumstances. They believed that God could not be indifferent to their fate, and they linked their belief to a fundamental change in society, willed by God, of which they would be the instruments. Gerrard Winstanley, the bankrupt mercer who was their leader, published in 1648 his pamphlet, *Truth Lifting Its Head up Above Scandals*. The prophetic, millenarian character of his ideas was clearly stated:

> The Father is now raising up a people to himself out of the dust, that is out of the lowest and more despised sort of People. In these and from these shall the Law of Righteousness break forth first.

In some ways Winstanley's ideas bore a haunting resemblance to those of Joachim de Fiore, for where Joachim had posed a realm in which the Father and Son seem to be superseded by the Spirit, so Winstanley threw overboard all the baggage of orthodox Christianity to equate God with "the incomprehensible spirit, Reason":

> Where does that Reason dwell. He dwells in every creature, according to the nature and being of the creature, but supremely in man. Therefore man is called a rational creature. This is the kingdom of God within man.

From this almost pantheistic conception of God as immanent reason, Winstanley derived a theory of conduct which suggests that if man acts in accordance with his own rational nature he will fulfil his duty as a social being. His most radical pamphlet, *The New Law of Righteousness*, is a series of essentially social and political propositions. Equating Christ with "the universal liberty," he begins with a statement on the corrupting power of authority and criticizes not only political power but also the economic power of master over servant and the familial power of father over child and husband over wife:

> Every one that gets an authority into his hands tyrannizes over others, as many husbands, parents, masters, magistrates, that live after the flesh do carry themselves like oppressing lords over such as are under them, not know that their wives, children, servants, subjects are their fellow creatures, and hath an equal privilege to share in the blessing of liberty.

61

But the "equal privilege to share in the blessing of liberty" is not an abstract privilege. Its conquest is linked with the attack on property rights, and Winstanley is emphatic in his insistence on the intimate link between economic and political power:

> And let all men say what they will, so long as such are rulers as call the land theirs, upholding this particular property of mine and thine, the common people shall never have their liberty, nor the land be freed from troubles, oppressions and complainings; by reason thereof the Creator of all things is continually provoked.

Winstanley insists that the only way to end social injustice is for the people themselves to act, and he talks with apocalyptic fervour of the role of the poor in regenerating the world, in the process showing himself a primitive historical determinist, though of a different kind from either Joachim or Thomas Müntzer or John of Leyden.

> The Father is now raising up a people to himself out of the dust that is out of the lowest and most despised sort of people. . . . In these and from these shall the Law of Righteousness break forth first.

The people should act, Winstanley contends, by seizing and working the land, the principal source of wealth. He does not think it necessary to seize forcibly the estates of rich men. The poor can settle the commons and wastelands (which he estimates occupy two-thirds of England) and work them together. From their example men can learn the virtues of communal life, and the earth become a "common treasury" providing plenty in freedom for all.

Shortly after *The New Law of Righteousness* appeared in January 1649, Winstanley and thirty to forty associates initiated their campaign of direct action by proceeding to St. George's hill, near Walton on Thames, where they began to dig the wasteland. Winstanley invited the local landowners to join them, prophesying that very shortly their numbers would increase to five thousand. But the Diggers seem to have aroused little sympathy even among their poor neighbours, and a great deal of hostility among the local clergy and gentry. They were beaten up by paid hooligans and fined by magistrates; their cattle were driven away, their seedlings torn up, and their flimsy huts torn down. Troops of soldiers were sent down to investigate them, but were withdrawn when a number of them showed evident interest in Digger teachings. Through all these difficult months Winstanley and his followers refused to be provoked into the violence they abhorred.

But even Digger endurance was not proof against unrelenting persecution, and their movement had disappeared by the end of 1650.

Destiny as Progress

The Diggers were an example of a movement that assumed the dynamic of the eschatological viewpoint, even to the extent of posing a variant of Joachim de Fiore's third realm of the spirit, metamorphosed into *reason*, yet that wholly lacked the extreme apocalyptic tendency to try and make their prophecies self-fulfilling by the elimination of those who opposed them and were not of the Elect. Far, in fact, from decreeing themselves as elect, they sought to persuade the rest of the population to help in creating their own better world.

How far they actually went beyond being an example of a group that rejected extreme apocalypticism yet sustained an essentially historicist search for a God-ordained and social revolutionary future, and wielded an influence on later similar tendencies, it is hard to say. Modern Marxists and anarchists alike have claimed them as precursors without establishing any real connection. Yet there is justification for speculating that Digger views may have survived among the many sects of the English Dissenting movement that continued after the restoration of the Stuart monarchy in 1660. In the eighteenth century these sects become a fertile seedground for a political radicalism that extended beyond the Whiggism of the great landlords, and mingled with rationalist trends in France to produce a world view that would largely dominate the writing of history during the nineteenth and twentieth centuries and develop an alternative historicism—a liberal historicism based on the notion of continuing progress and of the steady evolution of mankind towards perfection.

While this English liberal historicism long retained the marks of its religious beginnings, what emerged in France developed as part of a rapid secularization of intellectual interests on the continent of Europe, even in regions where the Reformation did not triumph. Here a double tendency emerged. First there was the attempt of legal and constitutional historians to investigate the origins of laws and governmental systems so as to provide a kind of intelligible continuity embracing the *status quo* and extending it into the future. In the search for material, many of the old chronicles of the more statically minded Middle Ages were recovered and took their place in a stream of history that was now future-oriented. But there was also the tendency, among the philosophic innovators of the Enlightenment, the Encyclopaedists and their successors, to see the study of the past as of minor importance in comparison with the other—and more exact—sciences that were developing so quickly at this time. Many of them, like Jean D'Alembert, declared that much of our knowledge of the past had become irrelevant to the contemporary task of understanding the world as it was and preparing for the future. And even the Marquis de Condorcet, that pure spirit, whose posthumously published *Sketch for a Historical Picture of the Human Mind* (1795) predicted the ultimate perfection of the human race (and whom the French Revolution first sustained and then destroyed), oriented himself so much towards the future of endless progress that he took part in a commission appointed by the assembly in 1792, shortly before the Terror, that destroyed part of the royal archives because they might remind men of their past servitude. Clearly, the rewriting of history, the elimination of events and persons from the records, was invented neither by the Stalinists nor by the Nazis, nor by the contrivers of the Orwellian memory holes, but by well-meaning liberal historicists with idealistic intent.

The concept of continuous progress, the liberal version of the utopian myth, was developed even more by economists than by historians in the mid-eighteenth century. Among its most influential advocates were Anne-Robert-Jacques Turgot, the brilliant intendant of Limoges, who attempted to reform the financial and economic policies of France during the reign of Louis XVI and was removed because of the opposition of vested interests which, as a result, reaped the revolution; and Adam Smith, the Scottish economist who became the prophet of laissez-faire capitalism. Men like these, and the philosopher Charles-Louis Montesquieu, whose extremely influential *De l'Esprit des lois* (1748) emphasized the importance of changing social institutions, were not historians. But they influenced social history by their confident belief in the inevitability of progress in the modern world, and most of all, perhaps, they influenced the great historian of their period,

Edward Gibbon, who wrote, as he himself remarked, "history related to and explained by the social institutions in which it is contained." His masterpiece, *The History of the Decline and Fall of the Roman Empire*, really had a double purpose. The first was to examine the causes of the decay of classical civilization—for the barbarization of Rome also meant a withdrawal into the shadows of a dark age lasting several centuries of the values and achievements of the Greek civilization where most that was good in Rome originated. But Europe when Gibbon wrote was beginning to go through a series of disturbances that would draw the continent near to chaos before the century ended. (The last volume of *The Decline and Fall* actually appeared in 1788, on the very eve of the French Revolution.) And thus *The Decline and Fall*, which described, in Gibbon's own words, "the triumph of barbarism and religion," became also a plea for the retention of what had been regained in the way of intellectual freedom since the Renaissance. To Gibbon, sceptic that he was, it seemed clear that the triumph of Christianity in the last great days of the empire had been retrogressive rather than progressive. He saw his own times as in contrast a period of progress, and in the last chapters of his masterpiece he inferred rather than stated that progress might have become virtually inevitable. When the French Revolution shook his world, he was already too ill to comment on it, and he died while the Terror was still in progress.

In *The Decline and Fall* Gibbon stated on a major scale the liberal and progressive view of history, and in this way—by suggesting that after the false start of the classical world progress had taken on a surer course—he was the predecessor of the British liberal historians of the nineteenth century with their Victorian confidence in the inevitability of progress which Alfred Tennyson (their laureate as certainly as he was the queen's) expressed so often, and nowhere in more variety than in "Locksley Hall." He dreamed of industry as an ever developing process whose heroes were

> Men, my brothers, men the workers, ever reaping something new:
> That which they have done but earnest of the things that they
> shall do.

The poet foresaw a time when humanity would have overthrown the savage need for conflict and

> . . . the war-drums throbbed no longer, and the battle-flags were
> furled.
> In the Parliament of Man, the Federation of the World.

Tennyson saw himself as "the heir of all the ages, in the foremost files of time" and ended declaring, "Better fifty years of Europe than a cycle of Cathay." His poem became as much a literary expression of liberal progressive historicism as Joseph Paxton's great structure of steel and light built for the Great Exhibition of 1851, a futurist artifact in its time, was its visual symbol.

The myth of progress fitted the mood of the industrial revolution and the Victorian age that followed it like a battle gauntlet. It accorded with the ruthlessness of the industrialists themselves and justified their crimes against their workers and the environment in much the same way as Marxist and Nazi historicism would justify similar crimes as the social price of progress. It suited the evangelical Christianity of the age, with its emphasis on widespread ameliorative measures like the Factory Acts and the abolition of slavery, and its armies of missionaries and Bible society workers who fervently believed that through their efforts all the peoples of the earth would in the end be converted into good Protestant Christians well covered with Lancashire-made cloth. Technology gave support to the progressivist view of history through its unbroken series of new inventions that rapidly changed the shape of daily life, and science added its emphasis with the evolutionary doctrines that were most strikingly embodied in Charles Darwin's *On the Origin of Species by Means of Natural Selection* (1859); vulgarized by secular evangelists like Thomas Henry Huxley, these encouraged a popular belief in an upward progress of the species through natural selection, which took on the form of a kind of historical law. This contributed to the transfer of the evolutionary idea to sociology—societies were soon perceived to be in the process of evolution—and hence to history, reinforcing the pattern of progressivist historicism. Finally, such developments had their effect on politics, introducing a progressivist utopianism shared by liberals and non-Marxist socialists alike; it is significant that in its early days the Labour party was in form and in fact the left wing of the Liberal party in England, its ideology more sharply defined than that of the radicals and crowned by the terminal utopia of the social-democratic state.

On the continent of Europe the eighteenth-century predecessors of liberal progressive historicism, and also to an extent of the totalitarian type, were the French philosopher and Encyclopaedist Jean Jacques Rousseau and the Italian writer Giambattista Vico.

In some ways Rousseau resembled Plato and Hesiod in seeing the process of history as retrogressive rather than progressive, but redeemable by wise men through various means, of which education and the development of a pattern of social contracts were the most important. Humanity, in

Rousseau's view of the past, was originally free, equal and innocent, living mainly in solitude as the animals do and coming together for purposes of reproduction. But natural disasters forced men and women to form groups in order to ensure their survival; this was at best a primitive version of the Golden Age of the ancients, a benign interlude of social peace until iron was discovered and, as in Hesiod's vision, turned the peaceful Golden Age into an age of conflict, complicated by the fact that the cultivation of wheat led to struggles over land and to the evil of private property.

Essentially, just as Plato and Hesiod believed that there had been a Golden Age which approximated—at least in Plato's view—the ideal archetypal harmony, in the case of Rousseau there was the "natural man" who had been corrupted by the material elements in civilization. Plato envisaged in the kind of totalitarian and sharply class-divided society he proposed a way of halting and perhaps reversing the degenerative process that seemed to him the inevitable direction of history, and Rousseau saw a similar reversion as possible through education and political reform. But both regarded history as a process that would continue, that could only be diverted and not halted, and in which the intervention of higher powers could not be ignored. Rousseau, for all his Enlightenment rationalism, viewed Providence as a rewarder of the good in social life and thus as an influence shaping the course of events which men, on one level, see as history.

Thus Rousseau had not quite reached the naive belief in the linear progression of history that later distinguished so many nineteenth-century historians of both the left and the right. In posing an idealized past from which decline had begun but could be halted, he saw like Plato a spiral rather than a linear movement, and so linked himself to the kind of cyclic historicism which in modern times has been a recurrent rival of the linear form developed under the influence of adopted millenarian doctrines.

In a different way from the Encyclopaedists, Vico departed from mediaeval and Reformation views of history as the extension of divine revelation, and from Renaissance views of history as the chronicle of the actions of great men; he began to seek its social roots and the laws which might be concealed within them, becoming the first actual historian since the ancients (outside the frankly prophetic tradition represented by Joachim de Fiore and his kin) to present a kind of history in which the past was shaped in such a way as to allow us to foresee a future in which the patterning might proceed in a generally predictable manner.

The pattern Vico saw was clearly that of the cycle, so prominent among Asian cosmologists, though perhaps he did not know that. For him, all civilizations developed and decayed in the same way. Starting at the "bestial" level—the less positive equivalent of Rousseau's "natural man," it continued into the "age of the gods," when men were ruled by fear of supernatural forces; then it emerged into "the age of the heroes," a time of great dynastic struggles like those of the early Renaissance cities, and ended in "the age of man," roughly equivalent with the triumph of egalitarian democracy. But the very liberties achieved might lead to corruption and disintegration and so eventually to the collapse of the society, as in the case of imperial Rome. Rather like Rousseau, Vico saw in Providence a force that might avert the repetition of such negative cycles, though he was no clearer than Rousseau as to how this might happen.

Vico's cycles anticipate of course the grand pessimistic circles of events that recur in two of the most remarkable—if not the most literally accurate—of historians' artifacts, Oswald Spengler's grand and gloomy *The Decline of the West* and Arnold Toynbee's *A Study of History*, perhaps the only work in our time to rival *The History of the Decline and Fall of the Roman Empire* as an example of the *art* of Clio, and of course as an example of one kind of historicist arrangement of the chaos of actuality.

But there is one important aspect in which Vico anticipates the linear historicists, and notably Marx, as Edmund Wilson so clearly showed in *To the Finland Station*, for he develops, perhaps more clearly than any writer since Plato, the element of class struggle as a motive force in history. During the "age of heroes," society would be divided sharply between plebeians and patricians; during the "age of man," the class conflict would result in the triumph of the plebeians and in the achievement of social equality. Marx's particular interpretation of history owed a great deal, though he hardly acknowledged it, to the economic elements in Vico's representation of social change and their importance in his masterpiece, *Principii di una scienza nuova intorno alla natura delle nazioni* (whose definitive edition appeared posthumously in 1744, the year of his death); Marx straightened out the Vico spiral to accord with the linear pattern of eschatological historicism, and he replaced the deity of "Providence" by an abstract "History" as the saving force.

It was, generally, the liberal progressive historians who paid tribute to Vico, notably after his "discovery"—eighty years after his death—by Jules Michelet, the French historian, who claimed him as "my own Prometheus." Michelet, who translated *Scienza nuova* in 1827, extracted from his master's book a highly romantic view of the role of man challenging with his sense of freedom the power of destiny, a typically Gallic concept later to be developed by Jean Paul Sartre and his fellow Existentialists and often to be wedded to a crude Marxism. An ardent nationalist, Michelet adapted what he learnt from Vico to present an epic account of the history of his own country, offered in two dramatic and many-volumed works, *L'Histoire de France*, and *La Révolution française*. Michelet was the kind of poetic historicist who helped to prove that history, which cannot be a science, is naturally an art, and a creative one.

Michelet sought the same kind of verisimilitude in his historical narratives as Daniel Defoe had done in his fiction; his aim was to piece the facts of the past together into a picture—rather like fitting together the fragments of an ancient mosaic. But many of the tiles have vanished and what is missing has been filled in by the archaeologist's own imagination, as Arthur John Evans fitted in so much of the frescoes at Knossos. Michelet's histories present the past as it partly was and the past as it partly may have been, but all so skilfully confected and united that we read it with the same kind of admiration we experience looking at Paolo Veronese's vast and splendid historical and biblical paintings, so amazingly authentic in spirit despite the numberless anachronisms in dress and gesture.

And this, really, is a return on Michelet's part to the world of myth, for oral myth too was based partly on past actuality, but presented in a fictional form, a pleasing and credible tale of gods and nymphs. Michelet's famous presentation of Joan of Arc, woman and symbol combined, was also myth so skilfully contrived to suit its time that it is hard even for the non-French and possibly impossible for the majority of French people to consider objectively the facts of Joan's life and deeds; her memory, far more than that of St. Louis, carries forward into our age the myth of Catholic and chivalric France. And Michelet's presentation of the French Revolution as the final stage in a Vico-like progression, with Justice triumphing over Grace, by which he meant religious and temporal power, was to echo through the revolutionary tradition, to be adapted by social philosopher Pierre-Joseph Proudhon in his masterpiece, *De la justice dans la révolution et dans l'église* and to re-emerge on the last page of the anarchist Peter Kropotkin's first book, *Paroles d'un révolté*, when he talks of Justice replacing Charity as the moving force of the revolutionary society.

Michelet was a superb practitioner of history considered as an imaginative art, the true realm of Clio, arranging facts for their effects as the poet arranges words. And perhaps, outside the bleakest of chronicles, there is no other way in which the chaos of actuality can be effectively presented, but the final result of Michelet's efforts was also a notable contribution to historicism, to the concept of a continually evolving progressivist or utopian destiny that dominated the historical view of both liberals and non-Marxist revolutionaries in the later nineteenth century.

British historians and ideologues were not unaffected by the heritage of Vico, which came to them through Auguste Comte rather than through Jules Michelet. Comte, who has been credited with actually inventing the name "sociology" for the quasi-science he largely created, began to publish his major work, the *Cours de philosophie positive* in 1830, shortly after Michelet's translation of Vico's *Principii di una scienza nuova*; the six volumes took twelve years to appear. Comte had already been associated, as a very young man, with the eccentric socialist aristocrat Henri de Saint-Simon, and from Saint-Simon he derived his notions of the importance of economic organization in human society. But it was from Vico that he derived his highly systematized views on human progression, and here he was—even more than Michelet—Vico's disciple. For he too saw societies developing in a series of manifestations and devised what he called "the law of the three stages."

Comte saw these stages in terms of intellectual evolution reflected in historical developments. It was a curious progress of expansion to transcendental vision and contraction to pragmatic realism that he offered. Humanity he saw emerging out of the tribal murk, and entering the "theological" stage, when life was interpreted in terms of the actions and the dictates of the gods and spirits. From this, people moved into a "metaphysical" stage, in which they believed they could understand the universe and interpret it in abstract and absolute terms, in terms of first and final causes, of essences and ideals. In Comte's own age people were moving into the final "positive' stage, in which the limitations on human knowledge are understood and accepted. Like Buddha long ago, Comte taught that the absolutes, should they exist, must be beyond human comprehension and experience, and are therefore better ignored.

Nevertheless, Comte shared with others of Saint-Simon's disciples a tendency towards the religious if not the metaphysical. If in his positivist phase he advocated an approach based on observation, hypothesis and experimentation that could be regarded as genuinely "positive," its incorporation into the "law of three stages" really meant the reintroduction of the metaphysical element; by the end Comte was advocating what was very near a religion of humanism, with its own eschatology and its own way to paradise.

It was this inclination that the English liberal philosopher John Stuart Mill criticized, while accepting much that Comte had to teach and incorporating it into what would become the most important of the English liberal progressive philosophies, Utilitarianism.

Utilitarianism began with Jeremy Bentham, who developed from the British radical philosophical tradition represented in the eighteenth century by David Hume and John Locke (with William Godwin on its extreme wing) a teaching that the aim of all social change should be the greatest happiness of the greatest number. The Utilitarians were political philosophers in so far as they advocated specific changes that would contribute to the larger goal of a happier society, and to that limited extent they were also utopians. Bentham's suggestions for changing the penal system were largely accepted, as were his proposals for prison reform. Though it has often been debated whether the Benthamite system really increased the happiness of English convicts, there can be no doubt of his universally progressive and humanitarian intent.

This can be said even more of John Stuart Mill, whose varied interests and activities extended far beyond his role as a political economist, for he perhaps more than any other of the English liberal thinkers of the nineteenth century found common ground with the social democrats of his time, and became deeply involved in progressive issues like women's rights, electoral reform, labour unions and agrarian co-operatives. Indeed, he was so eclectic a thinker that it is perhaps too restrictive to call him in any narrow sense a Utilitarian. It has been justly said that "every wind of doctrine of his time" blew through his head.

The last of the progressive historicists was Herbert Spencer, who showed the doctrine of historical necessity almost as extremely as Marx would do, for he coined the phrase that "progress . . . is not an accident but a necessity." Spencer, who carried on an extraordinary platonic relationship with George Eliot, and was friendly with both John Stuart Mill and the evolutionist Thomas Henry Huxley, was a generalizing polymath on the grand Victorian scale, as the titles of his works suggest: *Principles of Psychology, Principles of Biology, Principles of Sociology, First Principles, The Proper Sphere of Government* and *Man versus the State*. He was a kind of philosophic anarchist who warned people, having got rid of the power of kings, to make sure of "putting a limit to the powers of parliament."

Spencer was in fact one of the major Victorian thinkers, though his contribution was obscured by the extraordinary fame that Charles Darwin gathered for his rival evolutionary teachings. Spencer in one way was a throwback to the pre-Socratic philosophers, for like them he saw philosophy as a kind of compendium of scientific knowledge, a unified system whose main theme was what he called "the development hypothesis." This "hypothesis" rejected the idea of a special creation as taught in Genesis and accepted at least formally by nineteenth-century Christians. Yet in spite of his emphasis on the natural sciences, Spencer was at heart a metaphysician, believing in the kind of natural laws that can easily be translated into laws of history. Essentially, he believed that there were unknowable absolute forces at work that operated in every aspect of the natural world, from the solar system to the biological kingdom and to human society, and which inevitably produced the process of constant variation that was development, otherwise known as evolution.

Spencer was actually the predecessor of both Darwin and Alfred Russell Wallace in propounding evolutionary theories, for his essay, "Progress: Its Law and Cause," appeared in 1857, two years before *On the Origin of Species.* Contrary to popular belief, it was Spencer who, in 1864, coined the phrase "survival of the fittest," which has been so habitually associated not only with Darwin's teachings but also with the rather heartless doctrine, derived from Malthus rather than from either Darwin or Spencer, called "Social Darwinism." Spencer in fact was nearer to Jean Baptiste Lamarck than to Darwin, for he believed—as some biologists are beginning to believe once again—in the inheritance of acquired characteristics, though he did eventually admit the Darwin-Wallace theory of natural selection as one of the possible processes of biological evolution. He differed from Darwin not only in his continued Lamarckism but also in the generally teleological character of his teachings; he might not acknowledge the intervention of a personal god, yet he saw an immense purpose at work in the processes of the universe. Natural selection alone was too random a process for him to acknowledge it as the sole mechanism of an evolution that he saw manifest geologically and sociologically as well as biologically. Change moved forward by ineluctable processes, whose cause would never be known, but since one of the processes was endless variation, freedom might be held to be contained within inevitability. A consequence of progress was the emergence of individual consciousness as a form of variation, and according to Spencer, men would increasingly be able to make use of the process of development for their own benefit; it was one of Spencer's main libertarian tenets that society existed to serve men, and not men to serve society. Small wonder that many of the more individualistic nineteenth-century anarchists regarded him as one of their own.

Yet for all their liberal values, for all the dedication to the idea of freedom that made Proudhon so admire Michelet, for all the perceptions of defects in even the best governments we find in Mill and Spencer, they were all in their own ways historical determinists. They all saw progress moving forward in a grand flow of destiny, on which the efforts of individuals were merest ripples. They regarded themselves as the servants of progress, and

73

were shaped—each in his own way—by the great surge of optimism that, for all its horrors, the French Revolution generated.

Their attitudes to their time and to history can be compared with that of the pre-Revolutionary ironist, Voltaire, libertarian and pessimist at the same time. Historian though he was, he could say that "History is no more than a portrayal of crimes and misfortunes." And perhaps because he was a historian, and knew the game, he could also remark that "All our ancient history . . . is no more than accepted fiction."

The contrast is striking in moving from Voltaire, to whom the idea of History as a great, irresistible force in human destiny would have been laughable, to the historian laureate of Victorian England, Thomas Babington Macaulay. The author of highly risible heroic poems ("Lars Porsena of Clusium/By the nine gods he swore/That the great house of Tarquin/Should suffer wrong no more"), Macaulay was without rival among the liberal historians of his day. He taught that progress was inevitable, interminable, and led by England: "The history of England is emphatically the history of progress." Such progress, somewhat variously identified with humanitarian doctrines and industrial revolution ethics, was History as the liberals saw it. The totalitarians of a post-Victorian age would see it somewhat differently.

PART IV

•

HISTORY

•

AND THE

•

DETERMINING

•

PROPHECY

CHAPTER VII

Hegel and the
Hinge of History

As the recent events in Europe—which I shall later discuss more closely—
have shown, it was not only the followers of Marx and Lenin, of Hitler and
Mussolini and all the other totalitarian messiahs, who became hypnotized
by the teachings of historical determinism and continued to accept the
inevitability of regimes whose ideological basis had withered with their
modicum of practical success. So did many who professed to believe in the
open and pluralist society, the market society and generally in liberal
progress. They too, until events broke the mental ice jam, looked on the
Marxist regimes as manifestations of fatality that could only be removed, as
the Nazi thousand-year reich had been, by the kind of total war that nuclear
weaponry had rendered unthinkable. Thus the Western powers wrung their
hands instead of using them when the Russians carried out their brutal
repressions in Germany in 1953, in Hungary in 1956, in Czechoslovakia
in 1968, and when the Chinese submerged Tibet in 1951. Very few people
foresaw the intervention of the contingent, of unexpected events set going
by masses of individuals so angry and desperate for freedom that they could
no longer endure living according to those most portentous but insubstantial of laws, the laws of History, and therefore proceeded, above all in 1989,
to break them.

Undoubtedly one of the reasons the apostles of History turned out in
the end to be bad prophets was that they were primarily theologians or
religious fanatics or economists, and in later years sociologists and party
ideologists. Few of them were historians in the true and original sense of

chroniclers of the past, for the simple reason that to be historicists and to make a destiny out of History, they had to lack the sense of detachment and independence so important to true historians if their work were to emerge as a successful artifact, a convincing—if not wholly true—version of what may have been; their vision, like that of poets and novelists, must be free and their own. This is undoubtedly one of the main reasons why there were no historians of any significance in Nazi Germany or Communist Russia or China. The mind of the historian, like that of any other artist, must work out its constructs in freedom and without fear. We cannot, for example, imagine Michelet writing so well on the French Revolution if the year had been early 1794 and he had felt the chill of the guillotine near his neck. And in the same way we cannot blame for what seems their slavishness the Russian and German historians who wrote under the shadow of the walls of the concentration camp or the Gulag. The shape of History in such situations was dictated not by the historians but by the ideologues. The enemy of true history, then as always, has been History.

The great father of all the totalitarian party ideologues, though he himself belonged to no party, was Georg Wilhelm Friedrich Hegel, who in 1818 became a professor at the University of Berlin and eventually the rector. The rulers of Prussia had long been inclined to cultivate philosophers (there was the strange association between Voltaire and Frederick the Great). And it was into something very close to a court philosopher that Hegel metamorphosed as he began to develop his theories, and particularly on History that elevated the state—especially the monarchical state—into the supreme form of human organization, and the one fated by historical necessity to succeed.

It is perhaps not unfair to either Plato or Hegel to see in Hegel's theories and proposals something very close to what Plato might have developed had he been faced with the fluid political circumstances of the post-Napoleonic world of the Congress of Vienna. Liberal and revolutionary causes were in temporary retreat, though by 1830 they had recovered sufficiently for Paris to have its revolution and Hegel to become anxious that the sickness might spread to Berlin. But in the interlude between 1815 and 1830 the old monarchies that had survived or been re-established in Europe were conscious of the need to find a philosophic justification of their rule and the methods they used to sustain it. Thus rulers like Alexander I of Russia and Frederick William III of Prussia tended to show favour to safely conservative intellectuals, just as the tyrants of antiquity had found it useful to flirt with the political notions of Plato and his like.

But there was more to the resemblance between Hegel and Plato than a matter of similar circumstances and a similar relation to the political powers of their times. Both were idealists who, when they turned to the material and transitory things of this world, offered determined patterns of history and determined political solutions that diminished the freedom of the individual in favour of the all-wise and all-mighty state. The main difference between them lay in the extent and the immediacy of their success. For, while the democratic good sense of the Athenians prevented them from accepting the notions Plato had put into the long-suffering mouth of Socrates in the *Republic* (after all, they had experienced their own enlightened despot in Pisistratos), the teachings of Hegel spread insidiously in the volatile political atmosphere of nineteenth-century continental Europe, giving rise to the fatalistic historicism of reactionaries and totalitarians of the right and left, both of whose representatives eventually attained a malign and corrupting power.

Hegel, whose knowledge of Plato and Aristotle was unusual for his time, somewhat transformed Plato's doctrine of the ideal, substituting a kind of Deism modified by Lutheran orthodoxy. He envisaged, coterminous with the universe, coexistent with it, and guiding all reality, an absolute spirit, a kind of world-soul, of which human reason was one of the emanations. In earthly matters and in the affairs of people, this spirit manifested itself through a process of history that became known as the Hegelian dialectic.

The word "dialectic" in this instance is analogical. The dialectic in its original meaning referred to the logical process of reaching conclusions through argument and counterargument. Hegel shows History arguing with itself according to its own laws. Change—and progress in so far as it is desirable—comes about because one concept or condition of society (the thesis) inevitably generates its opposite, which is the antithesis. They interact and by a process of conflict and compromise produce a third concept (or situation), the synthesis, which in its turn becomes the thesis of the next triad.

At about the same time, the French philosopher Auguste Comte proposed his own triadic philosophy of history, which he called Positivism. He also saw history in three phases. The first was the theological one, in which myths were ascendant and priests interpreted them and gave them historic significance. The second was the metaphysical one, in which people sought to interpret human life and history through philosophic concepts. The final stage was the Positive one—materialist and, as Comte insisted, like Marx, "scientific," the realm of rationality facing things as they are.

Hegel's process of thesis, antithesis and synthesis is History with its pattern of inherent laws, by which the absolute is revealed in action; as process, History in fact acquires its meaning from revealing and fulfilling the purpose of the absolute. This means that we are in no sense free agents, the historicist view being that, as Engels would say in imitation of Hegel, "Freedom is the appreciation of necessity." Hence the historicists tend in their actions to mirror History as they see it, to believe, if only implicitly, and to act as if it were right not only as a record of the past but also as a projection of the future, and to support the creation of those structures like nations and states and eventually dictatorships of the elite or the proletariat that most seem to reflect the determined character of History as they perceive it. (It is impossible to imagine a historically determined theory of anarchism.) The state in fact was for Hegel an autonomous political structure prior to achievement of a theoretical abstraction, and far from the kind of structure created for the convenience of its citizens that liberals like Mill and Spencer envisaged. It was a structure as interdependent as a coral reef and reflected the laws of history as the coral reef reflects the laws of biology, both being aspects of the ineluctable laws of universal change.

Hegel's statements on history are scattered through the considerable corpus of his work, both in the volumes published in his time and in those curious collections of notes by his students which editors after his death cobbled into further volumes, of which the *Philosophy of History* is one. Often expressed, with little apparent editing, in the inflated language customary in university lectures, pages from these works express his sense of History as a process of Reason—which he otherwise interprets as "the Plan of Providence."

In the *Encyclopaedia of the Philosophical Sciences*, which he compiled while still in Heidelberg and published in 1817, he declared:

> That History, and above all Universal History, is founded on
> an essential and actual aim, which *actually* is, and will be, *real-
> ized in it*—the Plan of Providence; that, in short, there is Rea-
> son in History, must be decided on strictly philosophical
> grounds, and thus shown to be essential and therefore necessary.

The later Berlin lectures in the *Philosophy of History* represent Hegel's major attempt to give a rational form to his concept of History as Reason, and they owe a great deal to the Platonic original, though, considered as pure dialectical arguments, Hegel's statements have little of the arrogant precision attempted by the great Greek polemicist. Describing his belief as a "conviction and intuition," Hegel declares it no mere "hypothesis" but a proven truth, though he is somewhat short on the proof:

The only thought with which Philosophy approaches History, is the simple conception of Reason; it is the doctrine that Reason is the Sovereign of the World, and that the history of the World, therefore, presents us with a *rational process . . . .* That this "Idea" or "Reason" is the *True*, the *Eternal*, the absolutely *Powerful Essence*; that it reveals itself in the World, and that in that World nothing else is revealed but this and its honour and glory—this is a thesis which, as we have said, has been proved in Philosophy and is here regarded as demonstrated.

As Edmund Wilson remarked in *To the Finland Station*, when quoting the above passage, "This gush does not carry us very far." But it does put forward strongly the concept of History as actual process, as the instrument of a determined world destiny rather than as the mere record of events, and Hegel's sweeping and wholly unprovable generalizations appealed to a late Romantic generation on the continent of Europe that was seeking, like other postwar generations, to sweep away the debris of the past but at the same time acquire some new reassuring myth of humanity proceeding on the great train of History towards a utopian destination.

Idealist doctrines tend to spawn contradictory offspring, as in the case of a contemporary of Hegel who was not actually influenced by him, the English poet Percy Bysshe Shelley. Shelley started off a disciple of the great libertarian thinker William Godwin, but later he became an enthusiastic admirer of the great authoritarian thinker Plato, and in his own way managed to reconcile the two apparently opposite influences.

In a similar way the range of Hegel's admirers revealed the essential contradiction in his historical thinking, in that he endeavoured to impose on a dynamic dialectical process a final and contemporary thesis, the Prussian state as it had evolved under the Hohenzollern dynasty. So the people his teachings attracted were by no means all of them apologists for autocracy, Prussian or otherwise, but in many cases young intellectuals in full rebellion against the narrower orthodoxies of their time, rebels for whom the very grandiosity and vagueness of Hegel's teachings offered not only mental liberation but also a concept of political change that might be adapted, as Shelley adapted his Platonism, to notably unconservative ends. Thus, not only the authoritarian socialist Marx, but also his great libertarian rivals, Pierre-Joseph Proudhon and Mikhail Bakunin, fell initially under the Hegelian spell. Like his friends Ivan Turgenev and Alexander Herzen, Bakunin responded to the grand and stimulating wave of Hegelian doctrine that in the later 1830s defied the frontier guards of Nicholas I and overleapt borders to stir the hearts of the rebellious young in Russia. Bakunin left for Berlin in 1840 to study the doctrine at its source. He returned home as a political prisoner, in chains. Escaping from Siberia, he died a bitter enemy of the state Hegel had served. It was the sheer scope of Hegel's ideas that had freed Bakunin's grandiose mind. Proudhon spent whole nights learning the Hegelian dialectic from Marx in the dingy hotel rooms of the Left Bank. But in the end, by abandoning the thesis, he turned the Hegelian process into the dynamic equilibrium that suited his anarchist aims.

In his own field Hegel had his rivals and bitter critics, including the great pioneer existentialist Søren Kierkegaard—philosopher and theologian at once, and the maverick philosopher Arthur Schopenhauer, who had broken away from German metaphysics in the direction of Indian philosophy. Schopenhauer's *The World as Will and Idea*, published at the height of Hegel's ascendancy in 1818, posed the will of the individual against the collective forces of History, and drew a pessimistic conclusion from the picture of human existence as a gladiatorial conflict with no necessary plan or direction. If Hegel was the philosopher who transformed the laws of logic into the laws of History, Schopenhauer was the paradoxically realist philosopher of the imagination, whose influence percolated into the modern age through transmitters as various as Friedrich Wilhelm Nietzsche and Sigmund Freud.

But it was within the neo-Hegelian movement that the most striking contradictions of Hegel appeared, as social reactionaries and social reformers and revolutionaries began to interpret the words of the master according to their own inclinations. What Hegel had attempted in his idealistic scheme was to provide a single solution for all the philosophical problems, moral as well as speculative. What he did in fact was to envisage a rationally conceived mechanism of change that could be put to use even by polemicists who did not share his own religious or socio-political inclinations. He engaged philosophy in all the aspects of collective human existence, including history and culture and the organization of social change. But once that engagement had been made, there were many ways of sustaining it, and the followers of Hegel did not all come to the same conclusions about the destinations of History.

In fact Hegelianism—never a movement so much as a ferment of ideas—fairly quickly hinged into two directions: a conservative one that associated Hegel with evangelical Christianity, and a radical one, the "Young Hegelians" or "Left Hegelians," who set out to use Hegel's insight for purposes he had never thought of, much less approved. The concept of the universal motivating force of Idea lent itself to pantheistic interpretation and to radical religious conclusions that quickly moved towards atheism. The beginnings of the nineteenth-century rational reassessment of Christianity, the so-called "Higher Criticism," appeared in this group, in books like David Friedrich Strauss's *The Life of Jesus, Critically Examined*, which dwelt upon the proportion of the myth in the gospel narrative and the function of myth in the philosophic task of reconciling divine and human nature. Strauss's initiative was followed by that of Bruno Bauer, who edged his controversy from biblical criticism towards political radicalism.

Bauer became a leading figure among the Free Hegelians of Berlin, a group that included the anarchist individualist polemicist Max Stirner and the young Friedrich Engels, who provided a link with a more politically oriented Rhineland group that included the early Communist writer and orator Moses Hess, the poet Heinrich Heine, Arnold Ruge, who edited the influential *Deutscher Jahrbücher*, and, most important historically, Karl Marx. For it was through Marx—and the Nazi ideologues in imitation of him—that the one vital and ordering element in Hegel's vaporous teachings, the dialectical interpretation of History, would be transfigured into a fatally powerful system of self-fulfilling prophecy.

CHAPTER VIII

Marx Inventing the Spectre

Karl Marx did not possess the kind of original genius with which his
followers and many of his critics have credited him. He did not invent
socialism or even communism any more than he invented the dialectical
interpretation of history. Even if we dismiss Plato's *Republic* as the speculative fantasy of an idealist-philosopher applying his ideas to actuality, the
concept of communism (often condescendingly described as "primitive")
echoes down through the description of the early disciples in the Acts of
the Apostles. Essentially it means the having of all things in common and
the equal sharing of them. It was a feature of primarily religious movements
like the millenarian sectarians of the Reformation and the Hutterites and
Doukhobors of recent history as much as of utopian visions described by
Renaissance thinkers like Thomas More and Tomasso Campanella, and of
actual intentional communities of which there are clear records from the
seventeenth-century Diggers onward.

Socialism is something slightly different, the product of a scientistic if
not a scientific age, dating from the early nineteenth century when the
concept that wealth was generated by society, and therefore should be
administered by society for the general benefit, began to find expression in
the writings and even the social experiments of radical thinkers like Henri
de Saint-Simon, Charles Fourier and Robert Owen. But socialism essentially
directed itself towards the question of production and assuring a just reward
for the producer. Communism concerned itself with distribution as much
as with production. Socialism, at least according to Marx and Engels, could

be compatible with a class society, as the doctrine of the "dictatorship of the proletariat" clearly showed. There has always been a curious kind of perverted honesty in the avowals of "Communist" parties in power, that they are in fact administering *socialism* but that communism is their ultimate and future destination. Of course, they have never reached it.

Marx, in other words, took over socialism and communism as he had already taken over and adapted to his own purposes the dialectical historicism of Hegel. Of his sincere hatred of systems of exploitation, and notably of capitalism, there can be no doubt, and even if there was more anger than compassion in his observation of the sufferings of the workers, that too was genuine enough. He devoted his life to seeking a way to end these injustices, and combined, in a way Hegel and his more orthodox disciples never did, a historical perception that moved into prophecy with the beginnings of practical subversive organization through seeking control of the principal social revolutionary organization of his time, the International Workingmen's Association. As Marx himself put it: "The philosophers up to now have merely interpreted it [the world] in various ways; the real thing is to change it." And, indeed, one way of interpreting Marx's approach to the dialectic is to see existing society as the Thesis, change as the Antithesis, and History, the fusion of existence and change, as the Synthesis.

The combination of prophecy and practice involved in Marx's view of change takes us back to an earlier stage in our survey, that of the religious radicals of the Reformation period, of John of Leyden and Thomas Müntzer with their millenarian philosophies and their attempts at practical communism. Looking back to those sixteenth-century rebels who so fascinated Engels, we begin to see Marxism as the secularization of the whole eschatological tradition that stemmed from Zoroaster's teachings so long before the birth of Christ. Indeed, Marxism's early success among workers in Protestant regions may well have been largely due to the fact that its principal teachings ran parallel to those of Christianity and, even more, of the Jewish prophetic writings which, through the authority of the Old Testament recently translated into the vernacular, assumed much importance among the dissenting sects that flourished so widely among the poor and the repressed.

Arnold Toynbee, a modern historicist of another kind, has well analyzed the part Jewish traditions, which Marx abandoned in his daily life, continued to play in the pattern of his thinking:

> The distinctively Jewish inspiration of Marxism is the apoca-
> lyptic vision of a violent revolution which is inevitable be-

85

cause it is the decree . . . of God himself, and which is to invert the present roles of Proletariat and Dominant-Minority
in . . . a reversal of roles which is to carry the Chosen People,
at one bound, from the lowest to the highest place in the
Kingdom of this world. Marx has taken the Goddess "Historical Necessity" in place of Yahweh for his omnipotent deity,
and the internal proletariat of the modern Western world in
place of Jewry; and his Messianic kingdom is conceived as a
Dictatorship of the Proletariat. But the salient features of the
traditional Jewish apocalypse protrude through the thread-
bare disguise, and it is actually the pre-Rabbinical Maccabean
Judaism that our philosopher-impresario is presenting to
modern Western culture.

Edmund Wilson in his account of the origins of Marxism points to an
even older connection in the borderlands between mythical and rational
discourse, between metaphysics and pragmatism, when he refers to the
triadic character of the Marxist pattern:

He [Marx] still believed in the Triad of Hegel, the Thèse, the
Antithèse and the Synthèse, and this triad was simply the old
Trinity, taken over from the Christian theology, as the Christians had taken it over from Plato. It was the mythical and
magical triangle which from the time of Pythagoras and before had stood as a symbol for certainty and power and which
probably derived from its correspondence to the male sexual
organs. "Philosophy," Marx once wrote, "stands in the same
relation to the study of the actual world as onanism to sexual
love"; but in his study of the actual world he insisted on
bringing in the Dialectic. Certainly the one-in-three, three-in-
one of the *Thesis*, the *Antithesis* and the *Synthesis* has had
upon Marxists a compelling effect which it would be impossible to justify through reason.

Though one may question Wilson's quaint reference to male pudenda,
there is no doubt of the continuing potency of the triadic principle, which
manifested itself not only in the teachings of Plato and in trinitarian
Christianity but also in the Hindu concept of the Trimurti as expressed in
the great cave sculpture of Elephanta, the three-faced entity combining the
attributes of Brahma, Siva and Vishnu: Creator, Destroyer and Preserver.

86

Out of the conflict between what is and its negation emerges the synthesis of renewal. It was a potent myth that the elaborators of the Dialectic harnessed to their cause.

So Marxism itself was in a sense a working out of the Dialectic, a synthesis of modern philosophy and ancient beliefs dating from the age when the outlines of reason defined themselves out of myth. In such concepts as the triad we stand, as we do so often when considering the ideas enunciated by Plato and Pythagoras so long ago, in the seas where magic and mythicism and mathematics—the earliest and the most precise of sciences—mingle. The idea of the power of numbers runs through the traditions of East and West as much as it does through modern political myths. The Ten Noble Truths of Buddhism were potent because they were Ten as well as Noble, and the Eightfold Path because it was Eightfold, just as the Ten Commandments have through the ages sustained their authority because of their number (1 plus nought numerologically conveying Unity, the singleness of God), which suggested the unique power of the deity without even mentioning it. And the preoccupation with powerful numbers has persisted in and through Marxism not merely in the theoretical field through the Triad of the Dialectic (parallelled by Comte's contemporary triadic series of human conditions) but also in the practical field of Marxist-Leninist reconstruction, in which numbers and time were brought together in potent but often insubstantial images like those of the Five Year Plans.

What Marx did in adopting the Hegelian philosophy and adapting it to his own radical ends was to bring about a synthesis between the Enlightenment teachings of freedom, fraternity and justice, and a secularized idea of History as destiny, which, according to his teachings, would achieve the synthesis that is the third term of the French Revolutionary triad—Equality, which in his view and that of all the other varieties of socialists and Communists active in the early nineteenth century, would be won only by the mastery by the oppressed classes of the means of production. History remained the great self-fulfilling prophetic force, as it had been for Hegel, but the necessity under which it operated now became economic and material rather than metaphysical and ideal.

It was the steady process of economic transformation that, according to Marx and Engels, and even to their opponents Bakunin and Kropotkin, created the struggle of classes, sustained it, and used it as the mechanism of historical transformation. Thus, they claimed, the history of economic change in society ran parallel to the history of the liberation of humankind. The slavery-based economy of the ancient world gave way to the feudal economy of the Middle Ages, in which the peasant serf, though tied to the soil, ideally had rights to match his duties. As the feudal structure began to collapse, largely because of the caprice of natural causes represented by the Black Death and the other great mediaeval plagues, there began to emerge a literally bourgeois world in which the leading figures were the burgesses of the mercantile cities of Europe. The economic consolidation of their power was parallelled by the rise of monarchical absolutism, as the emergent royal dynasties of England and France, of Spain and Austria and Muscovy, allied themselves with the cities which they themselves had often chartered, or those that had risen independently on the advancing edges of civilization.

Once the nobles had been turned into tame courtiers going through their paces, the kings attempted to submit the cities to their yoke, and the period from the sixteenth to the eighteenth century became a time of strife and shifting allegiances. In England the nobility had protected itself by initiating a democratic process through the concessions it forced on King John under the Magna Carta, which was important less for what it granted than because it established a justification for the limitation of absolute rule. And this meant that during the revolutionary years of the seventeenth century, when one king was killed and another was deposed, the English nobility, allied with the country gentlemen and the city burgesses, maintained control of the governmental apparatus even as monarchs came and went and dynasties changed. The retention of land ownership (and through land ownership of power in parliament) sustained the great feudal and postfeudal magnates in England after feudalism ended in a way they were not sustained in France, where the peasants seized much of the land at the time of the Revolution and prevented a bourgeois-aristocrat symbiosis of the British type from emerging. (This analysis is not an exclusively Marxist one; it is based largely on that presented by non-Marxist revolutionaries like Kropotkin. The two trends agreed about the past; it was the future that would divide them.)

Britain was the setting for the social situation which Marx and Engels portrayed in their works and which they spent all their lives trying to elucidate and turn to the ends of History as they perceived it. The situation came about through the transformation of the mercantile burgess class of the late Middle Ages and the Renaissance into the industrial capitalist class, and the consequent disruption of social relations, urban and rural, at the same time. Capital gained in trade was invested in industry, which was largely fed by the coal and minerals that the landed magnates found and exploited on their estates. A series of inventions, the steam engine most important among them, mechanized the old handcrafts, replacing the traditional workshops with mass-employment factories filled by handweavers thrown out of work by the machines, by their women and children, and by country people forced off the land when the landowners enclosed the common lands originally shared by the local community and turned them into private grazing tracts. The old industrial relationship based on the guilds, which both protected the workers and guaranteed the quality of workmanship, disintegrated under the factory system, which created a proletariat in place of a community of independent workers, each master of a complex craft. A new kind of slave community was created in the raw towns that sprang up around the factories and the coal mines, more inhuman if not more ugly than the old city slums; they also came with instant pollution which spread even into the older cities and created the famous British fog.

Marx saw this situation as intensifying the class divisions which manifested the dialectic process at work in human history. While the rich were getting richer by robbing the workers of the surplus value of their labour, and the poor were demonstrably getting poorer, society was becoming polarized. The intermediate classes of clerks and skilled workers and professionals were being absorbed into the bourgeoisie and proletariat while the peasants were left on the sidelines to watch the last great struggle (*la lutte finale* of "The Internationale") as capitalism staggered from crisis to crisis until the revolution. Here was the prophecy that Marx had extracted by considering his time and place through Hegelian glasses, and he came to attempt his final transformation of the objective of philosophy from an explanation of the universe to changing the world.

Where Hegel had been absurd enough to accept, as the end of the dialectical process in terms of social transformation, the actual political structure of the Prussian kingdom in which he lived, Marx looked with a prophetic eye towards the future and, in a way that has ever since characterized all doctrines that call themselves Marxist, he assumed that his auguries were self-fulfilling. Still, following the old maxim that "God helps him who helps himself," he understood that a certain care had to be taken to make sure that the forecasts fulfilled themselves in the right way, which was why, from the Communist League in the 1840s to the International Workingmen's Association in the 1860s and early 1870s, Marx and his friend Engels attempted to form a movement among the workers to nudge events in the way they favoured.

Events, in fact, revealed that the shaping of the future was less certain and less easy than Marx had first imagined. He had envisaged the contradictions of capitalism building up until the economic structure collapsed; in the resultant struggle the forces of the revolution would take control under the leadership of the proletariat, whose dictatorship would usher in the new society and nurture it until an anarchist utopia emerged. All this was based on an assessment of social development in mid-nineteenth-century Europe, leading Marx to adopt a prophet's confidence and fall into the greatest of a historian's pitfalls, which is to assume that events, renamed History, will proceed in the direction that any particular time seems to indicate.

In fact, even when Marx began to write *Das Kapital* in the 1860s, events were moving in a different way from that he had anticipated. While it is true that the data presented in *Das Kapital* and earlier by Engels in *The Condition of the Working Class in England* showed the actual destitution of working people and the appalling quality of proletarian lives in industrial revolution England, the fact remains that they were derived not from the investigations of some Henry Mayhew or George Orwell pursuing his unofficial trips of discovery into the heart of English darkness, but from the actual blue books presented to the British parliament by its officials appointed in response to an urge—largely inspired by Christian evangelism—to remedy the abuses of the earlier generations of capitalism. A large section of the ruling class, whether from compassion or calculation, was already intent on removing the conditions that exacerbated class conflict. At the same time, far from behaving like slaves, the English workingmen were frequently rebels if not revolutionaries, through the Chartist movement, through Luddism, through the struggles to establish co-operatives and trade unions, and, even before Marx's death, through the creation of socialist movements, only some of whose members thought in revolutionary terms.

And the fact was that by the 1880s the catastrophic ending of the capitalist order was becoming steadily less imminent as English society moved into its Victorian prime. Capital survived its cyclic troubles, the condition of the workers slowly improved so that despairing socialists sometimes complained of their bourgeoisification, and the irreconcilable gap which Marx had foreseen opening wide between the rich and the poor was filling up with a growing middle class.

By the time Marx died he was beginning to wonder if History were in fact behaving according to its laws as he had seen them. He even admitted that the English might achieve social justice by gradual process rather than by revolution. And in 1901, after the death of Engels, the Social Democratic leader Edward Bernstein proposed with some success a "revision" of Marxism based on the growing power of the labour unions and the idea that all the socialists wanted could be achieved piecemeal and peacefully without resort to revolution.

By 1914 the working-class leaders of Britain, France and Germany all declared support for their respective sides in the first days of the Great War, and it seemed as though antimilitarism, the social revolution, all the old shibboleths of the left, had been shelved forever. Events had shown that history, however well it worked as a chronicle of the past, had little validity as an instrument for shaping the future.

Yet the most formidable manifestations of the power of historical doctrines were yet to come, in unexpected ways and places, and were to cloud the lives of whole countries for decades and even for generations.

CHAPTER IX

Lenin: Terror as the Servant and Master of History

As was customary among good North German bourgeois in the nineteenth century, Marx and Engels tended to despise the Slavs, especially the Russians and the Czechs, making an exception only for the Poles with their strong tradition of insurrectionary resistance to tsarist authority. Russia in particular seemed to them a land of peasant darkness that would have to move through the various stages of capitalism before the dialectic progression could be fulfilled and the rule of the proletariat be achieved. Certainly the antagonism towards Russia of the two founding fathers of Marxism was augmented by the vigour with which the great Russian anarchist Mikhail Bakunin, who believed strongly in the revolutionary potential of the peasants, led the opposition to them in the International.

Towards the end of his life, however, Marx was inclined to admit the possibility of a social revolution taking place in Russia. He based this modification of his views less on any change of mind towards the peasant masses of the country than on the fact that, with the introduction of railways and the spread of industry in the cities, a capitalist class and a proletariat were emerging side by side.

And Russia was to be, in 1917, the place where the first great revolution of the twentieth century took place. But it was not the kind of revolution that Marx had foretold, since it was carried out not by the proletariat itself but by a conspiratorial group of professional revolutionaries who manipulated the workers of Petrograd, and who would not have succeeded if the city had not contained thousands of soldiers and sailors, disillusioned with a mismanaged war, on whose numbers and weapons the Bolsheviks could rely.

The takeover of Petrograd, which committed Russia to what for long appeared a Marxist destiny, was mainly the work of that ruthless but brilliant revolutionary tactician who went by the name of Leon Trotsky. But the ideological basis of the revolution was the creation of Vladimir Ilyich Ulyanov, better known as Lenin.

The main difference between Marx and Lenin was that while Marx used an often brilliant economically based interpretation of social change—identified with History—not merely as a system of analysis but also a system of prophecy, Lenin set out to make the prophecy self-fulfilling: in other words, not only to understand History but to command it. Lenin's contributions to economic theory were meagre, consisting mainly of adding another stage to the dialectic process by borrowing from the English writer J. S. Hobson the idea that capitalism was about to undergo a final flowering known as imperialism. It was as the theoretician of conspiratorial insurrectionism followed by revolutionary dictatorship that he ensured the triumph of Marxist rulers for so long in so many countries.

Lenin did this by developing a method of interference in the dialectical process far more thorough than Marx ever contemplated or attempted. Marx thought in terms of mass working-class organizations, and in so far as he ever conspired, it was to influence their policies. He failed in these efforts, for Bakunin took the International out from under him, and in the great German working-class socialist movement he was challenged in his lifetime by Ferdinand Lasalle and after his death by revisionists like Bernstein. Marx, in fact, remained at heart a scholar, and he was far more at home in the British Museum, preparing the case against capitalism and promulgating the Jehovah he called History, than in playing the political game.

Lenin was convinced from the beginning of the need for conspiratorial discipline, and from his early days in the Russian Social Democratic party, before the split between Bolsheviks and Mensheviks, he worked on creating a tightly knit organization of revolutionary activists devoted not merely to advocating the revolution but to directing it as well as the society that would evolve. The myth of the dictatorship of the proletariat was always present in Leninism, but strictly as a myth; in practice the proletariat would dictate through the party.

Leninism as it emerged was a combination of original Marxism, so far as its economic side was concerned, with a strange variety of influences shaping its political aspects. In his thinking Lenin went back to Russian and

European revolutionary trends that had challenged Marxism and continued to do so. Among the most formidable groups in the Paris Commune of 1871, and also of the International, were the followers of Auguste Blanqui. Blanqui did not spend much time on socio-political doctrines. He was, rather, an influential revolutionary theoretician, and an energetic though not very successful practical insurrectionary.

Blanqui called himself a socialist, and indeed a socialist society was one of his ultimate aims, but he had no faith in the revolutionary capabilities of the undifferentiated proletariat. He believed that a revolution could be effectively carried out only by a small and disciplined minority which would establish a revolutionary dictatorship. The dictatorship—not the workers—would carry out the essential task of defeating and disarming the bourgeoisie, of expropriating the land, and of nationalizing industrial and commercial ventures. Then the dictatorship would set out on a vast task of education, which would lead the people to establish associations and co-operatives to administer the social wealth. Finally the dictatorship might dissolve.

Essentially it was a development in a socialist direction of the ideas and practice of the Jacobins during the French Revolution. Blanqui organized a whole series of conspiratorial secret societies, initiated a number of unsuccessful plots during the Restoration and Second Empire, and spent a total of thirty-three of his seventy-five years in French prisons. His influence has lingered in French left-wing politics down to the present day, re-emerging for example in the student revolt of 1968, but it also spread outside French borders, and his revolutionary programme reads remarkably like a sketch for Lenin's blueprint of the Bolshevik Revolution.

Mikhail Bakunin's influence did not die away after his death in 1876 and the virtual end in the same year of the International Workingmen's Association which had offered him and Marx so dramatic a battleground. The influence was not merely that of the anarchist theoretician advocating a free society to be achieved by the action of the workers and peasants themselves. Bakunin shared with Blanqui not only a taste for insurrections, for the smell of powder at the barricades, but also a passion for forming secret societies, which he began to found in Italy and Spain during the 1860s and used in his campaign against Marx in the International. He may not have believed in revolutionary dictatorship, but he did believe that revolutions must be prepared and led, even if not directed, by dedicated and secretive groups of activists whose deeds would inspire the people in general.

With his celebrated slogan, "The urge to destroy is also a creative urge," Bakunin was also related to the Populist tradition in Russia, which right down to 1917, when it was represented by the Socialist Revolutionary party, far exceeded the Marxists in popularity except among the industrial workers. The Populists sprang from the curious movement of political and educational missionaries during the 1860s, when thousands of upper-class young men and women, the "conscience-stricken nobility" of Russia, had "gone to the people," seeking to sow the seeds of revolt among peasants who often received them with suspicion and betrayed them afterwards to the police. Out of the Populists emerged the Nihilists, young intellectuals who, following Bakunin, presented themselves as deniers and destroyers, seeking to undermine all the moral as well as the political presuppositions of their contemporaries. Believing that the field must be swept clear for the inevitable appearance of a new world, the Nihilists were at heart as much revolutionary historicists as the followers of Marx. Yet the early Nihilists, of whom the most celebrated example in literature was Ivan Turgenev's character Bazarov in *Fathers and Sons*, were not practising terrorists.

By the late 1870s, however, the patience of the populist militants began to wear thin as Tsar Alexander II, who had liberated the serfs by imperial decree in 1861, delayed the further reforms, including a constitution, that he had promised. The activists formed a clandestine organization, Narodnaya Volya (the People's Will), whose executive committee blew up the tsar in 1881. The tsar's death led merely to increased persecutions, as Alexander III reversed the mildly reformist direction of his father's rule and committed Russia to the reactionary autocracy that would lead in less than a quarter of a century to the first Russian revolution in 1905. And the Draconian rule of Alexander's satraps led to an increasing number of plots against the monarch himself. One of the attempts against the new tsar was by a group that included Alexander Ilyich Ulyanov, the elder brother of the man who became Lenin; Alexander was one of the five inefficient dynamiters who were picked out for hanging. Up to this point Lenin had been politically inactive, but very quickly he too was vengefully involved, though he found his milieu not in the individualistic mixture of idealism and adventure that characterized the terrorist populists but in the Marxist movement where he could identify himself with History. In the end he would not only foretell but actually become History conceived as human power; he would utter the great millennial prophecy and at the same time pose as its fulfilment; he would be the apocalyptic but also the apocalypse.

But in order to create the monstrous body of teaching and merciless practice that became known as Marxist-Leninism and that shaped and shadowed—and still in many places darkens—the lives of millions in what so long seemed an irremediable destiny, Lenin needed more than the teachings of Marx. He needed to go beyond Marx's contempt for "bourgeois" morality to a rejection of all morality, and he found that total revolutionary amorality in the more aberrant corners of the populist movement, where nihilism was chained to its opposite in the liberation of the activist to act in any way necessary for the tyrannical triumph of destructionist revolution.

And here another figure entered on the scene whom Marx regarded with even more hostility than Mikhail Bakunin; the Sergei Nechaev who was the original of the ruthless Peter Verkhovensky in Fyodor Dostoevsky's *The Possessed*. A man of repellent yet charismatic personality, who captivated even the sly old plotter Bakunin and later turned the very warders of the Peter-and-Paul Fortress into his messengers, Nechaev was another inveterate conspiratorial fantasist who organized or invented many secret societies. He might have been wholly forgotten if he had not concocted an extraordinary document known as the *Revolutionary Catechism* which circulated in samizdat fashion in Russian conspiratorial circles. It set out the duties of the ideal revolutionary, who must lose his individuality and become a kind of monk of righteous extermination, a nineteenth-century *semblable* of that mediaeval Islamic sect of pure-hearted murderers, the Hashishim. Says the *Catechism*:

> The revolutionary is a man under vow. He must occupy himself entirely with one exclusive interest, with one thought and one passion, the Revolution. . . . He has only one aim, one science, destruction. . . . Between him and society there is war to the death, incessant, irreconcilable. . . . The revolutionary inhabits the world of the state, of the privileged classes, of so-called civilization, only to bring about its rapid and total destruction. He must not hesitate to destroy any property, place or person in that world. He must hate everyone and everything in it with an equal hatred. *All the worse for him if he has any remaining links with parents, friends or lovers; he is not a true revolutionary so long as he is swayed by such relationships.*

People were to be used and compromised without a second thought if they were of possible use to the revolution, and any means of destroying the ruling class or its supporters was admissible—"poison, the knife, the rope," treachery or open violence.

Even Bakunin shied away from Nechaev's expedient amorality when it was practised on him and his conspiratorial correspondence was stolen, and he warned other Russian exiles in Western Europe against his one-time protégé. Yet, though he achieved almost nothing as an activist, Nechaev gained a fine martyr's crown when he was imprisoned in the Peter-and-Paul fortress, and there, suborning the warders, kept contact with the Narodnaya Volya and other terrorists. He died in his cell in 1882. He built up an enormous reputation for his courage and steadfastness during his prison years and so, while for Dostoevsky he was a fascinating "monster" to be pilloried as the despicable Peter Verkhovensky, for Lenin he became a "titanic revolutionary" and a "genius."

In considering Lenin's later career, his writings, his actions in 1917 and afterwards, it seems clear that it was Nechaev's political amorality, even more than his courage, that Lenin admired and indeed appropriated, since it gave him the clue to his problem as to how the prophecies of Marxism were to be made self-fulfilling and therefore to be identified with History. He set out towards that fulfilment by the paradox of using unlimited violence, unlimited tyranny, to achieve the postrevolutionary end which he would portray with such startling naiveté as he wrote *State and Revolution*, a strange combination of Nechaevian ruthlessness and anarchist visions of paradise regained in a society of natural harmony. As in his earlier pamphlet of theory turned into action, "What Is To Be Done?," written in the aftermath of the 1905 revolution in Russia, Lenin wrote of conspiratorial movements leading the workers—who unled would content themselves with mere trade-unionlike action—into revolutionary activities where all would be permitted, since the task was one imposed by History, and imposed moreover as the prelude to social transformation. In "What Is To Be Done?" he expressed the historic duty quite clearly, and emphasized how much at the present time it was a Russian task:

History has set before us a task to be accomplished in the near future, which is far more revolutionary than all the immediate tasks of the proletariat of any other country. The fulfilment of this task, the destruction of the most powerful bulwark of European and (we may even say) of Asiatic reaction, would surely make the Russian proletariat the vanguard of the international proletarian revolution. And we rightly count on acquiring this honourable title, already earned by our predecessors, the revolutionaries of the seventies, if we succeed in inspiring our movement—a movement which is a thousand times broader and deeper—with the same limitless steadfastness and energy.

Lenin was creating the myth that is a necessary feature of any historicist vision. His was the myth of the militant proletariat that would triumphantly destroy the "bulwark of reaction" and thus lead on to the millennium—the ultimate synthesis—that is the goal of all historicist visions. But to become incarnate, the myth needed a structure of organization and action, and it was these that, with the relentless industry and ruthless energy of a man who feels himself destined for power as Napoleon did, Lenin built up. The organization consisted of creating a nucleus of like-minded men, ruthless yet obedient and willing to go to any extreme in seizing control of the state. As there was no revolutionary situation in Russia, the Social Democratic party became the first battleground; by dividing the party into the rival factions of Bolsheviks and Mensheviks and making sure that the Bolsheviks always took the initiative, Lenin succeeded in creating the tightly knit conspiratorial organization that was to lead the workers and in which Blanqui's and Bakunin's ideas would be developed.

When revolution did occur in Russia for the first time in 1905, the Bolsheviks, like all the other parties, were incompletely prepared—and Lenin as much as the rest; most of the initiatives were taken by Trotsky, whose somewhat romantic personality led to his being regarded very dubiously at the time by the hardcore Bolsheviks. During the 1917 revolution, the second chance that is so rarely given, the Bolsheviks established themselves as the party of the most militant groups of workers in Petrograd (though not elsewhere) and—more important—had won over some of the key army units and the sailors of Kronstadt. As in the case of most successful insurrections, victory owed less to the organization of the insurgents than to the disorganization of Alexander Kerensky's government and his military support. But the end for which Lenin planned so long had been achieved; the Bolsheviks were in supreme control, for though the Socialist Revolutionaries retained the loyalty of most of the peasants, they had no idea how to mobilize it in the situation of ruthless and audacious power that Lenin created.

From the beginning Lenin applied the morality and methods of Nechaev to the consolidation and continuation of his rule, and he more than any other individual is responsible for the shape that Bolshevik policies gave to History (and history) in Russia and in the countries that eventually accepted what later became known as Marxist-Leninism. Trotsky was merely the brilliant natural tactician who assured the success of the physical operations in October and in the subsequent civil war. Felix Djerzhinsky, the sinister and ascetic Pole who created the Cheka, turning the Okhrana from a tsarist into a revolutionary secret police, was little more than an enforcer who carried out the cruel will of his master Lenin.

Stalin, who was to be so greatly blamed for the brutality of the Communist regime and for the relentless elimination of all real and imagined enemies and critics, merely gave the coarse cast of greed and sadism to a ruthlessness that had been implanted in the Bolshevik regime by Lenin as theoretician and practitioner (though he never saw a man being shot) of terror in the cause of self-fulfilling prophecy. It was under Lenin that the Cheka was created, and on Lenin's instructions, sometimes open and sometimes tacit, that the tsar's family and the aristocratic hostages were shot. By the time of Lenin's death the slaughter had spread to the leaders and activists of rival socialist groups, including even the Mensheviks with whom the Bolsheviks had once formed a single party and the Left Socialist Revolutionaries with whom they had allied themselves for convenience in October 1917. And it was at Lenin's orders, and with Trotsky's enthusiastic participation, that the sailors of Kronstadt were slaughtered in 1921 when they demanded a return from Bolshevik dictatorship to socialist democracy.

These were the actions that set the mould of the totalitarian Communist state, and by their audacious atrocity created it in the image of a vast indefatigable state machine that consumed enemies and critics, ruthlessly remaking society in its own image. It was seen as the great consuming synthesis of the dialectic process; as history made manifest in unlimited power; as the prophecy self-fulfilled. And for seventy years, a longish human life, it would hypnotize one-half of humanity and inspire in the other half what turned out to be a groundless fear. Strangely enough, Trotsky—who played so active a role as Lenin's lieutenant—foresaw it all in a prophetic remark he made as early as 1903:

> Lenin's methods lead to this: the party organization at first substitutes itself for the party as a whole; then the Central Committee substitutes itself for the organization; and finally a single "dictator" substitutes himself for the Central Committee.

Trotsky left out one term of the process, that by which "the party as a whole" substituted itself for the proletariat it was supposed to serve as well as lead. But in general his perception was correct; from a very early stage Lenin was concerned to the point of obsession with gathering power.

Yet there was an extraordinary austerity to Lenin's drive to power, exemplified in the plainness and simplicity of his daily life even when he finally controlled for a brief period the whole of Russia. It was as if he had listened to the instructions given by Krishna to Arjuna before the great battle of Kurukshetra, to fulfil oneself in action but not for the fruits of action. Lenin, though he would never have given words to the concept, saw History as a recreating deity if not as a prime creator. And he saw himself, as all historicists do, as the minister of that deity, one of those chosen to prophesy and to fulfil the prophecy.

PART V

THE

AGE

OF

MONOLITHS

Rival Destinies:
The Totalitarians Try to
Create History in the 1930s

Like all those who imbue themselves with the sense of making History, Lenin was inspired by a kind of supermorality—not unlike that promoted by Nietzsche—that seemed to him and his disciples to justify all the killing and cruelty which, once he came to power, he initiated with the aim of creating universal human happiness. Though he may have doubted the men he had chosen to continue his mission, he seems to have died believing that his plans would be carried out by the will of History in all its rigour until eventually the wretched of the earth were liberated from their misery.

In fact, the opposite happened. The people of Russia were subjected to years of civil war followed by famine and continued oppression and misery from which, more than seventy years after the October Revolution, they emerged only in 1991. In developments resulting from the quasi-imperial direction assumed by the Russian state, people in China and Western Europe, in countries as widely spread apart as Cuba and Vietnam, Laos and Ethiopia, were subjected to Marxist tyrannies as oppressive as any rule they had endured in the past. If the prophecies of Lenin and Marx did fulfil themselves, it was only in cruel parody.

The custom in recent years has been to throw the blame for this disappointment of Marxist-Leninist hopes mainly on the shoulders of Stalin. The scenario runs something like this. Dominated by his greed, his jealousies, his fears, the Georgian monster Stalin lived for the fruits of power Lenin had rejected, distorting the ideal to which Lenin had sacrificed himself and so many others. But he invented nothing new; his proscriptions were merely greater and his elimination of rivals more coarsely and treacherously done than Lenin's had been. By squeezing all originality of thought and all initiative except bureaucratic initiative out of the state machine of communism, he turned the party, the great engine of history incarnate, into an *apparat*, a machine, a mere steamroller that crushed out not only the will of individuals but the spirit of the revolution itself. History under him became like a bleak landscape, the equivalent—and indeed the inspiration— of Orwell's London of *Nineteen Eighty-four*, in which all semblances of civilization were crushed down as they appeared.

We can accept the portrait of Stalin as a man without scruples and without vision, concerned with power *and* the fruits of power and not a little alarmed for his own life. We may grant that for the sake of his own ascendancy he transformed the party that was meant to be the vanguard of the revolutionary proletariat into an instrument of oppression. But even as we do so, there is the sense that Stalin and even Lenin were not entirely free agents in their pursuit of History but were caught up in patterns of events that negated the historical urge of Marxism and disturbed the dialectical equilibrium.

The assumption of historicists and of political activists who engage in prophecy and then seek to manipulate the fulfilment of their prophecies is that events will move in the quasi-eschatological direction they have chosen, that the results of their actions will necessarily be cumulative if not "progressive." But events do not always go as proposed or desired; once set in motion, they can—and often do—change course, and even do so more emphatically because of the ruthless tenacity with which activists seek to push them towards "the right" conclusion. The bloodstained Eden of Anabaptist Münster was an example; so was the French Revolution, as it moved inexorably towards the Terror and the negation of its proclaimed objectives of liberty, fraternity and equality, and eventually, by a complete historical reversal of direction, to an attempt at curing the troubles of the Republic by the ancient solution of Caesarism in a new Napoleonic form.

This in fact was what happened in Russia in the years following the October Revolution. The pull of a visionary future proved less strong than the example of a concrete past, and the revolutionary initiative died as autocracy re-emerged from its own ruins. Stalin's admiration for the ruthlessly innovative tsars like Ivan the Terrible and Peter the Great was reflected in his own autocratic policies, so that his real role in Russian history is equivalent to that of the barbaric tsars. He became an entrenched autocrat, while Lenin, even in his bewilderment with how to use power once he had gained it, remained to the end the revolutionary prophet and plotter. And it was as the successor to the Romanov monarchs rather than as the personification of world revolution that Stalin built up the structure of his state, with the various successors of the Cheka taking the place of the Okhrona but operating even more ruthlessly because of their inside knowledge of revolutionary tactics, and an official apparat closely resembling the elaborately ranked tsarist bureaucracy, just as tyrannical and just as corrupt. History did not lose its place in the Communist ideology; it was held to sustain and justify the Soviet state which, despite all appearances of stagnation, was represented as evolving towards true communism and in the meantime was impregnable.

The totalitarian Stalinist state was in fact autocracy adapted to contemporary circumstances, which means that it became tyranny in a rather classic sense, for the ancient Greek tyrants were, like Stalin—and in their own ways like Hitler and Mussolini—the figureheads of states that combined authoritarianism and populism. In modern times such states—Stalinist Russia, Nazi Germany and Fascist Italy—all claimed, no matter what their crimes against individuals and groups, to represent the people. They maintained that they were sustained not by the old-style ruling classes but by mass support, which was at least partially true, even though the later members of their party tended to be forced recruits. They also all claimed a monopoly of History, both as its prophets and as its heirs. Like their common ancestor Friedrich Hegel, they all saw war as an indispensable sign of a nation's vitality, and all of them dabbled in the Spanish Civil War during the 1930s to test their military powers.

But all of them encountered also what I call social factors rather than historical trends, and these factors confused their prophecies, frustrated their plans and eventually revealed History deified as a false god.

All three dictatorships quickly took on an imperialist form. Stalin promoted this by centralizing the Soviet state, which contained a dozen "autonomous" republics inhabited by non-Russians. And, having reinstated the tsarist empire, he developed the idea of socialism in a single state. This ran contrary to the aims and hopes of Lenin, who to the end of his life looked forward to revolutions in other countries to relieve Russia from its isolation and move History forward in great dialectic leaps; to this end he founded the Third International. It was also one of the main grounds of disagreement between Stalin and Trotsky, who to the end of his life (brought about by Stalin's agents) preached the neo-Leninist doctrine of "permanent revolution" (interestingly revived by the nominal Stalinist Mao Zedong in China's Cultural Revolution of 1966).

Trotsky was bound to be defeated over this issue because Stalin's idea of

105

socialism in a single country appealed to the latent imperialism of Russians and especially of the military class, who were increasingly essential to the survival of the Soviet state, and the *apparatchiks* (party officials) and secret policemen who controlled the country internally. The great parades in Red Square when the military might of the Soviet Union was displayed to the world were symbolic events at which the generals and the political leaders on their saluting stand personified an imperialist nation as certainly the entourages of Der Führer and Il Duce did on similar occasions in Germany and Italy.

Hand in hand with a revived imperialism went the related factor of tradition. Revolutionary Russia, by ritually slaughtering the tsar and his family, may have seemed to be casting off its links with the great imperialist rulers like Ivan the Terrible, Peter and Catherine (both ranked as "Great") and Nicholas I, and during the 1930s Stalinist Russia might seem to be passing up the chance of a Communist empire in Asia by betraying the Communists in Shanghai when it made a treacherous pact with Chiang Kai-shek.

Meanwhile, Italy (in the 1920s) and Germany (in the 1930s) had become subject to totalitarian dictatorships which were both strongly militaristic and led by men who believed as firmly as Lenin had ever done that they were both serving and shaping History. Benito Mussolini was a former left-wing socialist who had at one time translated the works of the anarchist Peter Kropotkin, and the ideological ancestry of fascism was indeed more respectable than that of nazism, sharing Hegel with the German movement, but also deriving from the political ideas of the Italian writer Vilfredo Pareto and the syndicalist theories of Georges Sorel. Mussolini had observed how, in exile in neighbouring Switzerland, Lenin and his associates formed a disciplined party which they presented as the vanguard of the disinherited. And later he observed how, in the October Revolution, a relatively small but determined proportion of the population had been able to seize power quickly and, once in power, had ruthlessly eliminated its opponents even when they belonged to rival socialist parties. In the same way Mussolini set out to seize power quickly and dramatically through his spectacular march on Rome in 1922, and got rid of his rivals with a ruthlessness equal to that of Lenin. Roughly the same pattern was followed by the Nazis in Germany during the 1930s.

The three dictatorships shared a great deal, for they were largely established by generations and classes that were disillusioned with the results of the Great War but not with the idea of war itself.

Russia technically avoided defeat in the Great War by concluding the humiliating treaty of Brest-Litovsk. Germany faced total defeat and the loss of its colonies while the Hapsburg dual monarchy was dismantled. Italy, which had chosen belatedly in 1915 to enter the war on the Allied side, hoped its colonial possessions would be increased at Germany's expense under the Treaty of Versailles, but went unsatisfied.

In Germany and Italy, old soldiers who were mostly young men formed the original cores of the Fascist and National Socialist movements. Though war had brought about their humiliation, they regarded it paradoxically as the means by which, if resolutely pursued, their nations (and/or races) could re-establish themselves and proceed towards the world power that would wipe out the humiliations of the past. Both Fascist and Nazi movements were fervently historicist, perceiving the control of the future as their proper task, and they were also fervently hostile to any kind of individualist thinking, for even freedom they considered as an attribute of the group; the German *Volk* (or people) could aspire to liberty, the German individual must fulfil himself as its servant, like a worker or a warrior ant within the hill. History, to the historicist has always, almost by definition, concerned the destiny of the collective; even the leader, in theory at least, is its mediator with the great forces that move the affairs of men, rather than its personification.

Perhaps the most striking aspect of the Fascist and Nazi movements, as of Stalinism before it declined into the stagnation of the Leonid Brezhnev era in the late 1960s, was the curious forward-backward movement they displayed. Their revolutions, if the campaigns and coups d'état that took them to power can be described as such, were carried out by young men, and in the structure that sustained them in power, the idea of youth was important; Stalinism had its initiatory Komsomol (Young Communist League) and nazism its Hitler Youth, while the very anthem of fascism was called "The Song of Youth." Despite this forward orientation, atavistic dreams and anachronistic ideas permeated the movements.

Just as Stalin and his followers looked back to the tsars to create their twentieth-century autocracy, so the Fascists set their historic sights on imperial Rome and attempted to match its conquests by the invasion of Ethiopia and its annexation, the last of the true African colonial ventures. As for the Nazis, their appeal to race and to ancient Teutonic tribal values led to a glorification of the Germany of the tribal leader Herman, the part that did not succumb to Roman invasion. More interesting perhaps, as an indication of the chiliastic historicism which united nazism with early German movements, was the harking back to concepts developed by radical heretics in the Reformation. The idea of the Third Reich, apart from looking

back to the Holy Roman empire and Bismarck's empire as its two predecessors, was an example of the kind of triadic thinking fairly universal in
human societies. But the alternative concept of the thousand-year reich was
one that had flourished, especially in John of Leyden's Münster and Thomas
Müntzer's holy republic of Mühlhausen (which had so fascinated Engels),
and the extreme anti-Semitism of the Nazis already had been evident in
popular religious movements in Germany as early as the late crusades.

In fact, as much as the Stalinists, whose eventual conversion to practical
anti-Semitism fitted in with their generally atavistic tendencies, the Nazis—
in planning their march into the future—were using History as they
conceived it to negate the natural process of events of which history—as a
record—writes. The latter form of history, the true chronicle of events past
and present, suffered in the process, since, like all other forms of truth, it
was regarded as dispensable by those engaged in the lordly tasks of
prophesying and shaping History to make their prophecies come true. The
Fascists, Nazis and Stalinists rewrote history to suit their own ends, eliminating whole successions of events and turning influential figures into
nonpersons whose names were eliminated from "historical" narratives and
whose faces were painted out of photographs. The "memory holes" of
George Orwell's *Nineteen Eighty-four* actually functioned over a large part
of Europe, and discredited the historicists as soon as they moved from
theory into action, for if the past must be changed to shape the future, how
can the predictability of the future be guaranteed? How can prophecy be
made with the hope of fulfilment? Whatever History may have whispered
to them, the prophecies of the totalitarians turned out to be wrong.

War as the Machine of History

Hegel, the great historicist, believed that although the individual mattered little in relation to the nation-state, the state itself had an evident collective individuality; it was the presence of such individualities that made conflict inevitable and admirable, and justified the permanence of a state of war or threat of war. Nations fulfilled themselves by victory, and to be victorious they must be externally sharply defined as well as internally cohesive. More perhaps than any of his followers, the Nazis extended Hegel's theories by declaring, as Sigmund Neuman pointed out in *Permanent Revolution*,

> that every race "is bound to have an intellectual and a moral standard peculiar to itself." There is no international science; even physics and mathematics have to accept their reinterpretation as being national and racial in character. This hypernationalism—again reflecting the psychology of war fever—that conceives sovereignty not only in its political aspects but as an economic and cultural phenomenon as well, is given added force by an uncritical acceptance of *social Darwinism*. The survival of the fittest in a continuous struggle for existence becomes the only maxim for action and the exclusive key to history. . . .
>
> Social Darwinism is further hardened and fortified into an active creed by the concept of the natural superiority of the Nordic man—a doctrine of extremely doubtful scientific

109

standing but extremely dynamic, especially in the hands of demagogical myth-makers.

The teachings of Marx, Engels and Lenin sustained the internationalism that was universally supported by socialists in the nineteenth century, finding its manifestation in the International Workingmen's Association, the First International, in the 1860s. After 1917 Lenin, and Trotsky later, banked on the possibility of world revolution for its own sake and as a means of protecting the victories of Bolshevism in Russia. Great Russian aspirations eventually complicated the situation, and in practice the Russians appeared as a master race in the countries they subordinated to Communist rule from the annexation of the Baltic republics in 1940 onward, but in general the moving force of dialectical struggle was class rather than nationalism. Ideally the enemy was a former land-holding member of the nobility rather than a German, but if he happened to be a Baltic German, all to the good! The prejudice and inverse snobbery thus created cost Russia dearly when that most useful section of the population, the intelligentsia, was largely liquidated, as would happen also, decades later, in China.

Whether it occurred in terms of nationalities or races or class, the dialectic of struggle initiated by the warring children of Hegel—as much on the right as on the left—led to an attempt at imperial homogenization, a kind of "synthesis" such as had not been attempted in the great empires of the past from the Persian to the British. Cyrus, though a Zoroastrian, is celebrated still by Christians and Jews because he not only released the Jews from their Babylonian captivity but also positively encouraged them to follow their own customs and live by their own beliefs. Alexander had seen his empire symbolically as a marriage of equal races. The Romans, going beyond active tolerance, followed the path of equalization. Everyone, regardless of race, who lived in the Roman Empire was entitled to say "Civis Romanus sum," and this concept extended so far that several of the emperors were not Roman or even Italian. And the British, for all their vast sense of racial superiority, followed a policy of noninterference in native customs, particularly in India, and often made use of traditional law and of native ruling systems to simplify the problems of imperial rule.

The deliberate pluralism of the Persian empire and its Alexandrian successor, and the idea—if not always the fact—upheld by the Romans and the British of the equality of all imperial subjects before the law, never became part of the imperial ethic of the totalitarian realms. Nazis, Fascists, Communists, all attempted to transfer their ideologies and to establish in the conquered or (very much more rarely) converted countries regimes that were merely extensions of the newly dominant power. The Nazis' pride of race, and their contempt for the customs and traditions of those they subdued, prevented the emergence of genuine Nazi parties or anything truly resembling them among the conquered peoples. The Reichswehr and the Gestapo sustained the presence of the imperial power in military and political ways. And, as in the classic example of Pétainist France, the ruling presence was manifested within the subjugated country by a puppet administration and perhaps a Quisling party. Since the adherents and even the leaders of such a government and party were members of a race that had been shown to be inferior by the fact of conquest, they could never become true Nazis, any more than a European could become a true Hindu, and usually they consisted of members of the traditional right, a large number of opportunists, and a few genuine intellectuals who believed their country should learn from defeat and from its victors.

The absence of a uniting ideology shared by conqueror and conquered distinguished the Nazis and the Fascists from the Communist totalitarians; they presumed that the conquered could not assume the virtues of the triumphant race or the ideas that sustained such virtues, since History had given the victors a determined role of their own. Even "sister" regimes in countries that were not actually subdued, like those in Spain or Portugal, were neither Nazi nor Fascist in any true sense. If the war had been won by the master race, they would have been added to the Nazi conquests as Pétainist France had been; even Italy, in the last stages of the war, found its own imperial destiny an insufficient protection and was reduced to a remnant, forced by growing military defeat to accept the domination of the embattled Reich. A Europe dominated by Nazi Germany could not have displayed the cultural plurality of the Persian-Alexandrian empire, since all other cultures would be rated as inferior to the Nordic and would be relentlessly homogenized. But no subject of that empire—however homogenized—would have been able to say, "I am a German citizen," because full participation in the Reich had become a matter of racial purity and those who did not belong to that extended tribal group, the "Volk," would be forever excluded.

Relying on what they believed to be the assurances of history, remembering ancient imperial dreams and uniting with them the illusions of those who imagined they could foresee and through foresight shape the future, the Hegelian regimes on the right collapsed in the very war they had thought would ensure their triumph. The great factor in their destruction was the clash of one historicist thrust against another; Hitler's opposition to the manifest destiny of the German people versus Stalin's conviction that

History had determined the triumph of communism precipitated the end of the Third Reich and involved the Fascist State—the New Rome—in its downfall.

The third great totalitarian realm, Stalinist Russia, was saved partly by the overweening arrogance of the Nazis, who believed that History would assure them victory as the dominant race, and who therefore, like Napoleon, forgot that geography—the sum of local physical circumstances—sometimes works against History as prophetic vision; General Winter would strike a second time across the Russian steppes. Moreover, there was enough of the pragmatic in Marxist-Leninist practice—if not in its theory—to allow Stalin and his machine to join with their great class enemies, British and American capitalism personified by Winston Churchill and Franklin Roosevelt, in the elimination of a common danger. And so, with a brutality equivalent to that of the horsemen of Genghis Khan and Tamerlane, the armies of the workers' fatherland marched into the empire the Nazis had conquered and seized much of it for their leaders. A gesture was made of liberating the countries of Eastern Europe, and then their briefly democratic governments were subverted or suppressed; a third of Europe and a good deal of Asia fell under the rule of the one remaining totalitarian power, the surviving heir of Hegelian historicism. The rule was partly direct, where the three small Baltic republics of Latvia, Lithuania and Esthonia were actually incorporated into the Soviet Union. Elsewhere, clones of the Kremlin system were imposed on the countries whose territories were contiguous to Russia, from Poland in the north to Bulgaria in the south and to Outer Mongolia in the Far East.

As often happens in wars to the death, Stalinist communism did not win without taking on some of the characteristics of the defeated enemy. The original opposition of a racial determination of History by a class one quickly began to erode in the circumstances of mass terror in which Russia conducted its side of the war. The numerical and economic superiority of the central mass of Russian-speakers in the Soviet Union gave them a power that the nation's many minorities long hesitated and even feared with good reason to challenge. And anti-Semitism began to emerge no later than the great Moscow trials, which were intended to reduce the high proportion of Jewish intellectuals in the Bolshevik old guard, thus bringing Jews in general into disrepute. And though the rhetoric of government in the European satellite countries was couched in Marxist class terms, there was no doubt of the tendency of ethnic power groups to emerge in both government and party levels, particularly in countries like Yugoslavia and Czechoslovakia that had been cobbled together out of various racial groups during the breakup of the Austro-Hungarian Empire in 1918. As for the termination of class warfare that had once seemed the goal of the Marxist dialectic, History was still far from achieving its ultimate task, and one ruling and privileged class was merely replaced by another, the nobility and bureaucracy of one autocracy succeeded by the commissars and cadres of another, with the military, as before, guaranteeing a status quo from which it benefited.

CHAPTER XII

The Failure of Fear

History, as conceived by Hegelians and Marxists, and by many of their hypnotized opponents, still seemed to stretch ahead even at the beginning of the 1980s, its manifest purpose ever waiting to be fulfilled, as the stage was slowly set for the drama that would characterize the fin de siècle period through which we are now living. In an ironic recapitulation of the failure of Christian millenarian hopes, the great eschatological drive of History had been delayed decade after decade by the contrary tendencies of that instrument of historical determination, the Communist party, towards procrastination and centrifugality.

Whether the Communist system of industrial management was naively conceived and intrinsically unworkable, or whether the economic circumstances of the countries in which it was attempted were unfavourable to its success, is in the long run irrelevant. Whatever the cause, and wherever it was tried, from the once industrially advanced areas of East Germany and Czechoslovakia to backward and traditionally poor countries like Ethiopia and Cambodia, communism in practice turned out to be tragically less efficient than capitalism had been in its primary task of improving the lot of the worker. In Western Europe and North America there was not a country in which by 1989 people in general failed to enjoy a way of living considerably more secure and comfortable than their forefathers had done seventy years before. With the special exception of parts of China, people in the Communist world were not merely no better off; they were actually worse off than they had been in 1917. In one of the English journalist

Timothy Garton Ash's marvellously illuminating essays on present-day Eastern Europe, a Polish worker summed up the situation with pungent irony: "Forty years of socialism and no toilet paper." And Russian miners put the lack of soap high on their list of grievances when at last they were able to strike. An Ethiopian under General Mengitsu Haile Mariam's recently deceased African variant of Marxist-Leninism could have made an even starker comparison between the mere hunger of the unregenerate past and the famine of the regenerated present. Throughout the Communist world we have seen a cruel story of hopes betrayed, of pie eternally hanging in the sky.

Procrastination is the inner vice of Communist and indeed of all bureaucratically dominated regimes. The great task of communism, of the dictatorship of the proletariat made manifest in the party, was in theory dual: 1) To expropriate the means of production and reconstitute them in such a way that the classic aim of socialists since Saint-Simon could be generously fulfilled; 2) To preside over that happy process envisaged by Marx and Engels, and even Lenin, the ending of the government of men by man through the withering of the state. Their great error was to seek the solution, by political means, of what Marx, through his interpretation of History as a process of *economic* determinism, admitted was a nonpolitical process; in doing so, Marx, and Lenin after him, sought to use the methods of the autocratic past to create the free future. We cannot be other than astonished by the accuracy with which, while not claiming to be a dialectical prophet, the anarchist Mikhail Bakunin foretold, at the time of the great struggles within the First International in the 1860s, the despotic and stultifying nature of Communist government. Here is what *le grand Michel* had to say in his time:

> But in Mr. Marx's popular State, we are told, there will be no privileged class at all. . . . Perhaps there will no longer be a privileged class as such, but there will be a government and, let me emphasize, an extremely complex government, which will not be content with ruling and administering the masses politically, as all governments now do, but will also administer them economically, concentrating in its own hands production and the "just" division of wealth, agriculture, the establishment and development of factories, the organization and operation of commerce, and, above all, the application of capital to production by the only banker, the State. All of this will call for an immense development of science, and for the

115

presence in government of many "heads overflowing with brains." It will be the reign of *scientific intelligence*, the most aristocratic, despotic, arrogant and scornful of all regimes. There will be a new class, a new hierarchy of real and pretend scholars, and the world will be divided into a majority that rules in the name of science and a vast ignorant majority. Then, let the mass of the ignorant look out!

Such a regime cannot fail to arouse formidable discontent among that mass, and in order to bridle it, the enlightening and liberating government of Mr. Marx will need a no less formidable armed force. . . . One can well see how, beneath all the democratic and socialistic phrases and promises of Mr. Marx's programme, there survives in his State everything that contributes to the truly despotic and brutal nature of all States, whatever their forms of government. . . . Externally there is the same deployment of military power, which means conquest; internally, there is the same employment of armed forces, the last argument of all threatened political powers, against the masses who, tired of always believing, hoping, accepting and obeying, rise in rebellion.

Like Orwell, Bakunin set out to warn rather than to prophesy. His warnings were surprisingly apt, particularly his suggestion that in the long run a Marxist rule could only breed rebellion. He did not say how long the rebellion would take to develop, nor the means by which it would succeed, but he might be surprised by the way it has come about in the 1980s and 1990s.

But what Bakunin saw, as an experienced revolutionary and former conspirator, was that the dictatorship of a party, even one claiming to represent the proletariat, could only be maintained by terror, and that terror meant the ascendancy of the secret police supported by the army. But military and police organizations by their nature are monolithic and resistant to change; administrations dependent on them, as Communist governments of every shade have been, will assume the same characteristics. Change can come only by way of conflict, according to Hegelian doctrine, and if the conflict is similar to that by which a revolutionary government (now turned conservative) was established, then the same kind of totalitarian government will succeed it. In practice, however, having come to power through violence and terror, totalitarian governments are well protected against such an eventuality; they know the revolutionary game beforehand even if they have ceased to play it. Their true enemy is not yet another violent revolution sustained by subsequent terror, as dissident Marxists, like the followers of Trotsky, still imagine. It is, as recent events have shown, rebellion by other means and principally by the widespread overcoming of fear which, as Gandhi showed long ago and the masses of the Eastern European cities have repeated in recent seasons, is the great solvent of terror. Even in Russia, so long terrorized by perhaps the most formidable twentieth-century secret police force, that fear seemed to vanish almost overnight on the occasion of the hard-line coup in August 1991. I was struck by a post mortem on television by a group of Moscow-based journalists after the people had supported Boris Yeltsin and ensured Gorbachev's release and return. All but one were Americans, experienced columnists, academic Kremlinologists, and they speculated on the various forces that might have affected a still obscure series of events. The single Russian present swept their arguments away. "There is only one real reason for what happened," he said. "We Russians woke up and found we had lost our fear."

Only by such spontaneous movements on the part of the people can the stream of events be set moving again and society begin to change in a positive direction. What this means in effect is that the methods by which historicist rulers strive to ensure the onmoving direction of History, which alone would seem to justify their actions and their existing dominant role, are the very means that negate such a progression.

The journey to the millennium is halted on its way in Communist countries as society stagnates, economically, politically, culturally. The reality of Lenin's terrible but genuine aims, and the ascetic dedication with which he pursued them, have been mocked by the privileged status of the cadres and the managers, by the grotesque greed of the party leaders, by the grim conservatism of the generals. But Lenin himself was responsible for the rule of terror that meant the halting of real change. As had happened in the stagnating Christian church, the grand eschatological pattern was forgotten; the ideal society would come in due course, when History chose. But History itself, the grand determining pattern of events, had stopped working; nothing progressed in the Communist countries except the perfecting of techniques of terror, surveillance and warfare to protect the ageing "revolutionary" status quo. The fulfilment of the people's needs and hopes was indefinitely postponed. Party members were happy with what they had, and the rest could wait. And so procrastination in the satisfying of urgent human needs became the first weapon—and a self-held one—that the historical rulers turned against themselves when they ruled by terror.

The tendencies that work like disintegrative organisms in naturally homogenous and stable societies are even more active and powerful in deliberately closed totalitarian systems, like dry rot, which flourishes in spaces deprived of the movement of air. These tendencies are—principally and customarily—traditionalism, regionalism and individualism, with all their various permutations and combinations; their manifestations tend to be local and dispersed, and therefore likely to be unnoticed in their beginnings, but difficult to control once they have emerged in maturity, as Mikhail Gorbachev in the end discovered.

But there is, as the poet Stephen Spender has pointed out, yet another element to be considered in the combination of antitotalitarian trends that have arisen in recent years, and this is one directly linked to the new community of awareness that, through the spread of television, has brought closer the peoples of democratic and totalitarian countries. Even the best-maintained of surveillance systems has been unable to prevent people in Eastern Europe from hearing what is said on Western radio or seeing what is shown on Western screens, or millions of Chinese from looking in on the television programmes emanating from Hong Kong and Taiwan. This has introduced an entirely new element of disintegration which the tyrannies of the past did not have to fear.

As Spender remarked in an essay in *Granta*'s Winter 1990 "State of Europe" issue, pointing to a historically unprecedented factor in the situation:

> This might be called the "boredom factor." Life under a dictatorship of old-style ideologists, whether in Russia, Eastern Europe or China, is extremely boring. Moreover, owing to modern systems of communication, people living under dictatorships are made aware of the boredom of the system; the flow of information from the outside is unstoppable. The Berlin Wall may have prevented East Berliners reaching the West, but it was leaped over and penetrated at a million points by TV and radio bringing East Berliners news and images of the lifestyle, vitality and competitiveness of the West.

Boredom may be considered a passive condition, but it is easily transformed into its more active counterpart of impatient discontent, an emotion all the more powerful because it is not a mass sentiment imposed by dogma or decree or propaganda but one felt personally by each individual. It eventually produces that shedding of fear, that ferment of liberation, which

118

created out of millions of wills and voices the great public demonstrations that in 1989 changed the political face of Eastern Europe and pushed the dictatorship in China to the verge of collapse, and that in 1991 frustrated the attempt at a coup in Russia by hard-line Communist party and military leaders.

Undoubtedly this shedding of individual fear is the greatest peril to totalitarian regimes, because it not only lessens the power of terror but weakens the will of the ruler by doubt. Gandhi demonstrated this double process in his great satyagraha movements in India during the 1920s, which dissolved the British will to empire as surely as they nourished the Indian will to freedom. Critics used to say that Gandhi won only because he had the "democratic" British to deal with, and that his methods would never stand up to ruthless totalitarian regimes. The experience of Europe in the 1980s proved Gandhi right and the "realists" wrong.

The forthcoming chapters consider these disintegrative processes at work by tracing the record of communism during the years of apparent triumph when it seemed to be spreading its power like the world revolution of which Lenin and Trotsky had dreamed, the years when American leaders were obsessed by the "domino theory." After the combination of military actions and political coups that assured its triumph in Eastern Europe in the 1940s, communism finally triumphed in China in 1949 and ended Tibet's independence in 1951. It won Cuba in 1959, the countries of Indochina in the early and middle 1970s, Ethiopia in 1973 and Nicaragua—the last and most fragile of its gains—in 1979. This was the era when the historicist myth grew strongest, when people inside and outside the Communist countries believed that History had declared its true form, that the dialectic was being fulfilled, and that—once established—the Marxist-Leninist model of utopia won and sustained by terror would never be superseded. Communist influence in the Third World grew steadily, as nationalist leaders like the Nehru clan in India and mere condottiere posing as nationalists like the rulers of Iraq and Syria accepted Russian aid and arms and willingly allowed themselves to be included in a Soviet sphere of influence and to support Russian policies internationally.

The Hegelian myth in one of its great manifestations seemed to be on the verge of fulfilment. Many people outside the Communist world began to accept, with joy sometimes but more often with dread, the prospect of an eventual worldwide triumph for totalitarian governments and historicist policies. Evidence of such trends emerging in all societies in the mid-twentieth-century world prompted George Orwell to write his great admonitory classic, *Nineteen Eighty-four*. For half a century that seemed the dominant probability, and the retreat from totalitarian communism seemed a historical impossibility. Only in the last decade have we seen the possibility of the impossible emerging and the end of the idea of History as a determined process. Once again, like Adam and Eve in the myth of Genesis, men and women have chosen freedom and uncertainty, and found

> The world was all before them, where to choose
> Their place of rest.

The walls of Eden, never more than a prison for the obedient, have fallen; the roads are open.

CHAPTER XIII

Export Communism

The true historian looks at the past to find the lessons in what has happened, not to foretell what will happen in the future, and in the rest of this book I shall be examining how we have reached the present stage of liberation from the age-old spectre of a foreordained History, and how we may be able to benefit from our new condition of freedom from the bonds of a determined vision of the future, our new acceptance of the possibility of the impossible.

What I am here concerned with is the failure of totalitarian regimes to live up to their own prophecies. Since the reigns of fascism and nazism as specific historic entities were so brief and left such a scanty heritage, I shall confine myself to discussing the record of communism from 1940 onward and showing how, by its very processes of expansion backed by the false assumption of historic certainty, the Communist movement weakened itself to the point of rapid and progressive disintegration in the 1980s and early 1990s, not merely as a political movement but also as a form of government—the dictatorship of the proletarian party which, Lenin believed, once established would never be replaced. Whatever History—conceived as prophetic myth—may have offered to Marx and his successors, history, as the actual trend of events, has negated and nullified.

The disintegration of communism as a system of power began as soon as it started to move out of the fortress established by success in the October Revolution and the civil war. During that war and the Stalinist terror, the powerful minority groups within the old tsarist empire were incorporated

121

into the Soviet Union by a combination of fear and fervour. In areas like Ukraine the deeply rooted traditions of regional identity were broken down—or appeared to be broken down—by such brutal measures as forced migration, systematic destruction of the traditional culture, and enforced famines in which millions of people—still uncounted—died.

Within this vast subdued area, Stalin and his associates could create and sustain, by the terror which Lenin had instituted, their massive five-year plans aimed at the creation of socialism in a single country. Initially impressive—as all the great works of tyrants from ancient Egypt onward have been—the grandiose dams and power stations and huge factories, centralizing the production of everything from heavy machinery to saucepans, were in the long run economically unviable, since they neglected the manufacture of consumer goods. At the same time the collectivization of agriculture diminished the production of food, so that the Soviet Union would eventually be unable, to adapt the phrase attributed to Napoleon, "to march on its stomach."

War saved Stalin and his government from the probability of an economic collapse and perhaps some kind of political upheaval that might have involved a loosening of the circle of terror imposed by the party and the GPU, as the Cheka had now become. But war also offered the parallel temptations of revolutionary imperialism and perhaps even of world revolution, temptations which would eventually destroy the monolithic strength and durability of socialism in a single country. In a strange, ironic way, Trotsky would finally win, and gain a Pyrrhic victory.

Lenin's original hopes of a general European uprising that would fulfil the dictates of History and incidentally support the Bolsheviks had been scantily satisfied. In the spring of 1919 a Soviet Republic was established briefly in Munich, with anarchists like Gustav Landauer and romantic revolutionary socialists like Ernst Toller collaborating with Spartacists (left-wing socialists) in what was by no means a completely Leninist venture. The Communists were more firmly in control in Hungary the same year when under Bela Kun they seized power there, but Kun's administration relied so much on Leninist terror that the Hungarians welcomed even their traditional enemies, the Rumanians, when they arrived as "liberators" and set up the autocratic regency of Admiral Horthy which lasted until the Nazis established their hegemony in Eastern Europe. After the end of the Hungarian adventure, no areas outside the Soviet Union were under Communist control until 1940, except for Outer Mongolia (the Mongolian People's Republic), which came into existence in the early 1920s and was as much the result of resurgent Mongolian nationalism against the Chinese as of a Communist victory.

As Japanese military autocracy began to strengthen its position on Manchuria during the later 1920s, and rival totalitarian regimes grew strong in Germany and Italy during the 1930s, Stalin's government found it necessary to intervene, more to adjust balances of world power than to spread the world revolution. In China the Russians played a consistently ambivalent role, sending advisers to the Communist insurrectionaries, yet at the same time supporting Chiang Kai-shek and his reactionary Kuomintang as a counterweight to the Japanese. Even when Chiang massacred the Communists in Shanghai in 1927 (so movingly recorded by André Malraux in *Man's Fate*), Russia did not turn against him, since the frustration of the Japanese, old rivals of Russia in Manchuria, was more important for the safety of the Siberian frontier and ultimately of socialism in one country.

It was on similar terms that Russia became involved in the Spanish Civil War in 1936, supplying arms to the Republican government and recruiting a foreign legion, the International Brigade, whose importance was propagandist rather than military. The Russian "advisers" (mainly secret police agents) who arrived in Spain were not interested in fomenting the "world revolution." They were more concerned with using Spain as a military testing ground in competition with their Nazi and Fascist rivals, and with infiltrating the Republican government with their own trusted men. A good deal of genuinely revolutionary activity was going on in Loyalist Spain at this period, including the great anarcho-syndicalist experiment of communalizing the villages in Catalonia and Valencia and the factories in Barcelona and other Catalan towns, but the Russians and their Spanish agents undermined such ventures, persecuting individual anarchists and revolutionary socialists. Stalin's intervention in Spain was in fact strategically motivated, like his Chinese policy, and directed towards the protection of Russia rather than the spread of world revolution.

Such strategically inspired political action was often conducted with so little sense of the reality of the world outside Russia as to be wholly self-defeating. This was the case in Germany, where memories of Marx and Lenin and of the Spartacist revolts led by great self-sacrificing insurrectionaries like Rosa Luxemburg and Karl Liebknecht gave the Russians a wrong idea of German revolutionary potentialities. It was a clear case of historicist myopia. Marx and Engels had taught that Germany would be the cradle of the Communist revolution, so the Bolsheviks must have believed that their own priority was accidental and that it was in the heavily industrial Germany that the dialectical process must be working itself out. Nowhere else in Western Europe were the Communists as arrogantly self-confident as in their contempt for the Social Democrats who controlled the German trade union movement and still retained the support of millions of workers. The German Communists believed that they themselves were sufficient to defeat the surgent movement of nazism and take advantage of the situation to bring about their own revolution; their masters in the Comintern believed this conviction could be used to Russia's advantage. Accordingly they denounced the Social Democrats as Social Fascists, and on occasion even sent their own hooligans into battle beside the brownshirts in attacking the Social Democrats. Only after they had helped Hitler in this way on his rise to power did the Russians realize their German policy had been strategically as well as politically insane, helping to create on their borders a totalitarian state with a rival historic mission; then Communists worldwide suddenly began to talk loudly of "popular" and "common" fronts of Communists, socialists and liberals, and Russia began to seek alliances with its enemy's other enemies and gained only cautious responses.

What followed was an extraordinary example of the use of realpolitik in ruthless hands. After the Western powers had stood by to observe the absorption of Austria and the progressive destruction of Czechoslovakia at the hands of the Nazis, the Soviet government decided to hedge its bets by concluding on 23 August 1939 the notorious mutual nonaggression treaty with Germany generally known as the Molotov-Ribbentrop Pact. Not merely a strategic agreement protecting Germany's rear while it engaged the Western powers in the war that began just over a week later, it was, for the Russians, an agreement that assured the temporary safety of socialism in a single country. It also prepared for the reconstitution of the old tsarist empire, since the secret protocols attached to it provided for Russia to act as it wished within its own sphere of influence. This meant that on 17 September 1939, a little over two weeks after the German invasion of Poland, Russian troops were able to cross the country's eastern frontier, and once again Poland was partitioned between great powers, Austria-Hungary alone not being present to take up its historic share. Shortly afterwards Russia invaded yet another former part of the empire, Finland; the Finns put up such a resistance that they came out of the struggle independent still, but with part of their territory lost. And then, in 1940, Russia completed its reconstitution of the empire by invading the Baltic republics of Lithuania, Latvia and Esthonia, formally incorporating them in the U.S.S.R. on the first of June. Six days later Russian troops invaded Rumania and reannexed the former Russian provinces of Bessarabia and Bukovina, forming them into the "autonomous" republic of Moldava.

In this way a phase of increasing Soviet power, in terms of both territory and influence, was begun. Most of the advantage would be temporarily lost when the German armies invaded Russia in June 1941, but with the help of several campaigns by General Winter, defeat was turned into victory. By the time of the Yalta conference in 1945 the decision to partition Germany into four zones, each occupied by one of the victorious powers, had set Russia on the second phase of its expansion, even now strategically rather than politically conceived—the creation of a series of satellite states along its western frontier, which as a secondary effect would become Stalinist clones in terms of the rule of terror and of Communist economics. Western nations, notably Britain and the United States, reacted with apprehension, and so there was the Cold War, and with it the rival NATO and Warsaw Pact alliances, as well as the so-called Iron Curtain, the line of closed frontiers behind which, having cut off contact between East and West, the Communists could go about remaking society in their own bleak image.

But always there was the world beyond the great power blocs, and it was here that communism expanded in independent ways, in insurrectionary movements powered by local forces of discontent even where the directing core of leaders was Marxist-Leninist and funded—as was often the case—by Russia. The most dramatic of these Communist triumphs began with the victory of the People's Liberation Army over Chiang Kai-shek's forces in China in 1949, but the first of the maverick regimes that threatened the unity of the Communist world arose in Eastern Europe. East Germany, Czechoslovakia, Poland, Hungary, Rumania and Bulgaria were all won for communism by the Red Army with relatively little help from local insurrectionaries. However, Yugoslavia and Albania were not liberated by the Red Army but by partisan forces subsidized and otherwise assisted as much by the British as by the Russians; this gave both of them a freedom of manoeuvre, so that Marshal Tito led his country out of the Comintern in 1948 to operate as an independent Communist country outside the major power blocs, and Albania cut its connections with Russia in 1961 and in an increasingly varied Communist world offered its allegiance to Mao Zedong's China.

The examples of Yugoslavia and Albania suggest what mixed blessings the emergence of independent Communist regimes offered to Russia as custodian and servant of History by way of the Marxist-Leninist dialectic. In its own way every new conquest offered the challenges of traditionalism and regionalism as threats to the homogenizing tendency of Communist historicism. The Russians might, though without lasting success, attempt to establish clones on their own system in the satellite countries of Eastern Europe. But the remoter revolutions, in countries where different original political conditions prevailed than those of tsarist Russia, produced different situations, and no Communist regime outside Europe and Eastern Europe has ever been like any other; still less have they resembled Russia except in their authoritarian governmental forms, their amoral use of terror (in which Cambodia's Khmer Rouge excelled even the Stalinists), and in their denial of human rights as irrelevancies unsanctioned by History.

China—that vast land where the most important nominally Marxist government still survives at the mercy of an unreliable army—forced its own nature on the Communist movement during the years before, after and during the Long March of 1934–35, when the People's Liberation Army and a rudimentary revolutionary government survived in the remoter corners of that vast land. Driven from the cities, the Communists under Mao Zedong had to adapt to a situation in which their ranks were filled by young peasants, and a curious alliance between countrymen and party cadres emerged in which the basic Marxist-Leninism was eventually adulterated by Bakuninist insurrectionary strains, so that Maoism was very different from Stalinism. Unlike Lenin, Mao acknowledged that the proletariat in his country was still a relatively powerless entity, and so Chinese Communist policies and tactics have been consistently concentrated around the peasant and the land, and the collectivization and privatization of land have continued to be major issues in Chinese economic policy.

Two other traditions affected the development of Chinese communism. One is the alternation of periods of rational, intellectual, autocratic government, government according to Confucius; the other is the violent pattern of book-burning and scholar-persecuting emperors and brutal peasant revolts like the Taiping and Boxer rebellions. In Mao's Cultural Revolution, it was the heirs of book-burning emperors and anarchic Taipings rather than of Marx and Lenin who combined in a movement that by its sheer nihilism seemed to rip apart the very structure of the Communist state.

If China, "liberated" by Communist armies with a great deal of initial military and financial help from Stalinist Russia, could lapse into patterns so reminiscent of the past, it is not surprising that Communist regimes in Latin American countries have followed the military revolutionary pattern that has existed in the region ever since the days of soldier-liberators like Simón Bolivar and José de San Martín. Whatever his origins, Fidel Castro quickly metamorphosed into a typical military caudillo, brutal, corrupt (in the sense of enjoying all the privileges and satisfactions of power), and parasitically surviving through the material support of Russia in the same way as right-wing Latin American caudillos have survived on similar support from the United States.

126

But the tradition of the Latin American caudillo is really at odds with the Marxist-Leninist concept of history, though perhaps not entirely with the aberration of that concept known as Stalinism. In the Latin American tradition the army takes precedence over the politician, which means that in Cuba and even more in Nicaragua the party has assumed a background role while the real leaders of the revolution have kept on playing soldiers. Latin American quasi-Marxist dictatorships resemble ancient Greek tyrannies more than anything elsewhere in the Communist world. They depend on the cult of the person, and like the right-wing dictatorships in the region—by Anastasio Somoza and François Duvalier for example—they are essentially dynastic, hoping to survive through the appointment of relatives of the dictator to key positions in the army and security forces. There was no room for brilliant rivals, and so Che Guevara in Cuba and Eden Pastora in Nicaragua departed, as Trotsky had done from Stalinist Russia. The highly personalized character of the Latin American military dictatorship— even a nominally Marxist one—makes it more dependent on the fate of individuals and also more dependent on popular tolerance than European Communist regimes were until very recently. Usually the dictator can court popularity by pointing to a predecessor even more shameless in his oppression, as Castro could point to Fulgencio Batista, and Daniel Ortega to Somoza. But even in Latin America the situation has been changing, and while Castro—an established dictator with a heavy military machine and a ruthless security service—still seems relatively unthreatened, a more recently established and insecurely based caudillo like Ortega found it impossible, like the East European Communist leaders, to resist the swell of popular discontent. His carrots were not good enough to support an inadequate stick, and the inability to create an unchallenged military superiority dissolved the basis of his power. He was all the more easy to topple because, in the typical Latin American way, he concentrated on creating the revolutionary army rather than building up the revolutionary party. He had slipped out of the world of preordained History into that of contingency, which of course is the unpredictable realm of true history.

The spread of communism outside the countries of the Warsaw Pact revealed that the difference between various national strains of communism could be as internationally disruptive as any other national rivalries. Yugoslavia withdrew from the Comintern in 1948, and embarked on a process of political decentralization and economic populism, including the abandonment of collectivization of the farms and the beginnings of worker control in the factories. Thereafter, though some features of Communist dictatorship remained, particularly the restrictions on intellectual freedom,

Yugoslavia withdrew from the official Communist bloc and played a leading role in the group of nonaligned countries in the United Nations. Communist regimes, like those in Cuba, Ethiopia and Angola, which were almost entirely dependent on Russian subsidies in cash and kind, remained loyal to the Soviet Union. But the most populous of all Communist countries, China, fell out with Nikita Khrushchev's Russia in 1960 and for many years the two countries were making military gestures on each other's borders, while, following the dictates of realpolitik rather than those of dialectical materialism, the Chinese community achieved a rapprochement with the America of Richard Nixon and the Canada of that other Machiavellian manipulator, Pierre Elliott Trudeau. Finally, as a trivial tailpiece to these momentous events, Albania renounced Russia in 1961 and allied itself to China, but in 1978 renounced that country too for its surrender to bourgeois values and stood out, a terror-ridden utopia of three million people, as the sole remaining representatives of pure Marxist-Leninism.

Communist states have not merely differed from one another and quarrelled among themselves, the later regimes rejecting their predecessors like adolescents rejecting fathers. They even indulged in war with each other. In 1979 Vietnam invaded Cambodia (renamed Kampuchea), and deposed the government of Pol Pot, which had carried Leninist terrorism to a ferocious extreme. In turn, the Chinese Communists, who had patronized Pol Pot and his fellow assassins, briefly invaded northern Vietnam, while threats rumbled along the Russo-Chinese frontiers.

Communist governments have in fact survived, particularly in international conflicts, by exploiting and even enhancing existing forms of nationalism, not excluding their xenophobic elements. Stalin's Russia survived the Nazi invasion only by calling on existing patterns of patriotism, whose manifestations carried a symbolism hostile to the idea of world revolution and to the forward march of eschatological politics. The "Internationale," song of the inevitable unfolding of the revolution and the final struggle between the workers and their oppressors, was replaced as the hymn of the Soviet Union by an anthem reaching deeply into the tradition of Russian folk music. A cult of the Russian land emerged, and of the great imperial leaders of the nation's past, who had often changed society with as much inhuman ferocity as Lenin and Stalin himself. Ivan the Terrible was suddenly rehabilitated as a great unifying force in mediaeval Russia, and Peter the Great as a noble modernizer. As early as 1938 the great visual laureate of Communist Russia, the filmmaker Sergei Eisenstein, had made an epic film on Tsar Alexander Nevsky, who had driven back the Teutonic Knights, and though this fell into temporary disgrace at the time of the Molotov-Ribbentrop rapprochement, it was revived with great effect after the Germans invaded in 1941. Only by turning the war into a great crusade for national survival and by calling on atavistic patriotic emotions was the Russian government able to repeat in the 1940s the extraordinary triumph of 1812–14, using the climate, the vast distances of the steppe (nightmare of French and German logistics alike) and the conservative instincts of a xenophobic peasantry to gain a victory of which the army alone, weakened by Stalin's massacre of its best generals during the Moscow trials of the 1930s, would probably have been incapable.

It was a magnificent feat of survival, for a regime as well as for a nation, but it meant an abandonment of the impetus of the Communist revolution. Henceforward it would be as rulers of a nation rather than as leaders of a revolutionary movement that the Communist party dominated Russia and played its part in world politics. Enough of the rhetoric of the past might still in the 1940s and even the 1950s inspire the surviving older Bolsheviks to talk about the eventual triumph of their system and Nikita Khrushchev to beat his desk with his shoe at the United Nations in 1959 and shout, "We will bury you all!" But under Khrushchev's sardonic successor, Leonid Brezhnev, and his modified revival of Stalinism, the transformation of Marxist-Leninism went so deep that throughout the world—even in Russia itself—those who most upheld the hard-line communism inherited from Lenin came to be called "conservatives" and not "radicals."

Thus two apparently contradictory features have been shared by world communism wherever it has emerged in the period after World War II. These are its atavistic lapse towards tradition and its inevitable tendency to fragmentation. The first came about partly through its necessary alliance with tradition everywhere, but partly through the internal rigidities of a monolithic doctrine. The second derived from its inability to throw off the consequences of geography, of people seeing their history in regional ways. Communism in China became Chinese communism, communism in Russia remained Russian communism, and when they met, it was the localizing adjective that counted more than the generalizing noun.

The Monolith Lurches

In the seventy years after the October Revolution we witnessed the transformation of communism from an apparently irresistible force into an apparently immovable object. Whatever may have happened in the peripheral realms paying service to the traditions of Marx and Lenin, the heartland of the Soviet Union and the European satellite countries seemed like a great monolith, so well contained internally, so well defended by its impermeable frontiers (the "Iron Curtain," the "Berlin Wall") that people both inside and outside what U.S. President Ronald Reagan styled "the evil empire" remained convinced of its durability. Only another world war, it seemed, could dislodge the rule of the party, protected by its vast army, by its security apparatus conducted on the principle of indiscriminate terror to strip the party and the country of all dissent and imbue them with that most negative of virtues, loyalty bred of fear.

The monolith was so well set that repeated attempts at rebellion failed to dislodge it when the Brezhnev doctrine was enforced by the marching of Soviet forces accompanied by secret police units. Marxist polemics justified it in the present and supported it prophetically as the opening out of the dialectical process of History; here, however slowly moving it might seem in revolutionary terms, was the stage of socialism that preceded true communism and even, it was still whispered in imitation of Lenin and Engels, the eventual withering of the state and the arrival at the destination of utopian anarchy.

But the very existence of the monolith meant that the revolution had lost its dynamism; the great lava flow of revolt that filled people's minds everywhere after the October Revolution and Bolshevik success in the civil war had long ceased to run. The magma had cooled, and the volcano, though it still sent up an occasional puff of rhetorical smoke, was virtually dead, for apart from being forced into a territorially defensive role, the Communists were ideologically spent, so that all they could rule with was the dead weight of fear rather than the élan of inspiration. It became like a church in which even the priesthood were unbelievers, intent only on maintaining their privileges. And what was true in Russia was even more so in the satellite countries, where the revolution had been imposed by conquerors rather than inspired by local urges.

To people who had fatalistically accepted the existence of this monolith and so played into the hands of the historical determinists, the events of the 1980s and of 1991 took on an appearance of the miraculous. Yet at the same time as the ossification of an ideologically dominated political structure, there was still the level of popular life at which people remained what their language and their land had helped to make them, Czechs and Hungarians and Poles, before they became Communists and nominal supporters of a party whose aims, to the populace of these countries, always seemed Russian and imperial rather than revolutionary. People at this level tended to be pluralist and individualist, paying lip service to what they rejected every hour of the common day, as portrayed in dissident East European novels like those of Josef Skvorecky, resolutely carrying on their "own lives" in spite of whatever may be imposed on them.

Still, more than three decades, a whole long generation from the mid-1940s to the early 1980s, passed without any successful effort to dislodge or even transform the structure of power. There were revolts, there were even palace revolutions, but they failed; perhaps we can get at the reasons by comparing the circumstances of the Cold War period with those of more recent years. Everywhere the period of Soviet hegemony started with the imposition of puppet Communist governments by a combination of force and fraud; always during this time, once Communist rule was established, its survival and its orthodoxy were sustained by the force of Soviet arms.

Let us move down the ladder of Eastern European countries from north to south and note briefly what happened in them during those years leading up to the annus mirabilis of 1989.

The end of the war saw Poland's re-emergence in 1945 as a nominally independent state, truncated to the west by Russian annexations but compensated by the acquisition of land at German expense in Silesia and East Prussia.

A Polish government-in-exile, conservative but perhaps representing the views of the majority of the preponderantly Catholic people of the country, had existed in London since the German invasion of 1939. Like much else, it was sacrificed in the name of "peace" by Roosevelt and Churchill when they met with Stalin at Yalta early in 1945. Instead, a provisional government containing some conservative politicians but mainly consisting of Communists and fellow travellers was instituted in Poland under the aegis of the Red Army in the spring of 1945. It signed a mutual pact with Russia in April that year and in June was replaced by a Government of National Unity dominated by the Communists and their allies, which took over the gigantic task of reviving a country that the war had stripped of most of its plant and its resources, including about six million people who had died or gone into voluntary exile.

Though a democratic government was at least nominally reinstituted, assimilation of the political and economic systems to a Soviet model proceeded apace. Large and medium-sized industries were nationalized, and successive changes in the constitution took the country along the path to becoming a people's democracy, which it did eventually in 1952, with a constitution based on that of the Soviet Union.

All this did not happen without resistance. The National party, revived from prewar days, became a focus of legal opposition, while an underground resistance movement treated the Russian intruders and their accomplices as no different from the Nazi intruders and their accomplices. It was devoted to the restoration of democratic rule and also to "Christian ideals," which meant that already the Catholic church was clandestinely offering itself as an alternative to communism. Under increasingly ferocious pressure from army units and powerful security forces, the resistance continued its struggle into the summer of 1947. It was up against not merely the physical powers of the state but also the political manoeuvres of the Communist leaders who, having suppressed the National party and other right-wing groups, called a managed election for the Sejm, or National Assembly, in January 1947. According at least to official statements, no less than 80.1 per cent of the electors cast their votes for a tame coalition of left-and-centre parties, later arbitrarily united into the Polish United Workers' party, virtually a Communist party built on a model exported from Russia.

Even before the establishment of the People's Republic in 1952, nationalization proceeded apace, as in other Communist countries, though with one significant exception. In Poland, agriculture was only partially collec-

132

tivized, and a very considerable section of the national economy thus remained in individual hands. Here at least the potential power of the peasant was clearly recognized.

Poland did not escape the renewed proscriptions with which Stalin and his entourage greeted the beginning of the Cold War in the late 1940s. Possible sympathizers with democracy were weeded out even within the government party and denounced as "right-nationalist" deviationists, and some of them, including Wladyslaw Gomulka, were imprisoned, making Gomulka something of a hero among the discontented populace. In 1953, after Stalin's death, there was a general relaxation of oppression, which was accelerated when Nikita Khrushchev denounced Stalin's policies and his cult of personality at the twentieth congress of the Soviet Communist party in 1956.

In Poznan and other places in 1956 discontent broke out in strikes and riots; it was significant that the first (and successful) opposition to the puppet regimes in Eastern Europe—as in Germany earlier—should come from the very people communism claimed to represent, the urban proletariat. To show a better face, Gomulka was brought out of disfavour to lead the Polish United Workers' party. All the other potential leaders had shown themselves irremediably unpopular. Gomulka still ran an autocratic state, but, like Khrushchev, he drew back in certain vital areas, and particularly in the arts; there was a brief renaissance in which some interesting avant-garde writing appeared, and during the late 1950s and the 1960s Polish films were among the most sophisticated being produced in Europe, under the direction of men like Andrej Wajda and Andrej Munk. Like the other early springs of Eastern Europe, this one waned quickly as Gomulka in his turn became more autocratic. Perhaps its most important legacy was the mini-concordat that Gomulka concluded with the Catholic church in 1956. It allowed the church to survive and gave it an enduring role in Polish society as the representative of an alternative concept of life and its meaning from the arid ideology of the ruling party.

As in regions like Latin America, the church in late twentieth-century Europe took on a quite unfamiliar role as the defender of popular rights against autocratic regimes; so in Poland it consistently sought the course that would ensure general advances in freedom without risking the return of total dictatorship. And if, in addition to the awakening awareness of millions of individuals in each East European country, at least one institution played a meaningful role in the destruction of totalitarian rule and of historicist philosophies in the late twentieth century, it was the Polish Catholic church, whose leaders turned out to be able tacticians in dealing with threats and promises during the time of unrest in 1970 when Gomulka was forced to give up his power to another pseudo-liberal, Edward Gierek. By counselling the workers to moderation in the crisis, the church succeeded in fending off the direct intervention on the part of Soviet Russia that had occurred in other East European countries. And so, doubtless with little premeditation, the way was prepared for the first even partially successful challenge to Communist authority, a challenge not from the church directly but from the emergence in 1980 of the first viable free trade union movement in a Communist country; this was Solidarity—first of the kind of spontaneous alliances of free individuals that have characterized political life in Eastern Europe during recent years.

One of the conclusions that follows from the nondeterminist view of history I adopt in this book is that all institutions and movements tend to change their natures according to their circumstances, as in the case of Communist movements outside Russia. The same may be said of the Catholic church. Although it was a force of reaction in Spain during the 1930s, it has become a force of rebellion in Latin America and Poland in the late twentieth century. Similarly, trade unionism (which so often in the West has become essentially reactionary, inspired by a narrow regard for the interests of limited groups) can become, in the context of an autocratic regime, a revolutionary impulse, as it was in the early nineteenth century when the movement began in England and as it became in 1980 at Gdansk, when the Cheshire cat–faced electrician, Lech Walesa, a longtime agitator, took over the leadership of Solidarity.

The surge of popular feeling that carried Solidarity forward was itself largely produced by two accidental but related circumstances. In 1978 the Archbishop of Krakow, Karol Wojtyla, was surprisingly elected Pope John Paul II, and in 1979 he made a pastoral visit to his homeland, where huge, enthusiastic crowds declared not merely their traditional allegiance to the Roman church but also—implicitly—their alienation from the Communist state. Here the relativism of true history was once again exemplified, for in visits to other countries John Paul emphasized the more reactionary and restrictive aspects of Catholicism, while in Poland he appeared as the personification of the concept of free choice and local autonomy.

Lech Walesa, as the worker driven from employment for his radical views and then rising to considerable power, demonstrated the populist basis of Solidarity, but his links with the Catholic priesthood and lay intellectuals were also strong. The shock effect of the rapid growth of Solidarity on the Communist government in Poland was great, and Rural Solidarity, a farmers' union movement, actually gained official recognition in May 1981. But shortly afterwards there was another change in the photographs in government offices, as Edward Gierek's face was replaced by the never-changing countenance of General Wojciech Jaruzelski, martial law was declared, Lech Walesa was arrested, and Solidarity was banned. The time had not come for open demonstrations, so Solidarity went underground and stayed there until the extraordinary happenings at the end of the 1980s.

Already, as I have been talking about events in Poland, the essential shapelessness of modern history will have become evident, as it will continue to be when I come to the other countries of Eastern Europe. None of the events I have mentioned was predictable in the way it happened; all that might be said was that the existing situation had become unworkable, so that a change must be expected, dramatic or otherwise. The general drift, seen in hindsight, suggests that dramatic change was perhaps in the offing, not from any positive revolutionary urge, since no revolutionary trends existed, but rather from a perceived failure of the various attempts to create a viable Communist rule. Perhaps, indeed, failure was a more active factor in change during this period than the pursuit of positive goals. Movements of rebellion among the people failed because they did not assume a workable form, and so other approaches had to be tried out. New attempts to shore up the regimes equally failed, and each such effort to reconcile the opposites of autocracy and popularity revealed the weaknesses of the mechanisms of government. We shall see these indeterminacies constantly at work as I slide my camera from north to south down the map of Eastern Europe during the years leading up to the early 1950s. And the sense of history as an undisciplined process—as opposite to History as the foreseeable destiny of peoples—will be enhanced as we find institutions, the Communist party and the Catholic church among them, assuming different stances and roles, just as individual human beings do, according to the places as well as the times in which their activities are set.

Germany differed from all the other countries under consideration in that it was conquered—not liberated—territory, divided in 1945 into zones of occupation among the four main allied powers—Russia, Britain, the United States, and a resurrected France. A Soviet Military Administration was established in the eastern zone, with the double purpose of organizing plunder and establishing power in a strategically important region. The Russians set about immediately collecting their reparations in cash and kind, confiscating currency and securities, transporting the plant of factories and the rolling stock (and even rails) of railways to help reconstitute the severely depleted Russian industries.

The Russian plan to impose a puppet government was encouraged by the past history of German political movements. A large proportion of the workers in the region that fell under Russian control, especially in the industrial quarters of Berlin and cities like Erfurt, had been ardent supporters of the Communist party in the years before the Nazi regime took power, and now—when "anti-Fascist" parties were allowed to operate once again, the revived Communist and Social Democratic parties came together under Russian pressure to form the Socialist Unity party of Germany. It was officered by men who had gone into exile in the 1930s and had been servile enough to survive all the Stalin purges. Wilhelm Pieck, Otto Grotewohl and the rigidly Stalinist Walter Ulbricht maintained in succession an autocratic rule that was consistently closer in its inflexibility to that of Russia than the administration of any of the other East European satellites. For the first few years they succeeded in this because the Communist party basked in the prestigious memory of having—unlike the Social Democrats—resisted the Nazis for at least a period. And there was also the fact that a decade under the Nazis had habituated the Germans to totalitarian rule; Nazi and Communist attitudes during the 1940s had so much in common that minor Gestapo employees had little difficulty taking cover in the security services of the German Democratic Republic.

East Germany, with its old Communist traditions and the stubborn loyalties to Stalinist values of its veteran leaders, should have been the easiest of all the East European countries to bring peacefully into the Communist fold. Yet here the first serious problems began to trouble the Communist leaders. Action after action of the government alienated new sections of the population, and it quickly became evident that the East Germans were more anxious to enjoy their liberation from nazism than to celebrate their subordination to Marxist-Leninism. Persecution of the churches raised up a Protestant opposition that eventually would become as important and disruptive to a good totalitarian state as the Catholic opposition in Poland. In 1945 a third of the country's large estates had been divided up between half a million peasant farmers; now all these small farms were collectivized, with no resultant increases in food production. Finally, the proletariat discovered what its dictatorship really meant when norms of production were arbitrarily raised at the same time as severe food shortages began. The workers, once so doggedly Red, were Red no longer, and on 17 June 1953 rose in a rebellion so violent and extensive that Russian troops had to be called to deal with it, a precedent to be followed later in Hungary and Czechoslovakia.

To the rulers of East Germany the prophecies and dogmas of Marx were

136

more important than the present reality of their own country, and, like Stalin, they took the course of repression and isolation. The result was that three million people left the country for West Germany. The consequence of this great voting-with-feet was that the German Democratic Republic established a patrolled cordon, the most dramatic manifestation of which was the barbed-wire barrier erected through the heart of Berlin, which from 1961 onward became the Berlin Wall.

What remained behind the barrier was a strange combination of two totalitarian heritages. The East German state built up the most efficient army among the military forces of the Warsaw Pact; it was, ominously and ironically, the only military force in the world that retained the old Prussian goosestep. And, combining the experience of the Gestapo with that of the GPU, the old men of German communism produced an effective, brutal and hated security force, the despised, detested and yet feared Stasis.

The presence of West Germany, fast becoming a successful capitalist economy, on the borders of the German Democratic Republic, and of West Berlin at its very heart, inevitably increased resentment against the Communist government, for despite the Berlin Wall the East Germans were able to see and hear for themselves on television and radio how well materially their fellows in the Federal Republic of Germany were faring. Yet despite the obsolete and inefficient factories that polluted the whole region with little attempt at environmental control, the East Germans were probably better off than most of the other peoples of Eastern Europe. Even if housing was scarce and decrepit and the roads were breaking apart, there was at least a sufficiency of consumer goods, though they lacked both quality and variety. The situation was superficially mitigated when the two Germanies began to draw together, thanks to the Ostpolitik initiated by Willy Brandt as the Social Democratic chancellor of West Germany. This very rapprochement, however, drew attention to the inequalities between the two half-countries and heightened the tensions that were growing in East Germany throughout the 1980s and were held in difficult check by the combined weight of both Russian and East German military and security forces. But even here, the people would in the end claim and win their freedom.

Assembled in 1918 as a patchwork of ethnic components drawn from the ruins of the Austro-Hungarian Empire, Czechoslovakia had been for its first twenty years the most thorough democracy in Eastern Europe. From 1939 to 1945 it was subjected to German occupation and the ruthless dictatorship which the Nazis imposed on "lesser" races. For a few years after the war it enjoyed the freest multiparty system in Eastern Europe, and the

Communists seemed for a while to be ruling as primus inter pares. But support for the Communist party began quickly to erode, and the other parties called for an election which they calculated they could win in the current state of public opinion. Following the Leninist maxim that Communist control, once gained, must never be surrendered, the party used the police and manipulated the trade unions to carry out a coup d'état in February 1948, when Jan Masaryk, the most popular of the democratic leaders, "fell"—according to official reports—from his office window; there was never any real doubt that he was brutally thrown to his death. This was the event, so obviously directed from Moscow, that convinced Harry Truman to begin the rearming of the West and that marked the beginning of the Cold War.

A densely unimaginative government of Stalinoid ideologues and bureaucrats gave Czechoslovakia during the 1950s and the early 1960s one of the most repressive of satellite Communist regimes, worse even than that in East Germany because it was less efficient. By 1967 an intellectual ferment began to stir among the people, shown in the works of the new Czech writers who were just beginning to appear and in unprecedented student demonstrations combined with a strong separatist movement among the Slovaks. Presumably with Moscow's consent, the party replaced the Stalinoid Czech Antonin Novotny with the reform-minded Slovak Alexander Dubcek, hoping in this way to placate students, intellectuals and Slovaks alike. Dubcek invented the magic phrase "Socialism with a human face" and set about restoring civil liberties, emptying the prisons of political prisoners, and planning important economic reforms. The old Stalinoids of Moscow reacted with alarm, and Leonid Brezhnev, enunciating the doctrine of Communist uniformity that has since borne his name, persuaded the other members of the Warsaw Pact (with the exception of Rumania, which refused) to send in forces to bring the "Prague Spring," as it became known, to an end. Most of Dubcek's reforms were withdrawn, and he himself was demoted to an insignificant bureaucratic post, while Gustav Husak, a reliable puppet of the old men in the Kremlin, reinstated a harsh rule.

The pathos of Czechoslovakia's history between 1945 and 1989 was emphasized by the remarkable generation of writers who, after the brutal crushing of the Prague Spring in 1968 by Russian forces, identified themselves with the cause of their country's liberation. Some, like Milan Kundera and Josef Skvorecky, went into exile and continued to write about their country and its repression by the Communists; Skvorecky operated from Canada the most important independent Czech publishing house, export-

ing large numbers of books clandestinely to his own country. Others, like
Ivan Klima and Vaclav Havel, the country's leading dramatist, stayed behind
to face imprisonment as they obstinately continued in various ways to resist
the restrictions placed on the freedom of speech and writing and to
denounce the Communist infringements on human rights.

The best known manifestation of this semiclandestine agitation was the
Charter 77 movement, started in 1977 to promote the observance of the
human rights clauses of the Helsinki accord. The supporters of the charter
showed a remarkable persistence, as Husak's harsh government periodically
imprisoned them, and it was the men and women, mainly intellectuals,
involved in this movement who sustained the legend and the spirit of the
Prague Spring. Vaclav Havel, whose plays were consistently banned, became a symbol of nonviolent resistance because of the time he spent in
prison, and largely through him the theatrical community was radicalized
so that in alliance with the students it would play a notable role in the events
of 1989.

But all this simmered mainly underground, and until quite late in 1989
Czechoslovakia gave the appearance of calm which a prison has on the day
before a riot.

Hungary stood in a unique position among the puppet countries of Eastern
Europe because of its ties of history and sentiment with Austria, which in
1955 was relieved of Allied occupation and allowed to go on its way as a
sovereign and neutral country. Relationship and friendship linked many
Austrians and Hungarians, and the barbed-wire barrier with its
machine-gun turrets which the Hungarian Communist authorities built on
the frontier did not prevent the news of Austria's growing prosperity and
political freedom from seeping over the border.

Perhaps because of the bad memories of Béla Kun's earlier (1919)
Communist dictatorship in Hungary, the Russians were slow to force a
completely Communist government on the country, so to begin a republican constitution was devised, with the secret intention of later subverting
it. It recognized civil liberties and private property, though banks were
nationalized and large estates were expropriated. In the elections of 1945
the Smallholders party actually received a majority of 60 per cent of the
votes and the Communists no more than 17 per cent, and this was the signal
for growing interference and compulsion. The Russian occupation authorities insisted that the coalition government should continue and that
Communists must hold important portfolios, including that of the Interior,
which controlled the police. The Smallholders were bullied into repudiating

and expelling their more democratic and nationalist members, with the result that in 1947 the Communists were able to gain power for a "workers' bloc" consisting of themselves and the intimidated Social Democrats, who were shortly forced to merge with the Communists into a "Workers' party." In 1949 all pretence of democracy was abandoned, and the Communist party general secretary, Matyas Rakosi, embarked on a decade of terror and oppression second only to that the Russians endured under Stalin. Not only were the minority opposition groups suppressed; in 1949 Rakosi and his henchmen instituted a Stalinoid purge within the party. Mass arrests followed, in the army and the judiciary, the civil service and the trade unions, and many people were executed on fake charges of "war crimes." The AVO, the state security police, became the true power in the land. All the churches—possible nuclei of resistance—were forced into subordination to the state, and Cardinal Josef Mindszenty, the head of the Roman Catholic community, who refused to accept this arrangement, was sentenced to life imprisonment.

The submission which Hungarians displayed was deceptive, as they went about their lives and allowed the great industrialization plans of the Communist government to founder in a morass of indifference and inefficiency. As soon as Stalin died in 1953, Rakosi was deposed in favour of Imre Nagy, a somewhat ambivalent figure, lacking conviction as a Communist and pushed on by the forces of contingency. Yet Nagy had his own kind of vision, and as early as 1953, to extricate his government from a chaos of unpopularity and unworkable bureaucracy, he proposed and started to implement some of the kind of reforms that would eventually be accepted in Eastern Europe during the 1980s.

This disturbed the Russians, and in 1955 Nagy was dismissed and replaced by Rakosi, who reinstated the old hard-line system. However, Rakosi quickly earned the disapproval of Khrushchev, the new Soviet leader; he was sacked in turn, and another detested hard-liner, E. Gero, took his place. Gero refused to make concessions. When the students took to the streets of Budapest on 28 October 1956, and the population joined them in mass demonstrations, Gero's security police fired on the crowds. The reaction of the Hungarians was immediate, violent and almost unanimous, showing how widely detested the Communist government had become. Even the army joined in the rebellion, and barracks and arms factories handed weapons to the civilian rebels. Nagy returned to power at the head of a coalition consisting largely of the old democratic parties that had reconstituted themselves virtually overnight. The outnumbered Russian troops withdrew from Budapest, and Nagy, miscalculating the situation, announced Hungary's withdrawal from the Warsaw Pact and asked for United Nations recognition as a neutral state. This was more than the Russians could accept.

The tanks and the Russian troops returned to Budapest. The rebels continued to fight for a couple of weeks longer, and the workers kept up sporadic strikes for another month. Over 150,000 refugees fled to the West; they included many of Hungary's intellectual élite. Imre Nagy, who had taken refuge in the Yugoslav Embassy, left it under a safe conduct from the Russian commanders, but was abducted and, with several associates, executed secretly and without trial.

Out of all this chaos and strife, which the Western world watched with fascinated eyes and without raising a hand to help (the plight of the Kurds in Iraq during the Gulf War brings the whole situation back vividly into one's memory), there emerged that insidious Vicar of Bray figure, János Kádár. Just after the return of the Red Army to Budapest, he announced the formation of a government with himself as prime minister. Why the Kremlin decided to back Kádár is uncertain, but the decision may have come from a realization of the power of Hungarian national feeling, which could stir even the army to revolt, and an awareness of the strength of anti-Russian feeling, for Hungarians had not forgotten how the troops of Tsar Nicholas I had helped to crush the Hungarian revolt which Lajos Kossuth led against the Austrian monarchy in 1848. Kádár was quickly reined in by Hungary's Warsaw Pact partners, who gathered in Budapest in January 1957 to lay down the law, which was that no concessions on matters of Communist principles would be allowed. Hungary was and must remain a dictatorship of the proletariat, and a Russian garrison would stay on "to protect it from imperial aggression."

Kádár turned out to be a better liberal and a more skilful manipulator of the political situation than most Hungarians had expected, and for many years he became the most popular of the Communist administrators in Eastern Europe. He made the strange declaration, for a Communist leader, that he would work on the assumption that "everyone who is not against us is with us." The power of the political police was gradually curbed, so that Hungary was perhaps the only place in Eastern Europe where, even in the 1960s, people felt they could speak freely and where they could write within broader limits than elsewhere. Farming remained collectivized, but the members of the collectives were allotted individual plots, from which a dramatic increase in consumer goods was derived. Small-scale and manufacturing enterprises increased the flow of goods in what became generally known as "goulash communism," and the standard of living, in contrast to

141

that of the other satellites, rose considerably and rapidly.

He was willing to sacrifice a great deal externally in order to maintain a degree of internal autonomy. When the Warsaw Pact countries moved against Czechoslovakia in the spring of 1968, he sent a Hungarian contingent into Slovakia, even though Dubcek and his followers were aiming at the kind of changes in Communism which Hungary was already achieving. But this concern for Hungary's interests over those of other countries fitted very well with the nationalism that made Kádár want to turn Hungary into a Communist country *pas comme les autres.*

Kádár's attempt to balance an orthodoxy that would preserve Hungary from Russia's application of the Brezhnev Principle, and at the same time a nationalism that appealed to the sentiments of the great Magyar majority, was bound to create stresses. Besides, as his rule stretched out over three decades, Kádár's mind began to lose its flexibility, and when an economic crisis occurred in the early 1980s, he quickly became unpopular. His ousting from the leadership of the Hungarian Socialist Workers party (as the national Communist party was now called) in May 1988, was one of the important early tremors announcing the great political quake that shocked Eastern Europe in 1989. Not that his immediate successor, Karoly Grosz, was in any way a democrat. He was in fact a hard-headed apparatchik. But the fissures that were now appearing in the Communist ranks prepared the country for dramatic changes before the end of the decade.

South of the old Central Europe and the Carpathian chain lies that rugged peninsula divided between five nations called the Balkans, which in popular legend became known as the home of vampires and vendettas, bears and bandits, and the absurd Ruritanian kingdoms in which Viennese operettas were often set. It was, even in actuality, a region of deep dynastic rivalries and strife between small ethnic groups, and this gave rise to a word—Balkanization—which signifies a condition of incurable political divisiveness. The instability of the Balkans was encouraged by the fact that in the late decades of the nineteenth century and the early years of the twentieth, the region was a battleground where Austrian emperors, Russian tsars and Turkish sultans fought out their imperial wars by proxy. A Turkish bridgehead—a remnant of those vast rivalries—still survives at Istanbul.

In 1945 communism seemed to be triumphant in four out of the five independent countries in the Balkans. Only Greece, thanks to the strong intervention of British and American forces, which helped to crush a strong Communist partisan movement, remained an intermittently democratic country.

By the 1980s the four Communist countries had followed strikingly different directions, and three out of them had in one way or another fallen out with Soviet Russia and its rulers. Bulgaria alone became and remained a model Soviet satellite, without a touch of originality in its administration or in its postwar history. Despite an elaborate republican constitution, power rested with the Communist party, and this meant with Todor Zhivkov, the general secretary of the Bulgarian Communist party, who became the virtual dictator of the country in 1954; it was a post he would hold virtually unchallenged for thirty-five years. He followed faithfully all the shifts in the Kremlin line, and appears to have been entirely unprescient of what his fate would be when the Bulgarian people eventually found their voices.

But awareness in the area of probabilities that involves actual events, as distinct from the generally inaccurate grand prophecies of Marxism, has rarely been a gift of Communist rulers, and Nicolae Ceausescu, the Communist ruler of Rumania, appears to have had no foresight at all of the fate, even direr than Zhivkov's, that awaited him in 1989.

Rumania had an unusual history among Communist satellite states, because in mid-war, in 1944, as the Red Army approached its borders, it changed sides, overthrew Ion Antonescu's Iron Guard government which was closely linked to the Nazis, and reinstated King Michael. For a brief while this anomaly of a monarchy within the Communist bloc was allowed to continue, but by 1947 the Communists had created a government of party members which nationalized industry and agriculture, forced King Michael to abdicate and declared a republic. The leader of the Communist party was Gheorge Gheorgiu-Dej, who increased his popularity and that of the party by obtaining the withdrawal of Russian troops in 1958. During the 1960s Gheorgiu-Dej began to follow Marshal Tito's examples in establishing a steadily more independent line. Rumania remained Communist, but not in the Kremlin style.

Gheorgiu-Dej died in 1965, but his successor, Ceausescu, continued in the same line, on a number of occasions markedly showing his country's freedom from Kremlin domination. He refused to send troops to crush the Prague Spring in 1968, declined—unlike the other Warsaw Pact countries—to break off ties with Israel after the 1967 war, and kept up close ties with Communist China throughout the period of Russo-Chinese dissension. This made him something of a hero in Western capitals in the 1970s, and for a while he was even popular at home. But in the end his rule became increasingly dictatorial. During the 1980s he established a rigidly policed state, systematically persecuted minorities like the Hungarians and the

Germans, and set out to destroy the traditional lifestyles of many parts of rural Rumania by eliminating the ancient villages and herding their people into soulless housing estates. Withdrawal from Soviet orthodoxy was no guarantee of freedom from Marxist regimentation, as Albania also demonstrated.

Yugoslavia, the remaining Communist country of southeastern Europe, shows the extremity of classic Balkanism in both its composition and its history. Formed in the aftermath of World War I, which Balkan tensions had instigated through the assassination of the Grand Duke Francis Ferdinand at Sarajevo in Bosnia, it consisted of the former independent monarchies of Serbia and Montenegro, with the addition of Croatia, Bosnia and Herzegovina, and Slovenia, all provinces of the former Austro-Hungarian Empire.

From the beginning, there were extraordinary reasons for dissension. The population consisted of several ethnic strains and spoke many languages. Even when groups shared a language, they might write it differently because of religious differences; the Croats used a Roman script and the Serbs a Cyrillic script for their common Serbo-Croatian language because one group was Roman Catholic and the other Eastern Orthodox. Many of the people of Bosnia and Herzegovina were Moslem by religion, and there were other linguistic minorities, like the Macedonians—heirs to a great past—and pockets of Albanians. All these groups were agitating for growing autonomy in a country where the dominant group was the Serbs, headed by a Serbian king.

During World War II Yugoslavia followed a course not unlike that of Rumania, first leaning towards the Axis powers and then proclaiming neutrality, which provoked an invasion by the Nazis. In true Balkan style, the resistance groups were divided into the royalist partisans or Chetniks (mostly Serbs) led by General Draza Mihajlovic and the Communists led by Marshal Tito. By 1943 they were fighting each other as well as the Germans, with Tito eventually coming out on top, largely because the British as well as the Russians supported him. Mihajlovic, as so often happens to the defeated, was treated badly by the historians, though he can hardly have been more ruthless than Tito, and his principal crime, for which he would eventually be executed, was anti-communism. The situation in wartime Yugoslavia was complicated by the fact that those Croats who did not follow Tito tended to support the neo-Fascist group called the Ustasha, which the Nazis had placed in control of a puppet state of Croatia. The feud between the Ustasha and the Serbian Chetniks still echoes in the strife-torn Yugoslavia of the early 1990s.

Tito was, in his own way, an old Bolshevik, and because of this felt he projected a Leninism truer than that of Stalin and his associates. A Croat peasant's son—by original name Josip Broz—he was active in the Communist party in the 1920s and 1930s, and eventually became secretary general of the executive committee of the Comintern. In 1941 he became the head of the clandestine Communist party in Yugoslavia and led the partisan movement that sprang up after the German invasion of Russia that year. As early as 1943 he was able to call an assembly of partisan delegates of his own persuasion, which fatefully proclaimed Yugoslavia a federal community of different peoples.

Though the eventual formal break between Russia and Yugoslavia was actually made by Stalin, who expelled the Communist party of Yugoslavia from the Comintern on 28 June 1948, the incident was certainly provoked by Tito's resolve to maintain Yugoslavia's independence and to develop communism within his own country as he saw fit.

Over the years from 1948 onward Tito developed a decentralized system in accordance with the divided history and geography of his country; economically, he rejected the doctrinaire Russian policy of collectivizing agriculture and initiated at least a measure of worker control in industry. But Yugoslavia remained a strict police state, and the misadventures of Milovan Djilas, the country's most brilliant political thinker and writer, jailed repeatedly for his dissident views, typify the plight of intellectuals and artists under Tito's rule.

Tito's varying stances led him into some strange inconsistencies: though Djilas was imprisoned in 1956 for supporting the Hungarian insurrection of that year, Tito denounced Soviet interference in Czechoslovakia in 1968 as a violation of the sovereignty of a socialist country. Tito's last bequest to Yugoslavia was an ambivalent one. Having ruled as virtual dictator almost unchallenged for thirty-five years until his death in 1980, he decided that a collective presidency, which would presumably reflect all the divisions of his country, must take his place in ruling the country. It was not an inappropriate beginning for the 1980s, that decade when the old certainties of the Communist world would all break apart.

PART VI

•

THE

•

CRUCIAL

•

YEARS

The Negation of Ideology

History, I have been arguing, does not proceed in a regular fashion towards foreseeable goals, yet there is no doubt of the emergence of collective shifts of consciousness which affect events and change society in social, political, cultural and personal ways. The kind of confidence that carried a conquest or precipitated a revolution can disappear entirely from a society—many empires have quickly and unpredictably lost their will to continue—but then, like a stream running underground, the will can appear elsewhere, in a movement of national vigour, in the rising up of a hitherto placid people. These are not the kind of events that can be programmed into self-fulfilling prophecies; they come from the heart of that chaos which the writing of history seeks to order and can be understood only in hindsight, and then not always very clearly. An astute observer can sometimes sense that a social earthquake is imminent, as birds are said to sense the oncoming of a physical earthquake, but what precisely will happen neither bird nor human can tell in advance. It is left for the historian afterwards to speculate on the facts that events have offered.

Of course there are people ahead of their time, in the sense that in every reformation or revolution the great event, the bursting of the dam, is preceded by lesser events then unrecognized as well as by statements of men and women who see farther than their contemporaries. Careful historians of world-changing events like the French Revolution, as Peter Kropotkin did in writing *The Great French Revolution*, would offer a whole prehistory of the symptoms which showed how, years before 1789, the rulers were losing their confidence and the people were developing theirs, the two conditions necessary for any kind of decisive revolution. Such historians must look at background developments resembling those that preceded the French Revolution and similar outbreaks to find explanations for what happened in the minds of men and women of Eastern Europe, and what led to the extraordinary failure of the rulers and the equally extraordinary courage and success of their subjects during the 1980s and especially during 1989.

The period between 1945 and the 1980s had not been without rebellion, some of it—in Germany and Poland and Hungary—violent, some of it even involving the bold insubordination of Communist leaders like Imre Nagy and Alexander Dubcek. But these actions had been at best forlorn hopes, doomed by the continuing ruthlessness and self-assuredness of the central Communist power in the Kremlin if not by its subordinate local agencies.

By the 1980s it seemed evident that the situation would change only when both the Russian "imperial" rulers and the local "colonial" govern-ments lost their will to dominate the people, and the people acquired the will to be free, exercising it with such nonviolent firmness as to render armies and police forces irrelevant. This had happened once, a couple of genera-tions ago and on another continent when, under Gandhi's challenge, the British will to rule dissolved at the same time as Indians became willing to sacrifice their lives, though not those of others, to be free. But it was an analogy that few people in either Eastern or Western Europe cared to draw in view of the dense fog of obedience that seemed to envelop the Commu-nist countries, especially after the destruction of the high hopes of the Prague Spring.

Yet the situation was changing steadily, even in Russia. There had been the so-called thaw which happened as a result of Khrushchev's contradictory policies. For though he suppressed the Hungarian revolt of 1956, he made his historic denunciation of Stalinist policies in the same year, and he patronized Alexander Solzhenitsyn, whose *One Day in the Life of Ivan Denisovich* fictionally denounced the Soviet concentration camp system, and generally initiated a cultural thaw in which censorship diminished and a brief literary renaissance occurred. It is true that Khrushchev's demotion by the conservatives in 1964 meant a return to Stalinoid attitudes and policies under the geriatric leadership of Leonid Brezhnev, including the renewed political domination of satellites (Czechoslovakia, 1968) and imperialist adventure in the borderlands (Afghanistan, 1979). Dissidents and artists who merely wished to follow their own vision were persecuted, but the great purges of the Stalin era were no more. The regime was no longer confident enough to repeat the great massacres. Dissidents might be put in psychiatric hospitals or harsh retraining camps. They were no longer shot in the cellars of the Lubianka prison. Many more returned to freedom and to tell their tales in the days of *perestroika*.

What happened was the growing negation of ideology in both its roles. It ceased to be a sustaining pillar for the rulers, and it ceased to offer a commanding faith for the ruled. And here we have to take immediate account of the two currents that were at work during this period. There were, on the one hand, the reform Communists, of whom Alexander Dubcek is representative in the earlier days and Mikhail Gorbachev in the 1980s. These were the people who were willing, like Khrushchev but with cleaner hands, to denounce and deny the methods used by Stalin as a perversion of Leninism and Marxism—not only his enforcement methods but also the economic centralism on which his regime had been based. They remained, nevertheless, Communists and even Leninists at heart, reluctant to admit that the very faults of the Stalinist regime lay in the heritage of historicism and terrorism it had derived from Marx and Lenin respectively, reluctant to admit that an antihuman political philosophy could not be given "a human face." None of them denounced the crimes against freedom and common humanity that followed on the October Revolution; none admitted the dark responsibility Lenin incurred in creating the Cheka and sanctioning the killing of hostages; none accepted guilt on behalf of their predecessors for the atrocity of slaughtering the revolutionary sailors of Kronstadt. None seriously offered to rehabilitate those great (even if in some ways detestable) Russians, Trotsky and Bakunin.

On the other hand, presenting with growing urgency and power their message of a world ruled by human values, were the true dissidents, increasingly surprising in their numbers and persistence. They bypassed the tired controversy of Stalin versus Lenin, reaching back into the democratic and the Christian traditions of European civilization for their own proposals to society, proposals that were not attached to ideological and historicist certitudes but to the improbable likelihoods, the impossible possibilities of real life.

In the end it would be these men, quietly protesting because loudness was not part of their undemonstrative firmness against power, men with no desire for office or fame, though they might and would gain both against their wills, who would stand finally in the world's eye as more realistic than all the Marxist-Leninists, conservative or reform-minded. When true historians look back over this era, it may well not be Khrushchev and Dubcek and Gorbachev, loyally trying to rehabilitate an amoral system in the eyes of moral people, who will be regarded as the most important figures of the strange interlude preceding 1989, but such mavericks as Havel and Walesa, Sakharov and Solzhenitsyn, who presented their own varying degrees of disassociation from Marxist-Leninist orthodoxy.

Let me quote some very germane passages from the clandestine writing which two of these men, Sakharov and Havel, issued during the years leading up to 1989. Sakharov, liberated from his legal disabilities by Gorbachev in 1985, died in 1989 still believing in the possible rehabilitation in practice of Marxist-Leninism. He was less a true dissident than a radical reform Communist. Vaclav Havel, who never accepted any such faith, read his history more carefully and devised his own libertarian alternative.

Both of these men, at the very time when they were being subjected to harassment and humiliation by their respective political police, wrote crucial essays defining the situation as they saw it and had them smuggled out and published abroad, after which they found their way back to other dissidents through the chains of samizdat publication that operated throughout the Soviet bloc.

Sakharov's essay, "Thoughts on Progress, Peaceful Coexistence and Intellectual Freedom," appeared in the *New York Times* as early as 22 July 1968. Its main preoccupations are with the possibility of a world-destroying nuclear war between the great powers, and with intellectual freedom considered as a prerequisite for a more general human freedom. I quote seriatim the essential paragraphs:

1. The division of mankind threatens it with destruction. Civilization is imperilled by a vast thermonuclear war, catastrophic hunger for most of mankind, stupefaction from the narcotic of "mass culture" and bureaucratized dogmatism, a spreading of mass myths that put entire peoples and continents under the power of cruel and treacherous demagogues and destruction or degeneration from the unforeseeable consequences of swift changes in the conditions of life on our planet. . . .

2. The second basic thesis is that intellectual freedom is essential to human society—freedom to obtain and distribute information, freedom for open-minded and unfearing debate and freedom from pressure by officialdom and prejudices. Such a trinity of freedom of thought is the only guarantee against an infection of people by mass myths, which, in the hands of

hypocrites and demagogues, can be transformed into bloody
dictatorship. Freedom of thought is the only guarantee of the
feasibility of a scientific democratic approach to politics, economy and culture.

The emphases, in the title and the text of Sakharov's essay, reveal the
limitations of his approach as well as the limitations of the possibilities as
he saw them in 1968. Like Dubcek, he is not rebelling against communism
as such; he talks not about a dissolution of Communist power but rather
of the achievement of "peaceful coexistence" between a reformed communism and the democratic societies which, as he remarks, have been shown
to be not as detrimental to the workers as Marx and Lenin predicted. His
own record as a scientist deeply involved in the development of Russian
atomic weapons (and aware of guilt as some of his American counterparts
became) made him lay an emphasis on the probability of wars of destruction
which today seems excessive. This gives a certain elitism to his approach
when he talks, like Marx, of a "scientific democratic" approach (how
Bakunin would have scoffed at the combination of science, which is
essentially aristocratic, and democracy!) "to politics, economy and culture,"
and attacks "mass culture," when one kind of mass culture, the "pop"
culture of jazz and rock, became a potent element in awakening people in
the Soviet bloc to revolt during the 1980s. His stance is essentially that of
the philosopher risking all for truth, much in the same way as Socrates.

To point out Sakharov's limitations of approach, and those of other men
of courage like Alexander Dubcek, is not to single them out for criticism;
all who are old enough remember how dramatic and inspiring Sakharov's
protests, like Dubcek's talk of "socialism with a human face," appeared
when the monolith of International Communism seemed so impermeable.

Vaclav Havel's splendid essay, "The Power of the Powerless," with its
populist, almost anarchistic approach, is remarkable not merely for its bold
step forward from reforming to rejecting communism but also for the time
at which it was written. His essay appeared in 1978, a year after Charter 77
was circulated for signature, and it allows us to relate that event and the
experiences of those involved in it to the later mass movements of individuals seeking freedom that would ultimately make Havel one of its half-will-
ing heroes.

I know from thousands of personal experiences how the mere
circumstance of having signed Charter 77 has immediately
created a deeper and more open relationship and evoked sud-

153

den and powerful feelings of genuine community among people who were all but strangers before.

Havel contrasts this kind of experience, on which the great East European revolt would eventually be based, with the attitude of what he calls the "post-totalitarian" state, by which he means the post-Hitler and post-Stalin police state which deals through the law, systematically misinterpreted, without a need for the gross mass brutalities of the classic totalitarians. Mainly, he argues, it rules by its psychological hold over even those who are its resentful subjects, and his passage on the way ideology is structured to dominate the wills of the rulers as well as of the ruled is an extraordinary view—from inside as it were—of the mental force that delayed so long an effective rebellion against the Communist state.

> Ideology is a specious way of relating to the world. It offers human beings the illusion of an identity of dignity and of morality while making it easier for them to *part* with them. As the repository of something "supra-personal" and objective, it enables people to deceive their conscience and conceal their true position and their odious *modus vivendi*, both from the world and from themselves. . . . The primary excusatory function of ideology, therefore, is to provide people, both as victims and pillars of the post-totalitarian system, with the illusion that the system is in harmony with the human order and the order of the universe.

Such a concept of ideology is linked to the leading argument of this book, for a system can only be "in harmony with the human order and the order of the universe" if it is seen to be determined by that order and therefore operating in the realm of foreordained and foreseeable history.

Having rejected as of proven impracticability the utopian idea that human societies can be shaped to fit a hypothetical future and the ideologies which support such a proposition, Havel offers his own proposal of an alternative society consisting of "structures not in the sense of organizations or institutions, but like a community." Rather than formalized political parties, he argues, "it is better to have organizations spring up *ad hoc*, infused with the enthusiasm for a particular purpose and disappearing when that purpose has been achieved." What he is talking about in fact is the structure of the "power of the powerless" and, as Herbert Read used to put it, the "politics of the unpolitical."

Havel, it seems evident from a look at his career, has received his perceptions and determined his actions perhaps less through rational planning than by means of an intuitive perception of what is going on within society. He is one of many, including the neo-anarchists, who have followed the lead of Kropotkin in *Mutual Aid* and have perceived an anti-state of voluntary institutions and movements operating within authoritarian and totalitarian political structures. This is the world of personal living, the permanent unorganized and invisible opposition that every society harbours against the will of its rulers, the underground of human normality which is at once anarchic and co-operative. It is this sense of the presence of an alternative way if only we will see it that emerges in the last paragraph of Havel's great essay:

> For the real question is whether the "brighter future" is really
> always so distant. What if, on the contrary, it has been here
> for a long time already, and only our own blindness and
> weakness have prevented us from seeing it around us and
> within us, and kept us from developing it.

Note that Havel is not, like the Marxists, talking in terms of History and its inevitabilities; he is, in the spirit of the true historian, looking on the present and speculating on it in relation to the past. And events during the following decade of the 1980s were of course to show his perceptions as astonishingly accurate.

But it was neither in Sakharov's Russia nor in Havel's Czechoslovakia that the first manifestations of the permanent opposition of people wanting to live their own lives began to show itself in dramatic forms and to destroy the empire of ideology. It was, rather, in Poland, and Poland is a special case historically and culturally.

The Poles are Slavs, like the Russians, but they were converted to Christianity by Catholic teachers from Western Europe and not by the priests from the Eastern Orthodox church of Byzantium, who proselytized in Russia and the Balkans. Historically they regarded themselves—and still do—as a bulwark of Western civilization against the barbarity of the East. And indeed, it was one of Poland's kings, John Sobieski, who effectively defeated the Turks outside Vienna in 1683, virtually saving Western Europe from an Ottoman invasion.

John Sobieski, like the other Polish kings, was elected, and at the height of Poland's independence, the Polish-Lithuanian Commonwealth (which ruled the borderlands of Russia from the Baltic to the Black Sea) had a remarkably different political structure from the old autocracy of Russia or the rising autocracies of Prussia and Austria, which eventually were to swallow it up. It seems to have reached a political stage similar to that of England before the Reform Bill, with power widely spread among all levels of the landowning community and the Sejm, or parliament, an active body. As writer Neal Acherson remarked, "It was not only the biggest but the most tolerant state of northern Europe," in which all citizens, whatever their religion or race, were treated as Poles, equal before the law.

Some of this old history was to be repeated in the new Poland, when in 1920 the Red Army under Marshal Tukashevsky invaded the country and had advanced almost to the suburbs of Warsaw by the time Jozef Pilsudski attacked with his largely volunteer legions and drove the Red Army back in disorder. Once again, the Poles could claim to have defended Western civilization against Eastern barbarism, for the Red Army was apparently about to enter East Prussia when Pilsudski struck it from the rear.

Outside Warsaw the Red Army had in fact encountered two of the great enemies of those who proceed on the assumptions of a determined History; the power of tradition, and the power of regional separateness, expressing itself in local loyalties. From the nineteenth century Polish political exiles who had taken refuge in Western Europe were celebrated and respected in revolutionary circles for their pride in their identity and the love of their land that made it hard for them to settle abroad; always they were awaiting the day of reckoning, of return and revenge. And, more than most people in the present age of widespread scepticism alternating with crazy fundamentalism, they have remained astonishingly loyal to their Catholicism, which in its turn has provided great national icons like the Black Virgin of Jasna Gora.

Nowhere but in Poland, perhaps, could the action of a conservative— even reactionary—pope precipitate a social revolution and by almost entirely unpolitical means bring an end to the political grip of communism. But the pope was a Polish primate whose unexpected elevation was hailed with pride by his fellow countrymen who were also his fellow Catholics. The Vicar of Marx on Earth, a stuffy and cruel old man named Brezhnev, might reign in Moscow, but for the Poles the Vicar of God on earth was one of their own, a man of comparative youth and great vigour who had insisted on breaking out from the old retreats of the Vatican and Castelgandolfo to take his assortment of messages to the world. And when in 1979 the pope returned for a pastoral visit to the country where he had been the Archbishop of Krakow, he forced the Communists to show their

156

weakness, for they dared neither prevent his visit nor hinder the enthusiastic crowds who attended him wherever he went. People had visions, they lived for weeks in a state of exaltation and exultation, and there is no doubt that the afflatus induced by the papal visit spilled over into the following historic year, when Lech Walesa led his fellow workers in a series of strikes that spread across Poland and led to the formation of Solidarity, the union whose very name came straight out of the syndicalist tradition.

There will always, no doubt, remain something enigmatic about the circumstances in which Solidarity was at least overtly brought to an end by a declaration of martial law on 13 December 1981, followed by its official abolition in December 1982. Most of the leaders of Solidarity, including Lech Walesa, were imprisoned or interned, but Walesa was set free in December 1982, and Solidarity continued as a clandestine movement that was capable of calling occasional strikes.

At the time it was generally thought that these happenings in Poland were directed by an actual threat of invasion from Moscow, where Yuri Andropov was continuing the hard-line policies of Brezhnev. But here again a doubtful element emerges in the enigmatic figure of General Wojciech Jaruzelski, who with the declaration of martial law became the virtual dictator of Poland. Was he a mere tool of the Kremlin? Or was he a Polish patriot saving his own country from the humiliation, so often suffered in the past, of Russian invasion, and confronting the Russians with the fait accompli of a "pacified" country where there was no excuse for them to interfere? The case for regarding Jaruzelski as a national hero was made in its most extreme form by the Bavarian poet Hans Magnus Enzenberger, who presented him as a figure of "almost tragic dimension":

> In 1981, he saved Poland from the inevitability of Soviet inva-
> sion. The price of salvation was the introduction of martial
> law and the internment of those very members of the unoffi-
> cial opposition who today run the country. . . . The resound-
> ing success of his policies did not spare him the wrath of the
> Polish people, a large number of whom regard him to this
> day with utter hatred. No one cheers him; he will never es-
> cape the ghost of his last actions.

In fact, of course, Jaruzelski's policies were not a "resounding success." Admittedly the Russians did not come; nevertheless Jaruzelski found the Polish people and the church united passively against him, so that Solidarity had no difficulty surviving underground, while one result of martial law was

157

a growing economic crisis that awakened the dormant spectre of industrial discontent. The pope appeared again in 1983 and demonstrated by the enthusiasm he aroused that, even under martial law, authority remained divided between the party and the church because "loyalty" was so divided.

The single most important event in the Communist world before the annus mirabilis of 1989 was the accession to power in Russia of Mikhail Gorbachev, who made his immediate task the ridding of Russia from the consequences of the rule of sick old men in the Kremlin that had continued from the last days of Brezhnev through the reigns of his two equally hard-line successors. Gorbachev represented the positive side of that disillusionment with ideology that was already manifesting itself within the Communist apparat by a cynical concern for privilege, profit and power, which led, in the interests of the *nomenklatura* (managers), to a continuance of Stalin's disastrous centralizing policies in the economic as well as the political life of the Soviet Union.

Gorbachev was a kind of political Proteus, hard to hold down for long enough to determine his true identity. Perhaps he can be described as a post-Communist rather than an ex-Communist. Though in the end, during the critical summer of 1991, he found himself forced to abandon the Communist party, he never denied the historicist tradition of Marx and Lenin and Stalin; he merely abandoned, with a fine understanding of the logic of events, the central and characteristic policies of Lenin and Stalin, those of unmitigated terror combined with unlimited economic centralization.

Gorbachev seems basically to have been moved by two considerations. The first was that Russia's disastrous economic situation made the imperial policies of the Brezhnev era unsustainable; so, while seeking ways to ease the burden of endless military expansion, he ended the unwinnable war of intervention in Afghanistan, abandoning the attempt to make Russia the successor of Britain and then America as policeman of the world. At the same time, with his home policies of *perestroika* and *glasnost*, he attempted the vast task of opening a society that had been closed for nearly seventy years since 1917.

Censorship virtually came to an end, criticism of the regime became free and abundant and was sometimes heard, art was released from the old Socialist Realist strait jacket. Losing its privilege of terror, the secret police ceased to be a political power. The psychiatric hospital as a penal institution began to follow the Gulag into the past. Opposition groups unheard of for decades—such as the anarchists and various nostalgic pro-tsarist forma-

158

tions—emerged or re-emerged, revealing how varied and vital were the traditions that had lingered so long in many people's minds.

At the same time, the other enemy of historical determinism, regionalism, was revived on a sensational scale. Greater Russia, the U.S.S.R., had always been a confederation of autonomous mini-states, theoretically sovereign. All in fact were ruled by branches of the same Communist party, NKVD and Red Army, though many, like Georgia and the three Baltic republics of Latvia, Lithuania and Esthonia, were there as a result of conquest since the revolution of 1917. Now demands arose for the sovereignty to be made realer; the recently seized republics began to declare independence unilaterally; even the vast Russian republic threw up a post-Communist leader more radical than Gorbachev himself in the person of Boris Yeltsin, who supported the small republics in their struggle for freedom. Having achieved the end of the one-party system in the U.S.S.R. as a whole and opened the field to an astonished populace and an astonishing variety of factional viewpoints, Gorbachev was faced with the problem of how to contain the great genie of independence he had aroused and so preserve the country that was more an empire than a nation. Eventually, to preserve it from the right-wing centralizers who devised the coup against Gorbachev in August 1991, the U.S.S.R. lost its very name and became an alliance of republics. But, miraculously almost, a unity of a kind remained.

It remained largely because Gorbachev was a pragmatist politician rather than an ideologue merely intent on helping predetermined History do its work through the minimal amount of Leninist terror necessary in the circumstances. He was clearly concerned, as few other Communist leaders since Rosa Luxemburg have been, with actual human misery, and it was mainly ill luck that made him unable to act decisively in reviving the Russian economy. In a strange way he resembled the "conscience-stricken" Russian noblemen, like Herzen and Tolstoy and Kropotkin, who moved out of the aristocratic ranks and "went to the people" during the nineteenth century. For, like them, he was a member of an aristocracy, the apparat of the Communist party, and stepped out with evident populist intent to involve the workers and peasants and intelligentsia directly in the affairs of the country. In doing so he went away from the certainties of the determinist view of history into the capricious world of actual events where the patterns, so obvious in hindsight, are in fact the products of chance association, human will always being one of the factors.

Never before had there been a Communist leader who moved so boldly into the unpredictable world of contingency, and this daring is what, when the tales are all told, will make Gorbachev stand out as a genuine hero.

159

Rather than sustain the greatness of the Communist party or the certainty of its prophetic statements, he sought a new way that accorded with the reality of existence. He was reminiscent, as he defended communism's revolutionary achievement while admitting the errors and crimes of Communists, of Antony standing beside Caesar's bier and saying:

> I come to bury Caesar, not to praise him.
> The evil that men do lives after them,
> The good is oft interred with their bones;

In actual history, those who demolish or dismantle old structures are often not chosen by events or by the people who always half hate them for destroying a kind of security, even when they half love them for creating a kind of freedom. And it may well be someone else, Boris Yeltsin perhaps, who will reap the rewards for what Gorbachev did—or most deliberately and fortunately failed to do by showing the peoples of the Soviet satellite countries how to make a choice of their own future.

His name will appear again in this book—but before I end this comment on his significance in the 1980s, let me arouse the speculation that Gorbachev was deeply influenced by the period when he served as a party boss in Siberia. From the late eighteenth century until very recently, Siberia was known, to the world as well as in Russia, as the home of political exiles and dissenters, as well as of common criminals. Some of the dissenters, like the Doukhobor settlers of whom Kropotkin tells in *Memoirs of a Revolutionist*, were simple peasants whose religious principles had set them in opposition to the imperial and militarist policies of the autocracy. But others were members of the intelligentsia, and they included some of the most remarkable of Russian writers and thinkers. Inevitably, their presence influenced the people who were associated with them in an official—even repressive—capacity; the example of Peter Kropotkin, who went there as an army officer with the prestige of a former imperial page, is not untypical. He entered a society where exiles, freed from prison but not allowed to return to Moscow, were so well respected that even high officials were affected by contact with them. One officer connived at Bakunin's celebrated escape from Siberia, while by the time young Prince Kropotkin left the region, he was almost the anarchist he very quickly became in Western Europe.

In addition to the fact that it was the kind of prison where the prisoners directed the way of thinking, Siberia was as much a zone of quick economic expansion as the Canadian or the American West, and has remained so.

From the beginning it produced notable entrepreneurs (though many of them took cynical advantage of the penal system to man their gold-mining enterprises), but also in recent years unorthodox economists, some of whom deeply influenced Gorbachev's way of thinking. Also, again like the North American West, Siberia became an unexpected land of worker militancy, with striking Siberian miners pushing Gorbachev to solve Russia's economic problems. Effective Communist leaders in the 1980s, like any other politicians, made their decisions in the world of contingency, not of determined History, and Gorbachev was the most formidable of them to do so. Their wisdom would be well tested in August 1991.

CHAPTER XVI

Miraculous Years

The response to Gorbachev's early announcements and initiatives in the mid-1980s was cautious, for people in the Soviet bloc remembered other times of inviting changes in policy, like Lenin's New Economic Policy and the Khrushchev "thaw" and the Prague Spring. The year 1985 was one of surface calm when people waited and a majority of the East European countries were being ruled on harsh neo-Stalinist lines by old partisans like Erich Honecker in Berlin and Gustav Husak in Prague. The Balkan countries seemed like a forlorn area of darkness. People rarely appeared anywhere on the streets to demonstrate, and when they did were beaten up; the main manifestation of dissent everywhere but in Poland, and to an extent in Hungary where some strikes were breaking out, was the constant hidden flow of opposition literature, some imported from abroad (West Germany naturally, and Canada notably for books in Czech and Slovak) and some reproduced internally by samizdat. Ideas were certainly on the move and occasionally were expressed in acts of protest—collective and personal at the same time—like those of the Charter 77 group in Prague. But they did not lead to widespread passive resistance. Indeed, people in the Soviet bloc countries of the early and middle 1980s were rather like Canadian people today, aware of impending crisis and of their duty to act in some way but not yet sure how to do so effectively.

In fact there were two tasks to be performed during these extraordinary days: the ruled had to discard their well-justified fear of the rulers, and the rulers had to reject the mandate of destiny by which they claimed to serve

History. And when the critical times began to arrive in the middle months of 1989, it was amazing how in country after country the growing doubts of the rulers and the growing confidence of the ruled came together to destroy the sense of a predetermined collective destiny that had seemed to assure the future of communism and to awaken in the people an awareness of the possibility of the impossible, in the sense that each age and each people and each individual had become able to create its or his or her own future.

In 1988 the uneasy peace of dictatorial rule in Poland that had lasted since the arrests of late 1981 ended, and this was the real beginning of the end of communism in Eastern Europe. In May of that year strikes began in response to the hardship among the workers occasioned by the poor and worsening economic situation, and although the strikes were mainly spontaneous, the slogan under which they operated was "No Freedom without Solidarity!" When the strikes temporarily died down, the government declared that "Solidarity belongs to the past for good." But in August an even larger wave of strikes swept across the country; the workers refused to be provoked into violence but were insistent that Solidarity should be re-established. General Jaruzelski, again playing his enigmatic role of Polish patriot, decided that he had no recourse but to call on that other noted patriot, Lech Walesa, and on 31 August a long historic day of talks took place between Walesa and General Kiszczak, who had once imprisoned him.

As a result Solidarity once again appeared in the public eye, trimmed down by the years of clandestinity into a leaner and more effective organization of militants, perhaps containing two million people as against the ten million in the euphoric days of 1980. Walesa called off the strikes, and several months of informal discussions followed between Solidarity leaders and those members of the apparat who had become aware of the increasingly rebellious mood of the people. Finally, the way was cleared when Jaruzelski once again intervened, at a crucial moment in January 1989, to insist that Solidarity must be recognized as a legal body with which formal discussions could begin.

The famous Round Table talks began on 6 February 1989 between Solidarity, the Polish United Workers' party (as the Communist party called itself) and the two lesser parties, the Democratic party and the United Peasants party, that for many years had survived as compliant partners in the government. A deal was finally worked out for a constitutional change by which the Sejm, or parliament, of 460 members would be supplemented by a new senate with 100 members. In the Sejm 35 per cent of the seats would be reserved for Solidarity candidates, and the remaining 65 per cent divided between the Communists and the other parties, but the senate seats would be decided by a free vote.

The Polish people, in the first free election in a Communist country for almost half a century, clearly made their will known on 4 June. Solidarity won every one of the seats it could contest in the Sejm and 99 out of the 100 freely contested seats in the senate. The inclination of Democratic and United Peasants party representatives to break away from recent loyalties meant that it was impossible for the Communists to form a majority in either house. The government that followed the election was a coalition, and, according to the tacit agreement reached at the Round Table, General Jaruzelski was elected president by a derisive majority of one vote. But very soon Lech Walesa would become president and the Polish people would set out to reconstruct their society—or perhaps deconstruct it—without any sense of being the beneficiaries or the victims of a predetermined history. The spectre called communism had ceased to haunt their land. And Gorbachev saw no reason to raise it again, even to the extent of dispatching a single Russian soldier. People in the other Eastern European countries took note.

June 1989 was to be a month of tragic but splendid significance in the history of the decline of world communism and of the reawakening, at least in Europe, of the libertarian vision. On 4 June two radically different and equally dramatic events took place, showing in the one case communism in the panic-stricken and murderous extreme of defensiveness, and on the other communism in full retreat before a revived and radical democracy.

On 4 June, after weeks of hesitation before the honest demands of the students in Beijing for greater democracy, which the population of that great city increasingly supported, the aged rulers reacted with fear and cruelty, massacring the militant marchers whose great processions had woven for weeks through the heart of the capital. When the People's Liberation Army decided to act against the people, the result was the temporary submergence of the democracy movement, but neither the students nor the populace of Beijing were pacified any more than the people of Budapest had been in 1956 or the people of Prague in 1968. The residue of bitterness remained, with the knowledge that the rulers had lost their confidence and that one day another passive opposition might strike at the soft underside of their will to power.

Meanwhile just over a week later, the Hungarians manifested their rejection of the recent past in their own country by a great symbolic gesture initiated by the Committee for Historical Justice. Its members, mainly survivors from the 1956 uprising and relatives of Kádár's victims, had discovered the plot where the murdered bodies of Imre Nagy and his companions had been secretly buried after their execution. The committee had begun in 1968 by holding a ceremony in the outlying cemetery where the bodies lay; the same day the police suppressed brutally a demonstration in the city. But in January 1989 the new leaders of the party, sensing that the ghost of Nagy would continue to haunt them if they did nothing to right the old injustices, declared that the rising of 1956 had not been a "counterrevolution" but rather "a popular uprising against an oligarchic rule that had debased the nation." Having, as historicists do, rewritten the past to suit the future they hoped to shape and control, they then announced that they would allow the exhumation and decent burial of the remains of Nagy and his associates.

As such matters usually turn out, the authorities set going more than they had bargained for, since the Committee for Historical Justice, working with the newly emergent opposition groups and with men like Imre Pozhgay, reform-minded pretender to party leadership, declared that it intended a "ceremonial burial and political resurrection" for the martyrs who had now become heroes.

This symbolic gesture took place on 16 June in Heroes' Square in Budapest (with all its memories of the rebels of 1848) and turned out to be a more dramatic occasion than even its organizers expected. Six coffins stood on the steps of the banner-hung Gallery of Art, five of them for Nagy and his closest associates, and one for "The Unknown Insurgent." People came in their tens of thousands, men, women and children carrying their single carnations or small bunches to lay on the coffins, and then the official delegations arrived, from town councils and foreign embassies and churches, from the opposition groups and schools, from Warsaw in the name of Solidarity, from the government and the parliament; the Communist party as such stayed away, perhaps fearing for the safety of its representatives.

They need not have feared, for the only mobs in Eastern Europe were the police they themselves had let loose; the crowd, which in the end swelled to 200,000, was one of the first of those great Eastern European gatherings whose appearance on the screen or in print during that marvellous summer so fascinated the world. Great assemblies, individuals of all types and classes, suddenly came to a common awakening: old men and old women (a surprising number of them), workers and intellectuals and professionals, teenagers and often children held in arms. Pacific but not silent, for they had their songs and their slogans and their cheers for speakers, with which they seemed to challenge the police to violence. But the police lay low, even

165

when the speeches began to challenge directly the legitimacy of party rule. At the end of the ceremony, as Timothy Garton Ash records in *The Magic Lantern* (1990), when a series of veterans and survivors had had their say, the representative of the Young Democrats stood up to speak, ignoring the caution of his elders:

> We young people do not think there is any reason for us to be grateful for being allowed to bury our martyred dead. . . . If we can trust our souls and strength, we can put an end to the Communist dictatorship, if we are determined enough we can force the party to submit itself to free elections, and if we do not lose sight of the ideals of 1956, then we will be able to elect a government that will start immediate negotiations for the swift withdrawal of Russian troops.

The wild and prolonged applause that followed this speech was shown on national television. Three weeks later the Hungarian Supreme Court declared the complete legal rehabilitation of the men of 1956. On the same day, with a melodramatic appropriateness that must have stirred the hearts of Hungarians, János Kádár died.

On such occasions it may seem, as Pierre Elliott Trudeau was fond of remarking, that "The universe is unfolding as it should." Even if we refuse to accept any doctrines of determined or destined historical development, we need have no difficulty in observing with the hindsight that is the essence of history that events may cluster in what afterwards appear to be significant patterns. The special circumstances of a time and place can propel individuals and communities to act in similar ways, and we can either consider this as coincidence (or what Jung called synchronicity), or we can find a significance in what they have in common, as an ancient historian like Herodotus did when he saw meaning in the fact that the earlier Western civilizations began in great river valleys and that many of their features were connected with the problems of benefiting from the flow of the rivers. But the Sumerian civilization of the Euphrates and the Egyptian civilization of the Nile and the Chinese civilization of the Yangtse, though they emerged from similar environmental circumstances, did not, in the end, resemble each other.

Similarly, in the Eastern European countries in 1989 the various revolts had a common background of rulers and ruled awakening from the nightmare of ideology, as one side began to lose its grip on power and the other to grasp for freedom. But in each country the revolt took on a special

166

form reflected in the key events and special directions of the various movements of rebellion, which harked back to the special traditions of the region. In Poland the deep Catholicism of the country and the often exaggerated egalitarianism of the old Polish-Lithuanian Republic were reflected in the unusual alliance of the church and the populist trade union that brought an end to Communist rule. In Hungary it was a tradition of revolutionary heroism that went back to Lajos Kossuth and the Year of Revolutions, 1848. Under the aegis of the honour done to the rebel hero Imre Nagy, the twentieth-century Hungarian insurrection took on impetus in the summer of 1989; the Communist party as such ceased to exist, and the nascent opposition groups formed their own Round Table to negotiate with the representatives of government. The constitution was suitably amended, and on 23 October the new democratic Hungarian republic was proclaimed.

Before this, even before the rehabilitation and reburial of Imre Nagy, the Hungarians had embarked on an earlier act of symbolic as well as practical significance. Long ago, after the East German Communists constructed the Berlin Wall and established a corridor of death along their western borders to keep out opponents and keep in their own people, the Hungarians followed their example. Some time in the early 1970s I visited Austria and saw the tall fence of barbed wire, at least three metres high, that had been built along the frontier, with decrepit-looking wooden towers, occupied by border guards with automatic weapons, dotted along its course. It was a menacing sight, among those peaceful woods and reedbeds, only relieved by the sudden appearance on the other side of the barbed wire of a jaunty little steam locomotive drawing a couple of decayed but imperial-looking coaches. They were full of passengers, but nobody responded to our waves. Obviously the great fence held for Hungarians the same kind of meaning as the Berlin Wall did for Germans, for shortly after Kádár's fall from power in 1988, the border guards put down their guns and picked up their clippers to demolish the barbed-wire fence.

And so the clippers snipped in the forests and the wooden towers were pulled down, freeing the Hungarians to pursue their old love-hate relations with Germans and Austrians. But the effect spread far beyond Hungary, and especially into East Germany where the glacier of Communist power had shown as yet little sign of the East European thaw. As the closed frontiers began to open all round Hungary, the people of East Germany began to show they had had enough, and they did so by turning Lenin's famous recommendation against his successors and voting with their feet.

167

As the fence opened the Hungarians first adhered to an agreement with East Germany and prevented the Germans in flight—most of them young people—from proceeding farther and set up special camps for them. But the flood continued and in September 1989 they opened the borders completely to allow the Germans to cross the borders into Austria and thence to West Germany, where they were welcomed; others found their way, claiming to be holiday makers, into Poland and Czechoslovakia, and took refuge in the West German embassies in Moscow and Prague.

In East Germany and later in Czechoslovakia, an important change began to take place in the movement against Communist domination. Great masses of individuals began to coalesce spontaneously in the streets, and by their sheer numbers and their sheer resolve struck mortal fear into the hearts of their rulers, so that regimes which had freely and unquestioningly applied terror in the Leninist manner suddenly ceased to do so and the whole rationale of Leninist procedure collapsed.

In East Germany the situation was symbolically resolved by the recognition on the part of those who took to the streets—men and women, old and young—that they formed a unity quite different from anything in the past, a unity that history had not led them to anticipate and that finally made the impossible possible.

For more than two decades since the Prague Spring, the Communist governments in both East Germany and Czechoslovakia had been rigidly and unimaginatively Stalinoid, and though the intellectuals continued to protest, they did so mostly from outside, represented by East German writers living in West Germany and by Czech writers living in France or Canada. Writers who stayed to defy and suffer, like Vaclav Havel, were the exceptions, though with poetic justice it was the Havels who gained the greater reward in respect and the greater penalty in responsibility. As for the people in both countries, through the decade up to 1989 they sustained a passivity whose ominousness nobody seemed to recognize; they reminded me of the English as G. K. Chesterton represented them in "The Secret People":

> Smile at us, pay us, pass us; but do not quite forget.
> For we are the English people that have never spoken yet.

When the people of East Germany finally did speak, it was loudly and menacingly. By and large it had only been the young who were ready to make their dash for freedom over one or another frontier. But the people who stayed began to demand a new kind of home, not there and tomorrow

168

but here and now. Leipzig became the first centre of open resistance to the regime, and within Leipzig the nerve centre was the Evangelical Church of St. Nicholas, where people gathered for small demonstrations after Monday evening services on the Karl-Marx-Platz.

To begin, in July and August 1989, the demonstrators consisted mainly of young people demanding easier emigration, though others protested the endorsement by the East German government of the massacre of Chinese students in Tiananmen Square. But by 25 September there were several thousand people, and on 2 October nearly 20,000 people came out, loudly singing "The Internationale" (since Tiananmen Square once again an anthem of rebellion), carrying banners denouncing the Communist regime and demanding legalization of a citizens' group called New Forum. The police dealt roughly with the protestors, and on 7 October, the occasion of the fortieth anniversary of Communist rule in East Germany, the riot squads used exceptional brutality, attacking not only demonstrators but also uninvolved spectators. The people of Leipzig reacted immediately, and everybody expected a major and bloody confrontation two days later, when police and army units stood ready to attack the 70,000 people who eventually assembled in the square, intent on offering passive resistance to official violence.

What happened to prevent a scene of vast bloodshed is not clearly known; the supporters of Egon Krentz, then in charge of the East German security forces, claimed that it was he who made the decision to renounce force. Others said that the famous conductor Kurt Mansur organized a group of like-minded people to warn the government of the likely consequences of harsh measures. The known facts are that the police and army units were ordered not to attack the demonstrators and that nine days later, in a palace revolution, Egon Krentz took the place of Erich Honecker as leader of the party. Honecker, who had endured the Nazi concentration camps, stood accused of massive nepotism and corruption, and the charges were probably true, so far had Lenin's cold but sea-green incorruptibility ceased to be a model for Communist activists.

Week after week in growing numbers, people came out into the streets— hundreds of thousands in the streets of Leipzig, and then, as the movement spread to East Berlin and other large cities, even greater and always nonviolent gatherings. The people called for free elections, a cry not heard in Germany for decades, but also, more significantly and in the menacing unison of half a million voices, they cried: "Wir sind das Volk!" It was a call that echoed far back into history, even prehistory. It is true that the Nazis often talked of the "Volk"—"Ein Reich, ein Volk, ein Führer!"—but they

169

were emphasizing the exclusive character of both state and people, ethnically limited and politically restricted. When the crowds in Berlin and Leipzig chanted "Wir sind das Volk!" memories far more distant than those of the short-lived thousand-year reich were stirring, just as a concept was emerging more profound than if they had chanted merely, "We are the people!"

For when crowds in Berlin and Leipzig proclaimed themselves "das Volk," and implied that being "das Volk" gave them a special function, they were reaching back into the ancient traditions of Germany, into the far days when the tribal leader Herman defeated the Roman legions with the power of free warriors among whom the chiefs were merely first among equals. Unlike nazism, early Germanic tribalism was an extremely democratic concept, of an assembly or army of free individuals united in a common cause. As among other great tribal peoples, like the Iroquois and the Blackfoot in North America, the leader led and was acknowledged only in so far as he projected the will of the folk. And this in fact is what happened in ancient Germany.

It was not a matter of *vox populi, vox dei*. The people did not see themselves as a god or evoke a god, either in the ancient past or in 1989. They expressed with sudden and inexplicable unity the will of millions of individual people who had been inhibited and silenced for too long and had suddenly broken out in immense collective expression. And as the people shouted, so the foundations shook beneath the structures of government, and a true revolution was achieved without the violence customarily associated with such an occasion. Communist authority virtually disintegrated in a few weeks. Travel abroad was freely allowed, the Berlin Wall was symbolically breached on 9 December, and East and West Germans mingled as brothers and sisters. The leaders resigned piecemeal and en masse, and their places were filled by election, as the Communist party declined dramatically and steadily. And there followed the rest of the astonishing history we all know, the restoration of democratic procedures for the first time since the 1930s, the abolition of the secret police, the liberation of political prisoners—and the wholly unexpected reunification of the Germany divided in 1945.

What seemed surprising to those who knew Eastern Europe, and who remembered the enthusiasm with which the Czechs and Slovaks had welcomed Alexander Dubcek's proclamation of "socialism with a human face," and how deeply they had resented the bleak autocratic rule established under the threat of Russian guns by Gustav Husak and sustained by Milos Jakes, was the tardiness with which Czechoslovakia joined the general movement against communism.

Even Bulgaria was inspired by events in Poland, Hungary and especially in Germany to break out in demonstrations, and on 10 November the Bulgarian party leader Todor Zhivkov, who had ruled the country for thirty-five years in a rigidly Stalinoid manner, resigned in the face of growing demonstrations which the police seemed unable to control, and his country started on the road to pluralistic democracy.

Czechoslovakia, on the surface at least, was calm under the watchful vigilance of its brutal security forces. In fact, a ferment was going on in the country that permeated more deeply than the principled protests of individuals like Havel and the writers in exile had done, though it was largely inspired by them. A rather shapeless opposition had built up, of shifting ad hoc groups—a form that remained characteristic of the Czechoslovak rebellion to its successful end. There were those who remained faithful to Charter 77, though by now they were probably too well known to the police to be effective on their own. There were the people connected with the clandestine publication and importation of forbidden texts of various kinds, political and literary. There were various degrees of subversion among church groups, Catholic and Protestant, for the rebellious tradition of religious reformer Jan Hus was by no means dead, especially among Bohemians. And, growing and proliferating like underground fungi, there were the groups of student radicals who provided a liaison between clandestine groups and individuals and who even infiltrated the SSM, the official youth organization.

The students were the ones who actually initiated the extraordinary rebellion that, without a touch of violence except at the beginning on the part of the authorities, led in less than a month to the complete dismantling of the Communist state in Czechoslovakia, and in about six weeks not only to the political resurrection of Alexander Dubcek as president of the Federal Assembly of a renewed democratic republic, but also to the emergence, as president of the republic and intellectual leader of the new order, of Vaclav Havel.

The chain of events began with the students obtaining permission to hold a memorial demonstration at the cemetery where Jan Opletal, a student martyr of the Nazis, was buried. On 17 November 1989 the demonstrators gathered at the cemetery in larger numbers than had been anticipated, and when the graveside tributes had been made, they decided to march on Wenceslas Square, the actual and symbolic centre of Prague. Shouting "Freedom" and bearing flowers and lighted candles, they advanced on the riot squads who were awaiting them at the entry to the square. They were immediately attacked, driven into side streets, surrounded and mercilessly beaten with truncheons—men and women, children and old people, who were there as onlookers. One person at least was killed; many were hospitalized.

That night broke the long patience of the Czech people. The students immediately declared a sitdown strike in their institutions. The actors and film co-operatives, already politicized by Havel's example, joined them in issuing an appeal for a general strike. The theatres were offered as centres for organizing the movement of civil disobedience, and in one of them on 19 November Havel convened a meeting of already existing underground groups, which created what from this point became the focus of opposition activities, the Civic Forum. Its initial demands were the resignation of Communist leaders, a public investigation into what happened on 17 November and the release of all prisoners of conscience.

Alexander Dubcek emerged on 24 November from twenty years of obscurity to ally himself with Havel, and a demonstration of 30,000 people hailed him with a thunder of applause. At the same meeting the ninety-year-old Cardinal Tomasek, leader of the Czech Catholic church, expressed his support for the popular movement. Everywhere the long-silent voices were sounding out of the shadows. And at the press conference held by Havel and Dubcek that evening came the news that the Communist hard-liners had conceded defeat with the mass resignation of the Politbureau and the Secretariat of the Central Committee.

The Civic Forum supported the call for a general strike on 27 November which the students and the theatrical workers had already issued. Meanwhile, at the same time in Slovakia, there emerged a parallel organization to the Civic Forum which bore the significant name of The Public Against Violence. These new insurrectionaries were not merely rejecting violence wielded by governments; they were also rejecting it as a possible tactic for themselves.

But the people in Prague did not wait for the general strike to project their demands and to test the resolution of the authorities. All over the weekend, crowds of young people had been forming and dissolving in Wenceslas Square, waving the flags of the old republic, chanting calls for freedom, lighting candles at the statue of Good King Wenceslas. By Monday, it was more than the young; even before the strike, the adults were leaving their jobs to demonstrate their solidarity with the peaceful uprising. Old and young, they packed into the historic square, shouting their calls for the resignation of the existing government and inventing their own special way of declaring themselves, the ringing of tens and later hundreds of thousands of key-rings which, as one observer remarked, produced "a sound like masses of Chinese bells."

172

In yet other ways the peaceful revolution that was developing under the bronze eyes of the good old king followed an original and slightly fantastic course. The nerve centre of the movement, where the leaders whom the rebellion had thrown up plotted the strategy of the Civic Forum, was the Magic Lantern Theatre. Timothy Garton Ash, in the account of the annus mirabilis in Eastern Europe which he actually called *The Magic Lantern*, describes the extraordinary kind of unstructured structure which the movement took on while he observed it as a privileged outsider:

> A political scientist would be hard pressed to find a term to describe the Forum's structure of decision-making, let alone the hierarchy of authority within it. Yet the structure and hierarchy certainly exist, like a chemist's instant crystals. . . . The majority of those present have been active in opposition before, the biggest single group being signatories of Charter 77. Twenty years ago they were journalists, academics, politicians, lawyers, but now they come here from their jobs as stokers, window-cleaners, clerks, or, at best, banned writers. Sometimes they have to leave a meeting and go and stoke up their boilers.

The Civic Forum was in form and practice almost the diametrical opposite to the trained, disciplined, ruthless party group that in the Communist pattern carries out the revolution by violence and consummates it by the discipline of terror, relegating the people or the workers to a symbolic and peripheral role. Here was a group of people brought together by emergency and opportunity, who had worked together sporadically in the past, if at all, but who now came forward of their own free will to form a loose but purposeful alliance; the very kind of organization Vaclav Havel had imagined a decade before in "The Power of the Powerless."

Nobody appointed or elected the members of the Civic Forum, but in the context of Prague in 1989 they legitimately represented the Czech people. They existed and acted, as Timothy Garton Ash also remarked,

> by right of acclamation. For the people were going out on the streets day after day and chanting "Long live the Forum!" In Prague at least, the people, the *demos*—were obviously, unmistakably behind them. In this original sense, the Forum was profoundly, elementally democratic.

173

And the movement centred increasingly on Vaclav Havel, not because of the power he wielded, for he had none; not on the ordinary charisma of a demagogic leader, for he did not have that kind of appeal either, but from the knowledge that had permeated the whole country, even when his name was concealed from the people and he himself was locked away, of his single-minded willingness to suffer, not in the name of highly flaunted ideals but in the name of a decent respect for the dignity and freedom of human beings.

Though it was in no sense a coup d'état, and proceeded by massive demonstrations of nonviolent power and by consensus won in hard negotiations, the Czech uprising* moved with remarkable rapidity. This of course was largely due to a failure of will and ideology among the local Communist leaders that was encouraged by the Kremlin, deeply engaged in the transformation of the U.S.S.R., withdrawing its support for hard-line policies in the satellite countries. Gorbachev made it clear to all the Communist rulers outside the borders of the U.S.S.R. that they could no longer expect either the intervention of Russian tanks or the supportive threat of forces waiting on the border. The rulers in Prague do not seem to have trusted the army in November 1989 to do with Czech tanks what had been done with Russian tanks in 1968, and given what happened shortly afterwards in Rumania, when the army turned against the regime, and what had happened in Hungary in 1956 when the local army joined the rebellion, they were doubtless justified. At the same time the security forces became less effective from day to day as the crowds grew larger and bolder.

From this time onward the momentum was sustained. Negotiations began between government representatives led by Prime Minister Ladislav Adamec and a Civic Forum delegation. The new situation revealed the disunity and rivalry in the ranks of the Communist leadership. At the same time the Forum itself and also its mass support remained confident and united. Its members seemed to owe their quiet resolution to an awareness that the capricious pattern of events had offered them an opportunity which might never recur, and the support of an awakened people who a few months before had looked like a cowed mass. Thus, while determined and prophetic History was breaking down as the Marxist myths disintegrated

---

* I have as far as possible avoided the use of the word "revolution" and even more the word "counterrevolution" in describing the extraordinary inversions of power that took place in the Eastern European countries in 1989, because "revolution" has long connoted the presence of violence. In fact, these nonviolent insurrectionary movements find a more fitting definition in the term "rebellion" as used by Albert Camus in his remarkable essay, *L'Homme révolté* (1951).

one after another, real history—the reign of contingency—was showing the unexpected splendour of its combinations, the wealth of its gifts for those who seize on them with confidence and gratitude.

By 10 December after discussions between the Communist incumbents and the representatives of the Czech Civic Forum and the Slovak Public Against Violence, a multiparty system was created and a new cabinet was assembled, most of them selected from the heterogenous group which in the early days of the insurrection had gathered in the back rooms of the Magic Lantern Theatre. One of them dropped a stoker's shovel to become Minister of Foreign Affairs, and the next week was standing with his Austrian counterpart, holding a gigantic pair of shears with which they symbolically cut the barbed wire that for so long had separated Czechoslovakia from the West.

Then, on 28 December, Alexander Dubcek, whom his fellow Communists had so cynically betrayed in 1968, was elected president of the Federal Assembly; the Kremlin had already apologized for the destruction of the Prague Spring by Russian tanks in 1968. However, for all the geniality with which he was received into the new movement of liberation, time had relegated Dubcek to a sad past of partial achievement. His role became the sanctification of his successors. Gustav Husak, the old Stalinoid who had ruled Czechoslovakia for the last two decades, had resigned on 10 December when he swore in the new government. And on 29 December, with Dubcek in the chair, the Federal Assembly elected the often-imprisoned Vaclav Havel as president of the Czechoslovak Republic.

Without violence and without humiliating compromises, the resolution of a few principled men and women and the consistent support of an awakened populace liberated Czechoslovakia in just six weeks. Following on events in East Germany, Hungary and Poland, it rang the final knell on the Soviet puppet empire in Eastern Europe, on the dream of world communism.

Nobody expected the future to be easy for Poland or Hungary, for East Germany or Czechoslovakia, when they threw off Communist domination and turned to a path of political pluralism and economic liberalization. And it has not been easy, except to an extent for East Germany, where reunification has provided an economic basis on which it can eventually recover; the other countries that have liberated themselves from Soviet political tutelage remain dependent on the good will and good sense of the democratic countries. However, the uncertainties of freedom are easier to endure than the certainties of tyranny. And if as much individual initiative and general patience go into economic recovery as recently went into political liberation, the four liberated countries may well in a decade or so assume a similar position to that of Austria, which climbed out of extreme poverty and economic disorganization through its unification with Western Europe and its neutrality (a vital point to which I shall later return).

For if History cannot prophesy, history can teach by example, and sometimes the examples are followed, as in the 1980s Hungary, East Germany and Czechoslovakia were clearly following the example of Poland, though with variations suitable to their own traditions, their own social identities. There were enough dedicated and perceptive activists to take a lead that was followed by those responsible groupings of individuals whom left-wing leaders so often insultingly refer to as "the masses." The members of such a responsive public, as distinct from the members of a mob, are not in fact cells in some vast human zoophyte, reacting mechanically; they are individuals who have simultaneously read the message of the times, which in the case of these countries was that the rulers had lost faith in their own system—and now was the time to rebel.

The failure to follow the right example in the right way explains why the Balkan countries, unlike those farther north, found their rebellions partly or wholly aborted. Neither in Rumania nor in Albania had a dissident intelligentsia been able to survive and keep up connections. Nor had the kind of accord between intellectuals, workers, students, even priests, developed, as in the countries in the north. A philosophy of nonresistance and nonviolent action like that developed by Solidarity in Poland and by Havel and the Chartists in Czechoslovakia did not exist in the Balkans. The consequence was that instead of the discipline of civil disobedience, Rumania lapsed into revolutionary violence when the country rose in proper indignation after the government initiated the massacre of several thousand protesting people by the Securitate (political police) in Timisoara, where most of the people were actually of Hungarian descent.

One compares with a touch of fascinated horror the photographs of the crowds that assembled in Rumanian cities with those that crowded the squares of Prague and the East German centres. The latter were true assemblies of the people, "das Volk" in all its majesty and genders and ages, demanding firmly and peacefully even if often loudly that right must prevail. The former were mob scenes, mostly of men and mostly engaged in violent action. The Securitate fired on the mob, and the mob hunted down and slaughtered men from the Securitate; eventually the army came out on the side of the revolution, suppressed the Securitate, captured Nicholas Ceausescu and his wife when they attempted desperately to flee the country, and arbitrarily tried and executed them. Yet because of the lack of real co-ordination among the rebel forces, Ceausescu's hard-line rivals within the Communist party were able to make their deals with the generals, form a National Salvation Front, and in a notably rigged election to gain power. So little co-operation had there been between the anti-Communist forces, and especially between intellectuals and workers, that the neo-Communists of the National Salvation Front were able to exploit the divisions. In June 1990, when demonstrations took place in Bucharest condemning the Front for failing to live up to its promises, hundreds of miners were persuaded to bus into the capital with their pick-staves to help the police rough up the demonstrators. By the kind of gross irony that persists in Rumanian political life, just over a year later in the early fall of 1991, thousands of miners from those same collieries swarmed into Bucharest to protest economies and overthrow the government they had violently supported a short time before.

Neither Albania nor Yugoslavia, having long severed their links with the Kremlin, was directly involved in the political perturbations that in Eastern Europe followed on the proclamation and implementation of glasnost and perestroika. But resentments were stirred by example, and in 1991 the people of Albania broke into a fever of rebellion. Great public demonstrations took place in Tirana and other towns. Tens of thousands of people attempted to make their way to Italy by whatever craft they could overcrowd or commandeer. The situation forced the Communist party to grant enough freedom for a multiparty election be held. The Communist party still had enough vitality to win the vote, though perhaps it was merely that the opposition groups had not yet creditably established themselves.

But the most ominous of all the Balkan situations is that which thrust Yugoslavia into virtual civil war. The origins of that country's problem lie less in the general Eastern European events of the 1980s than in the Treaty of Saint Germain, which in 1919 dismantled the Austro-Hungarian Empire and created Yugoslavia out of part of its debris. It was to become a land of the Southern Slavs, with fragments detached from the Hapsburg Empire— Slovenia, Croatia and Bosnia-Herzegovina—united to the existing precariously independent kingdoms, once under Russian protection, of Serbia and Montenegro. The pattern of related languages was deceptive as a sign of unity.

The great enmity between Serbia and Croatia, whose people resented their subordination to "barbarian" Belgrade, took on a tragic form during World War II when many of the Croats supported the neo-Fascist Ustasha and were blamed by the Serbians for the deaths of their anti-German partisans. The federal structure which Marshal Tito created at the end of World War II and eventually turned over to a collective leadership encouraged both the sense of an independent national destiny that inspired the Croats and the dominative nationalism of the former senior kingdom that motivated so many of the Serbs. Pessimists will perhaps say that it is too much to expect a group of peoples with such violent pasts as those who inhabit Yugoslavia to remain at peace together when a time of parting comes. But the dramatic events of the Russian coup of 1991 have called even pessimism into question.

There seemed indeed much reason by the summer of 1991 for a cautious rather than a pessimistic attitude towards the future of Russia's own liberation from the bureaucratic tyrannies it had endured ever since the October Revolution seventy-four years before. The NKVD might have been curbed, but it was by no means eliminated, and its leading officials were beginning to show signs of discontent with their diminished status, as were the Black Berets of the separate Ministry of the Interior Security Service. Even in the army some of the younger higher-grade officers were openly criticizing what they perceived as the disorder rampant under Gorbachev's administration and were beginning to make common cause with the industrial managers, who believed, with justification, that the centralized economic structure of Russia under which they had so prospered was endangered. Old and young apparatchiks jealous for their privileges, and old and young ideologues appalled that History was failing to observe what they regarded as its own laws, added to the potential forces of reaction, and when the first rumours of coups plotted on the right began to circulate, they acquired dimensions and turned into Brocken spectres in people's minds, precisely because of the uncertainty about the forces that might be involved and how they could be resisted. Who could defy the power of the Red Army? Who would stand up against the formidable NKVD, whose terror under various names had haunted Russian life for nearly three-quarters of a century?

As it turned out, the Russian people could and did. And a few days afterwards the Dalai Lama, with whom this book began, was able to intervene in the vein of the possibility of the impossible with a comment, as reported in the *Tibetan Bulletin* from Dharamsala (September-October 1991): "A little while ago, no one would have thought change possible. Now it has been shown that power rests with the word of the people."

What actually happened before and during the Soviet coup is obscure, and will probably remain so until the time for public trials begins. How was it that the three great institutions controlling physical political power in Russia could co-operate to such slight practical effect? What uncelebrated forces within the rank and file of their organizations applied the brake of inertia at the appropriate time? We shall perhaps never know, though it is certain that some army units at least rallied to the banner of democracy which Boris Yeltsin immediately raised in the Russian parliament. As for the Russian people, when the crunch came they showed that they preferred a certainty of freedom to a possibility of consumer goods combined with a return to tyranny. Young people and old came together in their tens of thousands to build the barricades and stand in a dense human shield at the White House (the parliament buildings), which acted as an inspirational and organizational focus for the resistance.

And though the preponderance of foreign correspondents in Moscow gave an appearance of special importance to events there, similar manifestations were taking place all over the country. One of my friends was in Leningrad as a visiting scholar when the coup took place. He noticed people hurrying through the streets, converging on some crucial point, and eventually he was swept with the gathering crowd into an open space where there seemed to be at least half a million people, cheering loudly as the mayor of Leningrad and other civic worthies exhorted them to stand up with civil disobedience to tyrannical force.

One incident struck him especially. A few shabby men habitually frequented the square with old gentle horses which they let out to people who wanted photographs of themselves in equestrian postures. Somehow the men had acquired some flags of the tsarist navy and, mounting their Rosinantes, rode them through the crowd, waving the colours overhead. Nostalgia moved the crowd to ecstatic cheering. (And a few days later, of course, the possibility of the impossible intervened again as St. Petersburg rose from the ashes of memory, a phoenix complete, and Leningrad was no more; at about the same time the people of Moscow pulled down the statue of Lenin's lieutenant, the cold sadist Dzerzhinsky who had founded the Cheka, and nobody emerged from the dread portals of the Lubianka to intervene.)

The abortive coup in Russia might have been, and events in Rumania, Albania and Yugoslavia actually have been, setbacks in the process of undermining Communist tyrannies, and those who merely saw their new history as a redirection of Marxist determinism were naturally perturbed. But the real world of contingency in which historical events actually take

179

place never offers such neatly completed progressions. Christianity, after all, did not convert the whole world, nor did Islam; the Reformation did not even convert the whole of Germany; the French Revolution broke on the unlikely rock of English pragmatism. No pattern in history is ever complete, yet its imperfect achievement is always an extension of the possible, and a declaration of the possibility of the impossible.

PART VII

•

THE

•

POSSIBILITY

•

OF

•

THE

•

IMPOSSIBLE

CHAPTER XVII

The Possibility of the Impossible

The possibility of the impossible! I claim no originality for this phrase, though when I first used it for an article in the Toronto *Globe and Mail* (whose editor presumed to retitle the piece—absurdly—"A blueprint for a better tomorrow"), I did believe I was the happy inventor. Later, as I began to study the events and utterances of the annus mirabilis 1989, I discovered that some of the participants in that movement, including Vaclav Havel himself, had used it to describe the success of their endeavours, astonishing even to them. I felt then a little like Charles Darwin receiving Alfred Russell Wallace's letter from Timur. But even in renouncing all claims to inventing it, I regard the concept of the Possibility of the Impossible as of great importance in studying the events of our times.

The phrase has negative and positive projections, and both are important in understanding and dealing with contemporary issues. Since it regards the future as always open, unconfined and undefined, the central concept of this book denies all the time-honoured doctrines of a History dominated by ancient and immutable laws. It declares that there is no divine plan for the universe. It declares that there is no eschatological movement leading to a millennium, a Last Judgment, a new Heaven and Earth—religious or secular. It denies the idea of unending progress, and equally of a utopian world where progress comes to an end. It declares that there are in fact no laws of history. It proclaims the anti-law of the impossibility of any laws of History and of the ever-present Possibility of the Impossible.

Such a view comes from my realistic attitude towards my task and my subjects as a historian. True history, as I have said, is first of all a matter of recording the past. In so far as it offers instances, it can also have an exemplary relationship with the present through what it purports to reveal about the past. The rediscovery by translators and historians of the achievements of classical antiquity, for example, had a profound influence on the Renaissance and the development of Western European humanism.

Historians, as recorders, are faced by a vast chaos of given facts, and to make this meaningful to their readers—or to themselves—they must concentrate and arrange it into comprehensible forms. Uncovering and assessing the facts may have something of the scientific about it; assembling but transmuting these facts into acceptable or even comprehensible form is the art of history (though no more an act of art than the writing of *On the Origin of Species* or *Relativity, the Special and the General Theory* or that highly imaginative as well as factual work, *Die Traumdeutung*, for all great theories are inspired arrangements—intuitively apprehended—of otherwise uncontrollable and often irreconcilable facts).

For each generation historians offer inspired versions of the past (a version for each notable historian), and just as much as totalitarian ideologues, historians rewrite history in accordance with the mindset of their times. Thus the patterns in which history is arranged for our understanding change constantly; in a religious generation historians may be primarily concerned with the alleged history of the faith and of the church that sustains it; in a conservative but less spiritual generation with the records of kings and dynasties; in a radically minded generation with the history of social discontent, of revolutions and rebellions. In recent generations we have become more concerned than our ancestors with the social and economic aspects of the changes within society and less concerned than they with the political and military aspects.

So long as history is oriented towards the past, as it must be to remain authentic, it remains tentative and to that extent true, an art of the possible, sometimes of the probable, occasionally of the certain, and on rare occasions of the impossible—or what till it happens has been thought of as the impossible. We may know of events that took place at a well-recorded time with sufficient witnesses, like the assassination of Caesar (though even there we shall probably never know the full details of the plot), or like the killing of Tsar Nicholas II and his family in 1917, which became widely known as a mere fact shortly after the event, but whose details even in an approximate way are only now beginning to emerge. And often, so that our sense of the map of history may be more or less complete, we have to accept hypotheses as working facts, as we do, for example, the existence of King Arthur

184

(possible) as a focus for our awareness of the British resistance (probable) to the Anglo-Saxon invasion (a certainty established by perceptible ethnic and cultural changes confirmed by archaeology).

This interplay of the possible, the probable and the certain, interrupted occasionally by the impossible, is what distinguishes true history from the exact sciences and makes it "unscientific"—unamenable to any known laws or to any form of experimental research beyond the givens of events that have already taken place. (I must point out how far the exactitude of even the "true" sciences has been shaken by recent discoveries in physics embodied in Chaos Theory.) And the fact that—despite the historicists from Plato onward—there are no demonstrable laws of history, is perhaps the very reason why true history, the chronicle of the possible and sometimes of the impossible, can have its uses while the historicism that strives to serve ideologies with false prophecies has only negative functions.

Implicit in my arguments is the consideration that we do not live in a world of determined events, and therefore of enslavement to what may possibly happen to us, but rather in a world of freedom within the limits of our mortality. It is an old dispute—the dispute that John Milton in *Paradise Lost* envisaged going on among the Fallen Angels after their rebellion had landed them in Hell, the debate between the advocates of predestination and free will.

Generally speaking, over the centuries, the predestinarians and the determinists have had their own way in the sense of dominating our historic thinking and have wielded immense power in our lives, from the Calvinists to the Communists and Nazis, by attempting to restrict them in narrow ways of existence. In terms of ruined lives and stunted societies, the temporary success of such doctrines is evident; in the long run they have universally failed. We are approaching the second millennium after Christ with no signs of millenarian events, and the Last Things of the various eschatologies seem far in the future. Even—indeed especially—in the countries where it has been tried, the vision of utopia faded in the process of attempting to realize it. The sublimity of the great historicist doctrines has been brought down to the ridiculous of everyday life when Russian miners complain that seventy years after the revolution there is not enough soap and Polish workers complain about the shortage of toilet paper. Thus the historicist doctrines, and the political structures they are designed to further and defend, have only proved false in themselves; more than that, the attempt to realize them, it has long become evident, is not merely futile in terms of achievement but also malignant in terms of effect. There are, I must repeat, no laws of history, and attempts to realize such phantasms of

185

the philosophic or theologic mind by means of autocratic government have been universally harmful. The sooner we shed them and face the world of contingency, the better, not only for humanity but also for the planet we inhabit.

In this world of contingency, history is no longer concerned with shaping paths into the future; it is concerned with chronicling and making some sense of what happened in the past for the benefit of people in the present. In so far as history exists as an entity outside the written record, it is a process, and the anti-laws that operate within it are change and chance and choice. It is a world whose possibilities are restricted only by the natural qualities of individuals and of course by their mortality. And because of the continually changing relationship between humanity and the environment, whether it is society or the natural world, impossibilities are constantly being transformed into possibilities.

For chance, by which we all live, is an ambiguous entity, destructive but also creative. It is uncertainty: the cholera that can kill in a couple of days; the anaphylaxis that can kill in a couple of hours; the electrical short that can kill in an instant; the landslide without warning that can drown a whole town and its people in mud. But chance is also opportunity, thought and circumstances coming together in a way that will benefit us, or, better, our fellow beings; it has often been observed that the great generalizations on which scientific theories are based are in fact intuitive, apprehended in sudden flashes of insight with Chance as their muse.

And finally, to complete the pattern and balance the factor of chance within the process of change, there is the factor of choice, which, as the Existentialists once insisted, constitutes our claim to free will. It is through choice that we define ourselves, for every day of our lives we are faced, like J. Alfred Prufrock, with alternatives, small and large, perceived and unperceived, and the awareness with which we make our choices determines the pattern of our lives and shapes our personalities, defining them against the background of our environment and in recognition and defiance of death. And the sum of our choices produces the vast chaos of events from which historians select their patterns. These patterns take place in the ever-changing Heraclitean present; that present advances into the future, but is not shaped by it, and crystallizes into the past, where historians find it. And when the choices of many men and women and children are alike, they come together, for the time being, as a collective will; when chance opens a way for that will, as happened in Eastern Europe during 1989, the result can be a situation of deep social and political change, even—in terms of the arrangements that historians observe in the past—a new era.

For, despite the pessimists, there are lessons to be learnt from history, and people sometimes learn them, as, for example, the Europeans in the Soviet bloc did when they learnt from the failure of the violent insurrections of the 1950s, and so in the 1980s and 1990s rebelled nonviolently with great success, at least in the immediate task of ridding themselves of tyrannical and monumental inefficient governments. Indeed, it is one of the most important roles of the true historians to search out in the past, their only province, those directions and conjunctions which may enlighten and assist dwellers in the present in their pragmatic tasks of sustaining and reshaping the institutions that bring them and keep them together. There is also a kind of seismographic element in the task of true historians which, at that crucial point when the past merges into the present, can detect the shifting of forces and hence the emergence of opportunities that can make what a year or so ago seemed impossible appear possible today. In other words, once we shed the assumptions of historicist dogma, once we cease to see progress as inevitable or utopia as part of our destiny, then our political and social senses are opened, and we perceive opportunities and conceive possibilities that never enter minds that are blinkered by ideology.

CHAPTER XVIII

The Monk's Message Vindicated

And that brings us to the Dalai Lama's vision with which we started this book; that vision is important because it takes us beyond the achievements of the annus mirabilis of 1989 and subsequent years into a concept that ultimately might liberate people and nations, small and large, from the threat of mutual destruction or of a return to the state of paralyzing fear that even a relatively remote threat of war can induce.

I suggest that the Dalai Lama's concept of Zones of Ahimsa offers an alternative in terms of political aim and also of political arrangement that could save humanity from wars and tyrannies and at the same time save the earth from further degradation. His proposals may relate specifically to Tibet, but they are capable of extension to other countries in other circumstances. Essentially, as he offered them, they were projections of the concept of neutrality, given an Asian cast by their relation to the Jain concept of Ahimsa, or non-harming—which had been one of the bases of Gandhi's teaching and successful practice of satyagraha, or nonviolent political action. The Dalai Lamai's proposals, coming early in 1990, were more closely related than they seemed to events in Eastern Europe, for the rebels there, at least until violence marred the movement when it reached Rumania, were practising their own form of Ahimsa. Specifically, the Dalai Lama thought of Tibet as a Zone of Ahimsa in three ways: there would be Ahimsa, or peace, between human beings through transforming the Tibetan plateau into a militarily neutral zone; there would be peace between humanity and the other species by turning Tibet into the "world's largest

188

natural park or biosphere"; there would be peace between humanity and the earth by abandoning technologies that produce hazardous wastes. All excellent aims—but can they really be achieved?

As noted, the immediate reaction of most people who read or heard of the Dalai Lama's proposals, even after the extraordinary events of 1989, was to regard them as impractical in view of the tight grip that the large Chinese army units in Tibet wield over its cowed population, and the apparent inflexibility of the Chinese regime there. But looking back over the record of Tibet and Tibetans during the past century, history offers us a number of reasons why the conditions of Tibet and the Tibetans may not be as desperately determined as many observers assume.

We have already seen that in the case of regimes dominated by ideologies of historical determination, two factors are at work: the strength or weakness of the ideology in the mind of the rulers, and the willingness of the ruled to continue accepting a manner of government that is justified only by a discredited ideology.

In this context we cannot think of the situation of Tibet, remote though it may be geographically, as politically isolated. We have to recognize, in view of the long history of Tibetan-Chinese relations, that the fate of Tibet has in recent generations been linked with the fate of China.

In the past, before the victory of the Communist People's Armies over the Kuomintang in 1949, the relation of China to Tibet had been one of suzerainty rather than sovereignty. The Mongols had been converted to Lamaist Buddhism, and when they themselves established rule over China as the Yuan dynasty, they developed a peculiar relationship under which the Mongol emperors became the patrons of Tibetan Buddhism, supporting the Dalai Lama, head of the moderately reformed Gelugpa or Yellow-hat sect (whom it may not be entirely ludicrous to describe as an Asian equivalent to the Church of England), as the temporal and spiritual ruler of Tibet, as well as the spiritual leader of the Mongols.

Under this never defined but always understood arrangement, Tibetan Buddhist society, with its elaborate monastic orders and its lay aristocracy, existed in virtual autonomy. Under the seventeenth-century Dalai Lama known as the Great Fifth, Tibet became strong in its isolation, no longer a country of invaders as it had been when the Tibetan king sacked Chang-an in the ninth century, but still a land that repulsed domination.

During the Ching dynasty, the reign of the Manchus, the Chinese made persistent efforts to establish at least their suzerainty over Tibet, and in this they were encouraged by the importance the highland kingdom achieved as the centre of the Great Game in Central Asia between Russian and British

189

imperial interests. Early in the twentieth century Chinese rule wavered, and it became evident that Tibetan independence would exist in inverse proportions to the strength of the power that ruled in Beijing. In 1903 the British intervened in Tibet, and the Chinese, in an effort to retain control of the territory, attempted to enforce a direct rule; the reigning Dalai Lama, the Great Thirteenth, fled to India in 1910.

But the next year, in 1911, revolution in China forced something like the withdrawal of the legions at the end of the Roman Empire. Chinese troops were pulled out or expelled from Tibet, and the Great Thirteenth declared his country independent. Unfortunately the greater powers delayed recognizing it, so that when in 1951 the Chinese renewed their claims to sovereignty and showed the strength to enforce them, they were able to return in the form of the People's Liberation Army without effective opposition.

So, Tibet's fate has long been clearly linked to that of China. But the links run two ways, for in 1911 it was not the mere fact of Chinese weakness that made the Tibetans so eager to claim their independence and rally around their spiritual ruler. It was also a will to preserve their unique mediaeval culture, with its spiritual intensities, its strange mingling of elaborate hierarchy and basic democracy, and its art of vivid form and fantasy that blossomed in one of the most rigorous terrains on earth.

Now, in Tibet, the situation is similar to that of the countries of Eastern Europe before 1989. The Tibetans are a people who, despite all the oppression they have endured, remain faithful to their special idea of nationality, to their religion, to their spiritual and political leader, so that the Dalai Lama functions from his exile rather like the pope and Lech Walesa in combination. Furtively, religious practices have been sustained, and so has the mystique of the Tibetan identity as expressed in the idea and image of the Dalai Lama. Only a minority, mainly of self-servers, has been attracted to communism despite the attempts at indoctrination. Tibetans still struggle for independence within their own country, led often by the surviving monks, and they are supported by a vigorous émigré culture in India, in Europe and in North America, presided over by the Dalai Lama, who has become something of a world figure since winning the Nobel Peace Prize. They are also supported by a considerable phalanx of Western converts to a proselytizing Tibetan Buddhism, and also by others, like myself, who are not interested in becoming devotees but are concerned for the fate of a unique culture and for the struggle to preserve their way of life by a people for whom the endurance of hardship seems cheerful second nature.

Up to now the sporadic risings in Tibet—hardly more than town riots—have failed, in part because the Tibetans let themselves be provoked into violence but even more because the imperial will in Beijing has not weakened as its counterpart has done in Moscow. Just as the fate of the countries of Eastern Europe was dependent on what happened in the Kremlin, so the future of Tibet and the other outlying parts of the Chinese empire is dependent on what happens in Beijing.

In this connection the key event of recent history that may throw a light on the possibilities of the Tibetan-Chinese situation is not anything that happened in Lhasa, but the democratic demonstrations in Beijing during the spring of 1989, and their conclusion by a massacre on the part of the People's Army, resulting from an alliance of conservative elements in the Communist party and the military services.

What happened before the massacre is of more importance than the massacre itself, which was in the nature of a cutting of the Gordian knot, the application of sudden violence to a situation that seemed otherwise insoluble. The Communist party itself, through Deng Xiaoping's reforms, had changed the political atmosphere in China, even though they were—as he and his followers insisted—primarily economic in character. I was in China in 1987 (see my account: *Caves in the Desert*, 1988), and it was quite evident that with the economic changes there had come about a change in the tempo and temper of life. The individual was, as it were, reborn, as the great communities and collectives were dismantled and peasants and artisans were allowed to work and trade for their own benefit. The changes from the preceding Cultural Revolution period were striking, the reversion to tradition in the popular arts, like opera, being as remarkable as the attempt in the fine arts and literature to absorb international influences. Talk, even with foreigners, was amazingly free, and many people were ready to speak of the way in which their own lives and their aspirations had broadened. Very often they would say, in tones that seem plaintive only in retrospect, "We only hope that it will last."

Clearly the students of Beijing were acting on real possibilities when in the spring of 1989 they began their demonstrations in favour of democratic changes in the Chinese political system. Their action brought to light important rifts within the Communist party, and also important shifts in popular attitudes towards the government, the result of the individualization of Chinese society in the preceding years. Though the gerontocrats like Deng Xiaoping and the old Long-Marcher president Yang Changkun demanded the final say, and got it by manipulating the generals, the party itself was divided between a "liberal" faction ready at least to hear and consider the students' demands, led by the incumbent secretary-general

Zhao Ziyang, and the conservative hard-liners led by the ruthless Li Peng.

In the end, and at great cost to the party, the hard-liners won, because they had the support of the old leaders and because within the army a parallel struggle had resulted in a similar triumph of the hard-liners, closing ranks around the nepotistic Marshal Yang, members of whose family held key military positions. The stories of the execution of six or seven generals because they were unwilling to move their troops against the people of Beijing have been too persistent over the past two years to be ignored entirely. If nothing else, the fact that they are given credit widely suggests that there must have been tensions within the army as well as within the party, which itself abandoned its independence and weakened its image by calling on the armed forces to solve problems that should have been solved politically. Any further crisis might well result in the establishment of a kind of Napoleonic communism led by generals, as happened, for example, in Ethiopia. But the most important point, so far as the structure of government is concerned, must surely be that both the internal struggle for power and the vagaries of policy have left a party in which, from the leaders down to the humblest cadre, faith in the ideology has thinned away. Neither the leaders nor the members of the party have that confidence and loyalty which inspired the Long March and led the marchers to eventual victory.

But if faith in ideology is leaching out of the party in China as elsewhere, it has also evaporated from among the Chinese population, as was shown by the support given to the demonstrating students not only by the intelligentsia but also by the ordinary people of Beijing, who saw that their own hopes for a decent life lay with the protesters, and who organized themselves spontaneously to offer passive resistance to the soldiers sent to repress the students' nonviolent insurrection. Since that time, popular resentment towards the government of Li Peng and his associates has not diminished in Beijing, Shanghai, Canton and the other great centres of population. The Chinese are a pragmatic people in any case, and though they did not strongly resist ideological lessons brutally forced on them at times of militancy like the Cultural Revolution, they have moved steadily in recent years towards an individualism that rejects dogmas and doctrines and seeks a broader and freer scope of life.

Without making any prophecies, and dealing with possibilities rather than the certainties of the historicist, true historians can nevertheless point to the analogies between China and Eastern Europe, the similar and simultaneous collapse of ideology among the party and the people, and declare that here also the impossible may have become possible. And if the Communist state in China continues to rot at the centre, and the Dalai

Lama's people persist in their will to freedom, Tibet may yet, and perhaps sooner rather than later, emerge as an independent society existing in a great neutral zone in the very heart of Asia and serve, if the Dalai Lama's proposals are followed, as a model for other countries for which neutrality is the obvious direction in a world dominated still by great powers that lurch across the earth like diseased dinosaurs.

CHAPTER XIX

The Local and the Particular in True History

In their implications the Dalai Lama's proposals extend far beyond Tibet and offer a way of conduct for nations everywhere that could not fail to make the earth a more serene and beneficial place for all its inhabitants. Yet his proposals are not entirely novel. Countries in the past have deliberately withdrawn themselves from international alliances and the conflicts they foster, to become militarily neutral without necessarily becoming pacifist. Switzerland and Sweden are examples in Europe, and Costa Rica in the Americas; Austria became neutral for the convenience of the great powers, but it has flourished on neutrality ever since.

Costa Rica is the most interesting of these countries, since it has not only declared itself neutral but has also cast doubt on the alleged perils of neutrality by abolishing its army and still surviving in the war-prone setting of Latin America. Sweden and Switzerland have protected themselves heavily, but the experiences of two world wars suggest that they need not have troubled. Neither Nazi Germany nor the Stalinist Soviet Union attempted to invade either of them, because they were so necessary, even for rogue totalitarian empires, as buffer countries to sustain communications in a warring world.

Following an independent policy without becoming militarily involved, the neutral countries have not only been left in peace. They have prospered. Costa Rica is one of the better-off countries of Latin America. I have at first hand watched Austria developing from poverty to prosperity since it declared its neutrality, and the Swedes and the Swiss have lived for generations high on the world's scale. But the aims of such countries have never been wholly selfish; they have always responded to the responsibilities implied by their neutrality. Costa Rica has been tireless in its efforts to promote peace in Central America, and Switzerland has been host to a multitude of international agencies and conferences. Moreover, countries such as Costa Rica with its imaginatively conceived wildlife refuges, and Switzerland and Sweden with their legislation against factory farming, have been pioneers in the ecological struggle and the humanitarian one. And forest management in neutral Austria is far in advance of that in Canada or the United States.

Clearly, neutral states—our existing Zones of Peace (or Ahimsa)—are useful members of the international community, and today, with the breakup of the Warsaw Pact and the steady weakening of NATO, the possibilities for the neutralization of small and even medium-sized countries are growing. And the likelihood of the emergence of new areas of neutrality increases the options in terms of complete Zones of Peace as the Dalai Lama conceived them.

All such zones would obviously, as a first requirement, become disengaged militarily and renounce the manufacture of arms as well as the production of hazardous substances and wastes that are so often the result of militarily based economies. But beyond the narrow field of military considerations there is a great role which neutral countries might play in the struggle to save the earth and its natural life from the destruction that threatens not only the surface of the earth but also the atmosphere vital for our survival. Here conventional alliances for military purposes might be replaced by survival alliances, in which ecological zones of world importance would be defined and defended through individual states agreeing to sacrifice a degree of sovereignty in exchange for help in establishing and maintaining natural resources as well as in sustaining neutral resources that are of value and indeed of urgent concern to all of humanity.

For example, the Amazonian, the African, the Indonesian, the Madagascan forests, with their climatic importance and multitude of unique species, could be supervised and conserved for the benefit of all humanity, which desperately needs them, by an international co-operative (*not* an "authority") to which countries like Brazil, Peru and Indonesia might assign, without any sense of losing dignity or territory, the supervision of lands that ecologically are of world importance. High Arctica and Antarctica, where sovereignty cannot in any case be exercised effectively except at great expense, should be conserved by international agencies, whose aim would be to monitor military as well as polluting intrusions.

The environmental aspects of a world of spreading neutralism are in fact closely linked with the military aspects. The progress in reducing nuclear armaments that has resulted in declining belligerence between the great powers has led already to diminishing requirements of dangerous metals like uranium, which can be left to follow their benign unprocessed existence within the earth. That is a gain environmentally as much as it is a gain antimilitarily.

But of course the fight for the health of the earth interlocks with the fight against militarism in many other ways, and here past history, and especially that of the recent past, offers more than one lesson. And all the lessons have a particular bearing on our own country of Canada during its present extended political crisis. Hence at this point I propose to change from the general focus to consider what special relevance the issues of the day, like the fate of the nation-state, like the direct role of the people in political events (so dramatically highlighted in 1989), like neutrality itself, have on Canada today. For I believe the way that Canada absorbs and deals with these questions may greatly influence their effect on other countries.

CHAPTER XX

Zeroing In: Canada's Impossible Possibilities

Canada is in 1991 at a stage of crisis that will affect not only its own political structure and the interrelationships of its many territories and communities but also its relations with the outer world. And by the way it conducts itself in this crisis, Canada may well offer an example that will influence other countries and help in the politically urgent reshaping of the world.

Perhaps the fate of the nation-state is the most important of these issues, since what Canadian politicians are mainly attempting to do these days, with their misapplication of the idea of national unity, is to seek a perpetuation of the nation-state; they cannot see unity in other than such ultimately divisive political terms.

The nation-state is an idea and a political form that developed between the seventeenth and nineteenth centuries as the feudal order disintegrated and monarchs gathered control over large areas of territory, often including, as the Austrian empire eventually did, peoples of varying cultures like the Czechs and the Slovaks, whose own national feeling actually developed under imperial control. To the simple minds of rulers and functionaries, the tight centralization of the nation-state seemed an easy way to deal with the problems of social and political diversity.

The era of republicanism, beginning with the American Revolution, did not change the situation. Indeed, if anything it worsened it, since it led to the creation of idealistic myths of nationality to replace the selfish and dynastic motivations of kings. Because of these myths the republics became even more centralistic than the monarchies had been; France called herself a "Republic One and Indivisible," and the first major war that the United States fought after 1814, the Civil War, had very little to do with the issue of slavery; it was basically concerned with the unity of the nation-state. The idea of the nation-state is of course deeply linked with the whole problem of a determinist, future-dominated view of History that is the principal concern of this book. Hegel, the great champion of the Prussian monarchy, was after all the greatest advocate of such a view. Manifest Destiny, the doctrine of the God-given right of the United States to control the whole of the North American continent, flourished in the same period as Hegel's nationalist fantasies and Marx's declaration of the History-given right of the proletariat (or those who claimed to represent it) to rule the world. To this doctrine were related such aberrations of national pride as the proclamation of the nineteenth century as "America's century," and Laurier's speculations—so pathetic to remember at the fin de siècle of the 1990s—that the twentieth would be Canada's century.

Of course, there is no Manifest Destiny for any of the numerous claimants, whether capitalist America, Nazi Germany, imperial Japan, or Communist Russia. Every century, even metaphorically, belongs to all the people of the earth, and the nation-state is a harmful abstraction, dangerous in terms of the belligerent pride it induces, and entirely undemocratic in its restriction of the role of the people—both as individuals and collectively—in the arrangement of their lives and their freedom. One of the most fortunate features of the current situation in Eastern Europe is that though traditions are re-emerging and varieties of nationalism are reforming in reaction to the imperial homogeneity of communism, there is little evidence of the old nineteenth-century centralized nation-state rearising. Even Russia, after generations of monolithic state-worship, became a confederation of culturally different peoples, with the right-wing coup of 1991 apparently only a ripple in the process.

Canada, of course, started in this context with an immense advantage which its political leaders, driven by ambitions to power, have chosen largely to ignore, either because they have been infected with the pride of nationalism or because of the doctrinaire follies that make a pseudo-radical party like the New Democratic party cling to outdated dogmas of nationalization plus centralization. The lessons of the past of course reveal the perils of both, for the ideal economy, as over seventy years of world experience since 1917 have shown, is not a state-controlled but a pluralistic one. And the ideal polity is a federal one, which theoretically at least means that every region, every cultural group, ultimately every individual, will participate, directly rather than through representation, in the political process.

198

The economically pluralist and politically federalist idea is not dominated by determinist historical models. Rather, it is based on that experience of the past whose consideration is the historian's true province. Here history has two lessons to teach, one negative and one positive. The negative lesson, of course, is that political and economic centralization, tending always towards homogeneity, have failed to do what they should do, which is to provide people with material sufficiency, with freedom and control of their own lives, including their cultural lives.

Looking back over the Canadian past, I cannot be other than appalled by the opportunities that have been neglected to create a new kind of polity, an anti-nation, a true confederation that might have been an example to all countries whose geography is home to as many streams of history as ours has been.

In fact, in the first approaches to the emergence of Canada as an independent polity, there were the elements of true confederation rather than mere formal federation. We still give the name of Confederation (which means a union of sovereign entities) to the act of coming together in 1867 of the two Canadas and the Atlantic colonies of Nova Scotia and New Brunswick. This Confederation, though it may incidentally have been convenient to the imperial government in Westminster, took place on the initiative of the British North American colonies who petitioned the British parliament, and it is important to stress this point, because it means that the Canadian parties to the arrangement were regarded as sovereign bodies negotiating the terms of their independence, which emerged in a confederal form embodied, however imperfectly, in the British North America Act. Provincial sovereignty within Confederation was what provincial premiers like Oliver Mowat of Ontario and Honoré Mercier of Québec defended in the later nineteenth century, and what the Judicial Committee of the Privy Council largely accepted in a series of crucial decisions in the area of provincial rights.

There were always enemies in high places of the concept of confederation as the basic principle of Canadian political structure, and none more persistent than Sir John A. Macdonald, who from the beginning, with his National Policy, sought to transform the confederation of Canada into a nation-state. Equally invidious was the influence of Pierre Elliott Trudeau, who in his young manhood, in the *Cité Libre* days, wrote as an eloquent advocate of free confederation, and then, when he tasted power as Liberal leader and prime minister, adopted a new pattern, announcing himself a *federalist* in opposition to the Québécois *separatists*, and virtually declaring that in Canadian terms *federalism* (which in political terms ever since

199

Pierre-Joseph Proudhon has meant decentralization) was equivalent to "strong central government." Such has been the perfidy of Canadian politicians that for more than a century they have sought to extract political power out of a situation whose outcome should have been the devolution of power.

Inevitably, such policies have militated against the living realities of Canada: its vast geography, its widely differing traditions. Combined with the moralistic urges of Canadian Christianity—the dour Jansenism of Québec and the even dourer Calvinism of the Protestant regions—they have led not only to major cultural differences which built up into a political conflict between Québec and the rest of Canada but also to persecutions of small minorities—the Doukhobors perhaps the most striking example— revealing how incomplete our democracy has been and how narrow the limits of our tolerance. And, tramping with the relentless tread of da Ponte's Commendatore in *Don Giovanni*, there is the inescapable spectre of our treatment of the native peoples that will grow in moral even more than in physical magnitude until in some honourable and harmonious way we solve it.

It is through ignoring the great variety of Canadian life and its special hierarchy of loyalties, through failing in the courage to recognize that the extreme devolution of true confederation would solve all our conflicts and make us a great example to the world seeking new examples as empires and nation-states crumble, that we are in our present impasse. And our fate is in the hands of the very political leaders who have led us into this Slough of Despond.

There are two things in the world of the early 1990s that Canadians must recognize. One is that, as a land of many cultures, we have ignored the possibilities offered by our geographical distances and our historical divisions. Even more, we have neglected the impossibilities, those great challenges to go beyond the past into an untrammelled future with which our great land confronts us. But also we have failed to see beyond ourselves and to recognize the lessons that the events of the 1980s have for us.

For what distinguished the annus mirabilis of 1989 and the other year of 1991 in Russia was not merely the possibility of the impossible in a world that had shed the spectre of a determined History. It was also that power of the powerless of which Vaclav Havel spoke so eloquently.

The concept of the power of the powerless is present, of course, in all democratic thinking, which implicitly bases itself on the will of the people. In practice, democracies have dissipated that power by the political arrangement of what is called "representative democracy." It may indeed be representative in the sense that the rulers are picked by vote, but its practical arrangements, embodied in whip-driven political parties and parliamentary caucuses, are the reverse of democratic, curbing the independence of the representative legislator and thus creating a rigid barrier between the people and real power.

When the power held by politicians begins to disintegrate, when those who hold power cease to believe in the ideologies by virtue of which they hold it, then the power of the powerless begins to grow, and the people, gathering in the streets, can blow a regime away with the thunder of their shouts and the ringing of their key-rings. Today, in Canada, the political parties are in disarray, and even those leaders not wholly discredited in the eyes of the people are weakened by an appearance of failing to understand, let alone having the power to overcome, the crisis in which we are involved.

That crisis is in fact a crisis of power and how it should be distributed. Claimants abound—the Québécois, the Acadiens, the native peoples, the West, the poor, are only the more prominent among them. As a democracy, Canada has not been successful in preserving or creating equal rights, yet it has equally certainly not been successful as a nation, since by entering power blocs like NATO and NORAD, it has squandered the international prestige it might have gained as an honest broker. Those who still cling, with their babble about "a strong central government," to that outdated concept can only be suspect of cherishing the last remnants of a system that has provided them with power and often profit as well.

To put the matter plainly, we cannot trust the politicians to devise a new political system that would dramatically shift the balance of power within Canada towards the people. We cannot trust them to take as a principle of action the possibility of the impossible and to devolve power so that the genius of the people may be released to renew the land and save it from economic and ecological disaster.

So, though, like everything else in Canada, our predicament is under-stated, we are in fact in a situation resembling that of the East Europeans in recent years. We have a government and opposition parties whose proposals are ineffective, who have no faith in themselves, and who inspire no lasting trust. Yet these hollow men—and hollow women too—strive to keep the dead hands of a past of failure on the new country they propose to offer us. Meech Lake, when eleven men met in secret to try to agree on our national fate, was surely a lesson in the undemocratic nature of their kind of formal democracy. In fact, on that level, Meech Lake was a remarkable demonstration of the closeness of such a system to fascism, for here were leaders transforming themselves into führers negotiating from positions of power and relying on the support of their parties to carry out changes on which the people would never be asked to offer opinions, let alone participate in a vote.

But paradoxically, Meech Lake, which showed the path that politicians must be prevented from following ever again, also showed a path for the Canadian people—or peoples—to take: the path of the power of the powerless, of the possibility of the impossible. By ingeniously bringing strict legality to the aid of nonviolent resistance, that one just man, Elijah Harper, halted the process virtually agreed on by the eleven leaders and threw the future of Canada's constitution into a morass of doubt from which the people must rescue it before the politicians are again allowed to control it.

Elijah Harper showed what a single determined individual, acting with the moral support of great numbers of Canadians, can do against the presumptions of power and the insolence of office. In one way it was important that Harper was a Cree chief. He brought the native peoples of Canada into the heart of a process from which in the past they had always been excluded. But it was even more important that he acted as an individual, setting an example for individual Canadians who can call a halt to the whole process of politicians presuming to rearrange our polity without a special mandate from the people.

How can we go about this? No better way, I suggest, than to follow the example of those who have succeeded in their fight against political leaders, the inhabitants of Poland and Hungary and Czechoslovakia and the former Soviet Union. In the process we may learn the true uses of history.

For even here there is no question of prophecy. I can only repeat that history has no plan and no laws, and that the future is merely the tabula rasa on which the past writes the present. How that present is written is where our possibility of fruitful action lies. And history, which is no more than the process of our lives moving through the past and present towards the future, limited only by our mortality and our courage, can offer us by example and analogy the possibilities within which we may operate, the old and new forces and correlations that contingency offers; it shows us also, like mountains seen at the end of some long valley, the peaks of the impossible that the resolute can sometimes climb. It is up to us to choose what chance and change may offer as opportunities for improving on the past. It is by choice that we define ourselves as human beings and save ourselves from being the slaves of destiny, natural or political.

In Poland, Hungary, Czechoslovakia and Russia itself, the recent radical changes in society depended mainly on the strong initiative of the people and of activists like Walesa and Havel and Yeltsin who defined their aims

202

and orchestrated their nonviolent strategies. In Canada we shall only have changes of lasting value if we make sure that the people are involved, and for that to be achieved the people must awaken from the condition of having things done for and to them, to that of doing things for themselves. If the politicians refuse us a constituent assembly where all views can be talked out, we should arrange it ourselves. If the government will not hold referenda on various points of the constitution (as is already customary in Switzerland and some other countries), we should recruit the technicians and the facilities and proceed on our own. And if the government does not effectively return power to the people, we should strike and march and fill the streets and clog the roads with cars and tractors until our peaceful manifestations secure a political arrangement that satisfies us. The peoples of Berlin and Leipzig, of Prague and Budapest, of Moscow and St. Petersburg, have given us an example abroad; the native peoples with their nonviolent confrontations are giving an example at home. They have acted according to the ancient right of dissent against governments that fail to meet their responsibilities to guard the rights and freedom of the people.

One can safely say, I think, that the people of Canada, like those of Eastern Europe, desire above all more involvement in controlling their own lives, in arranging the polity and the economy of their country, and in protecting its natural heritage. The movement for participatory democracy which swept through North America in the 1960s, and to which career-making politicians like Pierre Elliott Trudeau once paid lip service, never really died out, and a strong libertarian remnant survived in both Canada and the United States. And the governmental effrontery of Prime Minister Brian Mulroney and the provincial premiers at Meech Lake, and incidents involving native people, like the surprisingly bloodless standoff at Oka, made millions of people in Canada more aware than ever before that the strings of government, which mean control over the people who control our lives, have too long been slipping out of our hands into those of politicians and of the stone-faced bureaucrats who manipulate them.

The general wish has long been for less government, and this, more than any other of its promises, was the reason why the Conservative party was returned so decisively to power in the most recent parliamentary elections. In office the Tories interpreted this mandate to mean little more than the deregulation of industry, and the federal government virtually conspired with the provincial ones of all parties to retain as much power as possible in their hands. That is why the Tory party in 1991 stands so low in the polls, and why the Reform party, suspect though its promises may be, has gained so much ground recently across the country. People, whatever their origins, long for more control over their own affairs, and only a radical devolution of power will satisfy them.

Here we are perhaps fortunate in confronting a factor unparalleled in the countries of Eastern Europe, that of the native peoples and their aspirations towards self-government. Some of these native peoples, like the members of the Blackfoot and the Iroquois Confederacies, have old and sophisticated political traditions of their own, forms of confederal and participatory democracy in which women often played a leading role commensurate with their contribution to the economy of the community. The native demands for sovereignty to be granted to each aboriginal "nation" or language group to conduct its own affairs and develop its own political structures are equally important, since once they are granted they will offer precedents for small-scale organization, which among the general Canadian population would devolve power by transferring more control of their own affairs to municipalities and even to small communes through town meetings. In this way power could be made to spread upward rather than widening downward, and the politics of freedom might begin to take shape.

I talk of these things hesitantly, realizing that ideals and realities never correspond, though they can distort each other; perhaps what we must hope most of all is that whatever political arrangement may evolve in Canada, it will remain tentative and open-ended, ready to embrace new possibilities and to convert old impossibilities into reality. We must resist the temptation of the final solution. Utopia—need one repeat the warning?—represents an assumption of perfection, and perfection is the end of change, and therefore is death. Rigidity makes all constitutions seem the enemies of freedom, and so a constitution should never be complete, never be cut in stone. Far better for it to be writ, as the poet John Keats desired his name should be, in the water of people's memories so that it will be fluid and ever-changeable. Since that is perhaps impractical, constitutions should be simply stated and quickly and easily amendable by referendum if a sufficient number of citizens so demand, as happens in Switzerland and some other countries already; but only the people, wielding their power directly, should be able to change it.

These proposals—*modest* I might have called them but for Jonathan Swift—are drawn from a pragmatic study of societies in the past and present, and of the endurance of voluntarism and of mutual aid even in totalitarian settings; they presume a society in which power will not only be diffused among individuals and groups but will also be localized, brought to the level of practical living in the community. And this fact brings us back to the Dalai Lama and the ideas he put forward through his concept of Zones of Ahimsa. Political arrangements that emphasize and reinforce the idea of locality lead inevitably to the matter of the environment, which is generally conceived in local terms: a locality, indeed, is usually an ecosystem as well. Emphasizing the regional or local quality of a community also emphasizes its intimate links, economically, culturally and in terms of personal feeling, with the physical character of the land where it is situated and with the wild creatures that inhabit it, as well as with the basic industries, such as farming, fishing and forestry, that its soil maintains. Protection of the environment will necessarily become a growing element in politics as it is increasingly localized.

But the localization of politics faces people directly with the responsibility for solving their own predicaments, offering them an opportunity to develop habits of conservation and in the process to find the human community and the ecosystem growing more intimate, the links with the animal kingdom more concerned and more compassionate.

Militarism, particularly where it involves the manufacture, distribution and use of nuclear weaponry, is almost by definition hostile to the natural environment as well as to humanity. And its advantages, to all but rogue powers like Nazi Germany and present-day Iraq, are dubious and always temporary.

In the modern world, small and medium-sized countries cannot defend themselves with what in effect are ornamental armaments; even the elaborate defence plans of the Swiss citizen army envisage falling back on the infertile mountain core for a last stand. Canada, with its vast area and long frontiers, is even less defensible than most other countries, and for the doubtful privilege of American protection in the event of war it would pay the as yet unimagined cost of being the actual front-line region on which all the weaponry destroyed in flight would land. Defence alliances are in fact worse than useless to the lesser powers; they merely draw them unnecessarily into the quarrels of the great powers, who still dangerously flourish the threats of nuclear aggression.

So circumstances encourage us to grasp the nettle and bite the bullet and fulfil all the old warmongers' metaphors in a different way than they imagined by accepting the last of the Dalai Lama's conditions and turning ourselves into a Zone of Peace, where our young people may be encouraged to satisfy their desire for adventure by serving humanity peacefully, and the armed services may be reduced to a busbied ceremonial guard at Rideau Hall, preserved for old time's sake.

These then strike me as the possibilities and the benign impossibilities for Canada, seen from the standpoint of history read only as a chronicle of the past and a source of examples for survival. They are perhaps also the most viable possibilities for the whole world if we are to survive long into the twentieth century as a civilized community of nations. War and the manufacture of the tools of war, and the cost of it all, must end; the demands of human society and those of the natural world must be harmonized; people must be allowed to determine how they shall be governed and have the right to change their minds and hence their choices by easy amendment. These minimal demands for survival in the present and in the proximate future accord with the great anti-laws of human life: Change and Chance and Choice. They need no Laws, no Providential Plans, no Eschatological Prophecy, none of the determinist and futurist rubbish with which historians as the servants of the powerful have marred their vision and their craft.

Index

GEORGE WOODCOCK is one of Canada's most respected men of letters. A biographer, critic, essayist and poet, his more than forty books include *Anarchism: A History of Libertarian Ideas and Movements*, a subject in which he has held a lifelong interest, *British Columbia: A History of the Province* and *The Doukhobors*.

His biographies include *The Crystal Spirit* about George Orwell which won the Governor General's Award in 1967; *Gabriel Dumont*, which won the University of British Columbia Medal for Popular Biography in 1976 and *Thomas Merton: Monk and Poet*.

He was the founder and for twenty years the editor of Canadian Literature, and his writings on that subject include *The World of Canadian Writing: Critiques and Recollections, Strange Bedfellows: The State and the Arts in Canada* and *Northern Spring: The Flowering of Canadian Literature*.